Toxicity

Out of the Box, Book 13

Robert J. Crane

Toxicity
Out of the Box #13
Robert J. Crane
Copyright © 2017 Ostiagard Press
All Rights Reserved.

1st Edition

1.

"Romeo and Juliet. Bonnie and Clyde. That's our kind of love story, baby. That's who we are. That's our destiny." June Randall laughed as she said the words aloud, brushing her strawberry blond hair back over her shoulders and kicking the beach sand between her toes.

Elliot Lefavre—she called him "Ell" because it was simpler than saying his whole name every time she wanted to get his attention, and because it was uniquely her way of calling him—brushed back his own hair in reaction to her motion. His was shaved on the sides and long on the top, slicked back usually, though not here, in beachfront paradise. Here it was the sheen of the Atlantic's waters still shining in his hair from when they'd gone for a little swim just a few minutes earlier.

The sea salt felt sticky on June's freckled skin, drying as it was in the warm air. Florida in March felt a lot better than Ohio, where she was from. "How is this compared to Nevada?" she asked, moving the conversation along as her last comment hadn't elicited the response she was looking for.

"Hotter there," Ell said, looking darkly pensive. "The air's drier." He sniffed, like he was taking stock of the environmental conditions around him. He probably was, she knew by experience.

"I bet the nights are amazing," June leaned in against his shoulder and found it satisfyingly sticky, her hair draping itself over his shoulder in wet ringlets as she crunched sand beneath her ass, snuggling in against his warmth. They were in a town called Melbourne, on the east coast of Florida, for the moment. It didn't have the best beach she'd ever seen, but it was pretty decent. Growing up in Ohio, she hadn't gotten to see ocean beaches, so this was a welcome change. "All bright and lit up and gorgeous." The opposite of the way things had been in Westerville, where the only lights were the chain stores that kept their signs on all night, and the lamps that shone down on near-abandoned streets during the vampire hours she liked to be awake.

"On the strip and in old downtown, sure," Ell said, staring down at her where she rested on him. The skies above were abundantly blue, and the ocean stretched out over the horizon with only a few small boats to clutter it. The slow, dull roar of the tide coming in was soothing, almost lulling her to sleep. Sleep by day, live by night, that was her idea of life. But this wasn't so bad, either.

"Could we head that way, bae?" she asked, draping her arms around his shoulders. He had a few stray strands of hair sprouting out of his shoulder. It made him self-conscious when she twirled them, but it always made her giggle to do so.

"It's a long way from here." Ell didn't sound convinced.

"Please." She hugged him tighter. "I want to see the West."

"Not much to see in the middle of the country." He felt rigid against her, his discomfort with being here now palpable.

"Well, we can't fly," she said, giving him a *Duh!* kind of look coupled with a smile to offset the needle of scorn she added.

"I think we should head south," Ell said, scratching the back of his forearm. "Get to the Keys, head for Cuba—"

"Ugh," she said, breaking from him. "I don't want to go to Cuba. Have you seen the cars? They're so old. It's like they don't have anything made in this century. It's pathetic."

"There's a reason for that," Ell said in that dry, infuriating way he had when he was lording it over her that he knew something she didn't.

"I don't care," she said, pursing her lips together. She might have to not speak to him for a while if he kept this up. He always got the point when she stopped talking for a while. Eventually. "I don't want to go there."

"It's not safe here anymore," Ell said, scratching his forearm again.

"For them, maybe." She looked at the people with their towels and blankets spread up and down the shore, flecked across the beach like islands in the sand. Behind them lay a sea of green vegetation with a boardwalk path over it, and somewhere beyond that, their car waited. "We're fine."

"For now," Ell said, his head hunching over further, like he was trying to put his own head in his lap. "But June … the things we've done—"

"Who cares?" Yeah, he was getting the silent treatment. And soon.

"I–I car—"

A ball smacked into the beach, showering them with a spray of sand. June's mouth fell open in shock as grains dusted her cheek and chest, falling down the front of her soaked tank top where it bubbled and failed to cling to her skin. She felt the hot surge of rage and sought out the bastard who would have dared to do this to her, to *her*—

"I'm sorry," said a little girl, probably no older than eight, her eyes downcast and fixed on the soccer ball that was cratered into the sand between June and Ell's feet. The girl sounded like she was steeling herself for a furious rage, the contrition as obvious as the little freckles on her nose.

June felt the tension bleed out of her shoulders. How could she be mad at that? "It's all right," she said, almost laughing. "It was an accident." Ell's hand was anchored on her wrist, and she looked at him and patted his cheek. "It's all right," she said again, this time to reassure him. He unclenched his fingers slowly.

The ball was just sitting there, the girl making no move to retrieve it, so June leaned down and grabbed it. "What's your name?" she asked the girl, spinning the patchwork on her finger. It spun at high velocity, making a singing noise against the tip of her finger. June had played volleyball in high

school all the way up to her senior year—last year—and she'd gotten pretty good at this, even before her powers had manifested.

Now she could serve a volleyball hard enough to kill a man. Not that she'd killed a man that way. Or at all.

Yet.

"Sara," the little girl demurred, still fixated on the ball. She didn't show much amazement at the blur of white and black spinning on June's finger.

Crunching of feet against sand caused June to look up. A man approached from behind little Sara, looking cross. A dutiful father, she figured, here to warn his little munchkin about the rudeness of pelting strangers with a ball.

He opened his mouth, and she assumed an apology was forthcoming. "Why don't you just give her back her ball?" he asked instead.

"Excuse me?" June said, feeling that flare of anger return.

"You're excused. Now give her back her ball." The man's accent was northern, a little like Boston or New York. Way out of place here.

"Make—" June started.

"June." Ell's hand found her wrist again, but not hard enough to jar loose the ball that she now clutched between her fingers.

"—me," June finished.

The man almost seemed like he might pass on the challenge. She could see the gears turn, spinning as he tried to decide how best to handle the challenge thrown down in front of him. She could feel the heat under her collar, her freckled skin warm, and not just from the sun now. She felt like she might have boiled the ocean if she'd gone for a swim now, cheeks burning as she stared him down. There was, too, this little thread of worry in the back of her mind, and it sounded like Ell—*Are you sure you should be doing this?*

She ignored it.

The man's shoulders dipped and he strode toward her, swiping out a long, ungainly arm for the ball—

"Dick!" June said, and sprayed him, a cloud of purple toxin billowing out of her hand. He didn't stop in time, didn't see it until his head was engulfed, and his swarthy face disappeared into the plum-colored cloud, emerging a moment later with his eyes squinted shut, coughing and sputtering wetly.

"June!" Ell lifted his own hand and blew the cloud out to sea, dispelling the toxin in a thousand different directions. He was on his feet, trying to grab hold of the guy who'd come at them—at her. "You can't—"

"I just did," she said, as Mr. New York sank to his knees, coughing, his eyes already bloodshot when he opened them briefly between fits. He would have been fine if he'd kept his distance, but the dumbass had come right at her, gotten too close, and she'd given him a snootful of her own personal toxin. It was only a fraction of what she could make, but he'd run right into it. She wasn't entirely sure, but she figured it was fifty/fifty whether he lived or died.

Her hand shook as she let it drop, that feeling like she might have pushed a little too far diminishing. What did it matter, anyway? He was asking for it, coming at her like that.

"Daddy!" Little Sara wasn't so dumb as to think that nothing was wrong. Seeing her father cough and choke and drop to his knees wasn't the sort of thing even a kid could easily ignore.

"Here," June said, responding to Ell's panicked pressure on her arm. She tossed the soccer ball next to Sara's feet, but the girl ignored it, too focused on her father, who was now turning a lighter shade of lavender himself, his tongue swollen and hanging out of his mouth unnaturally.

"We can't just—" Ell said, lifting his own hand.

She grabbed his arm and started to drag him away. "Yes, we can." She didn't care about the blanket, the towels they were leaving behind. They were all stolen anyway. "This is a good lesson for him."

"If he dies, he's not going to learn anything!" Ell pushed back against her and broke free, dropping into the sand next to the downed man. With a raised hand, he shoved his palm into the man's face. The air stirred around them and Ell drove oxygen into the man's lungs, his power over wind being used, once again, to counteract what June had done.

She stared at him for a second, feeling stricken, watching Sara with wide eyes, over her father. What could she do, though? Best to leave. June turned and started stalking off over the dunes toward the boardwalk. This was Ell's thing now, not hers. She shook the sand out of her tank top and wrung out the bottom of it. She could see her nipples through the wet, wrinkled fabric, and she giggled a little to herself at the mere sight. She didn't care.

June was up on the boardwalk when Ell caught up with her, feet thumping against the planks. "I don't want to hear it," she said warningly, taking care to keep her back perfectly turned to him.

"You can't just do that, June," he said, trying to catch up. Even when he made it to her side, she turned her face away, trying to give him her shoulder as much as possible. "That little girl—"

"I don't care," June said as she descended the boardwalk steps on the other side. It was better this way; better to put up a wall, not think about what had happened back there. Hadn't he seen? That man had forced her into a corner, coming at her like that.

He deserved it.

June's feet were covered in white sand. When she stepped off the boardwalk ramp onto the hot asphalt, she cringed, but kept facing away from Ell so he couldn't see her.

Cold shouldering him always shut Ell up. This time was no exception, and she made for the car where she got into the passenger side as he climbed into the driver's seat wordlessly. He was so damned weak, she wondered if he'd start crying on her again. That happened sometimes. This time, she'd be indifferent to it, because she was pissed as hell at him over everything that had just happened on the beach.

And maybe, just a little, tiny bit that she wouldn't have admitted even to herself … she was pissed at herself for letting her anger run away with her.

"Where to?" he asked.

"I don't care."

"I'm gonna head south," he said, starting the engine.

"Fine." That stung her even worse. She was already mad

at him, and he was going to do this shit? He'd be lucky if she ever spoke to him again.

"It's not fine," he said gently.

"Just do whatever you want," she said, keeping her eyes fixed out the window. She felt the sting at the corner of her eyes, and her voice cracked a little.

He backed the car out of the space, his shoulders slumped. She was almost positive she knew what he was going to do now, just by the bearing of his body. He sped the old Pontiac Parisienne out of the parking lot toward A1A, and she knew that the turn he took would tell the tale. If he went left, he'd be heading south, toward Cuba. And she wouldn't speak to him again, maybe ever. At least not for a couple days.

But if he headed north …

He drove up to the stop sign and sighed, shoulders slumped. He lay his head on the steering wheel for a few seconds and she did not say anything, not a word, because she needed not to.

The turn signal clicked on after a few seconds, and she knew the decision was made, one way or another. She held her breath, waiting to see which direction he'd choose.

When the car turned north, she smiled, just slightly. She blinked against the sun shining in through her window, blinding, but kept facing it, and away from him. She'd start talking again in about five minutes.

After all, how could she stay mad at him for long?

2.

Sienna

The breakfast room in my resort in St. Thomas was wall-to-wall windows that overlooked the blue ocean. As a result, I had to eat with my sunglasses on every morning.

It seemed a fair trade-off on those mornings when I actually decided to go down to the breakfast room and brave possible human contact. The rest of the time, I just ordered room service and sat unsociably by my lonesome, watching the TV news and browsing the internet, as I tended to do when I had an abundance of time to kill. Which was every day.

When I'd arrived in the Virgin Islands a couple months earlier, it had been right in the middle of the dead season post-Christmas. Within a few weeks, though, business at the resort had picked up, and now the breakfast room had gone from a few isolated, mostly old souls into a surplus of wealthy spring breakers and families, all enjoying their little slice of tropical paradise and oblivious to the dangerous fugitive who sat right in their midst.

Yeah, that was me. Dangerous. Mostly because I hadn't had my coffee yet.

"Ms. Gracie," said Hannah, my usual server, showing up with the blessing of coffee already steaming, cream and sugar neatly mixed within the wondrous bounds of the cup. "How you doing this morning?" She was a peach, that Hannah. It was always a struggle for me on the days when she didn't work. Fortunately for me, they were few. Fortunately for her they were few, too, because she'd already told me I'd doubled her pay for the entire year since I'd been here.

Because Ms. Gracie—my assumed identity while I was staying here—was as benevolent as she was blond. And Ms. Gracie was definitely blond, my long, faux locks ending just above my shoulders. Yikes. At least the color went with my new tan. Hard-working Sienna Nealon, always pale as snow from spending so much time indoors, would have looked like an albino with a blond wig. Fugitive Sienna had actually picked up some coloration, so I didn't look quite so mismatched.

"I'm lovely, Hannah," I said from behind my immense, dark sunglasses, wrapped up in a cottony robe. I just showed up in a robe to breakfast. Not because it was comfortable, not because Sienna Nealon would have done it (I wouldn't have; it's kind of mortifying) but because Ms. Gracie was the sort of person who simply didn't care. Rich heiress, spoiled all her life, never had a worry, never been in a fight.

Pretty much the opposite of me. It was tough getting into character for her. Ms. Gracie probably wouldn't have tipped as well if she'd been a real person, but that was the advantage of being Sienna beneath it all, I guess. At least for Hannah.

"Are you doing the buffet this morning?" Hannah was asking out of politeness. Ms. Gracie always ate the buffet for breakfast, because Ms. Gracie had a problem putting down her fork when she should have.

Coincidentally, it was a problem Sienna Nealon might have had as well, though it had become a lot more obvious since I'd come here and had occasion to be more idle than I'd ever been in my entire life. And better fed as well.

"Oh, I don't know," I said, trying to act like I was thinking about getting a fruit bowl or something. The buffet had fruit. I assiduously avoided it, though, because who wanted fruit when you could have pancakes covered in real, thick Vermont maple syrup? And don't give me that crap about how pancakes are good with fruit; pancakes are good with syrup. Maybe a fruity syrup, if you're in the mood. Save the strawberries for burial under a mountain of whipped cream, because that was the only way I liked them. And I honestly would have rather just had the whipped cream.

Yeah … Ms. Gracie had a problem.

"I'll just take the buffet," I finally said, tossing the thin, one-column paper menu aside. Hannah nodded, projecting an aura of calm acceptance. Inside, I was not calm nor accepting. I was raging a little bit at myself, but it was tempered with the desire to go hit the omelet station and request every single kind of cheese in my breakfast, including the aged, pickled feta and the creamy goat cheese.

"Very good," Hannah said, nodding her head. "Do you want anything else to drink?" Her islander accent was still strong, even after years of being around about a million mainlanders.

"Milk," I said.

"Whole or skim?"

I warred with myself. "Whole," I said, giving up the fight quickly. If I was going to drink skim milk, I might as well have just stuck to the water.

Hannah nodded and vanished, threading her way across the full room. I sat there for a few seconds longer in self-loathing, then sighed and started to get up to make my way to the buffet.

I filled my plate with other goodies, like buttered toast, a blueberry muffin, some juicy sausage, hash browns and a custom-made omelet before picking my way back over to my table.

As I did, I noticed a guy in a muscle shirt with his arms exposed was staring at me. His stick-figure girlfriend next to him paused with a bite of cantaloupe the size of a pinky finger hanging off her fork, inches from her mouth. They were both looking at me with the same gawking expression on their faces, though his was laced with smugness, his arms folded in front of a black shirt that said, "5%."

Their whole manner irritated me, because it was as rich with scorn as my pancakes were with syrup, so I nodded at his shirt and said, "5%, huh? I could have guessed that was how much of your brain you were using just by the dumb look on your face." I spoke with a northeastern accent, long-practiced, because there was no accent like Bahston for being an asshole.

His smugness died in an instant and he looked down at his shirt like he'd forgotten what it said. "That's my body fat percentage," he said, expression darkening. He had a plate of lean proteins in front of him, and I could have believed the 5% figure, if I actually cared about such things. "And since most people only use 10% of their brains, 5% isn't so bad." He tossed that one my way like it was a stunning refutation of my insult.

"It's half," I said, blinking in surprise. "Half as much. That would be bad. And even if it weren't, that 10% number is bullshit. But in your case, I believe the 5% of your brain in use is entirely in the stem."

"Not funny," he said, face darkening further. "And not true."

"Way to prove me wrong by using your wits to rebut, there, guy," I said, letting the back of my robe brush my chair as I sat back down to start devouring my breakfast.

"What are you eating that for?" Mr. 5% asked his girlfriend, and I heard the clatter of a fork as he slapped the eating utensil out of his companion's hand. I could hear him plainly without the aid of my meta enhanced hearing.

"I was—"

"You don't need it," he said with supreme, asshole snippiness. "You think I haven't noticed the disgusting cottage cheese forming on the back of your thighs? You need to stop eating."

This was greeted with a choked sob, and the sound of his girlfriend leaving the breakfast room via the nearest exit, which led to a walkway to the beach.

I ate in silence, ignoring the hell out of Mr. 5%, who was stewing and trying to catch my eye, probably looking to continue the fight I'd just picked with him and that he'd promptly continued with his girlfriend, the douche.

I savored my meal, staring out at the ocean in the distance. There were some clouds on the horizon, which I took to mean, based on my boundless three months of experience, that we'd see rain come rolling in later this morning, and it'd be gone by noon. I sighed and looked around the breakfast room. I liked it here, but it was starting to get a little crowded for my taste.

After finishing my breakfast in silence, aided by my incomparably delectable omelet, I drank the rest of my coffee and left, without a further word from Mr. 5%. Which was good, because his companion might not have been insulted to the point of violence by his asshole behavior, but I was insulted enough to consider doing some on her behalf.

"We see you tomorrow, Ms. Gracie," Hannah said as I signed off on her tip on the way out. I smiled at her and gathered my robe close, stepping out onto the path to the beach.

The air was warm, the sea running across the sand in the distance a harmonious sound that was way, way better than the noise of horns honking, or people shooting at you. I walked with bare feet toward the beach, which was sparsely populated this morning, only a few people hanging out in the white chairs with blue cushions that rested all along the beachfront. They had canopies you could pull up if the sun got to be too much, and even a little flag you could raise in order to signal some kind waiter to bring you a drink of your choice.

I'd gotten lots of drinks here over the last couple months. Lots and lots of them. Too many to count. They had helped balloon my waistline to the point that I'd been forced to go up a size or three.

I walked past the infinity edge pool, listening to the gentle splash of water running over its edge, as though it ran directly into the ocean beyond. Sometimes I sat here, too, because you couldn't just hang out on the beach all the time, after all. A change of scenery was occasionally necessary, because … I dunno. It really wasn't that necessary, because it was all just variations on a theme—blue waters, white sand, white concrete decking. Umbrellas, beach chairs, and flags up so you could booze yourself into oblivion.

I shook my head. It was going to be another day of boozing myself into oblivion here at the pool or on the beach, I knew, unless I decided to go on one of the boat expeditions. Then I'd still booze myself into oblivion, I'd just be doing it on the open sea instead of here at the pool or on the beach. I could also have done the same from my patio back in the hotel, but … I had done that yesterday.

"Ugh," I said, and then heard a footstep behind me, turned, and said, "Ugh," again, but louder.

"I saw you looking at me back in there," Mr. 5% said with a grin that really proved my brain stem observation true. "And I came out here because … let's face it … you couldn't take your eyes off me."

3.

Scott

Scott Byerly could feel the ocean drawing nearer as he drove his borrowed government sedan toward the Atlantic. It loomed behind the vegetation at the edge of the parking lot, a boardwalk platform rising above the patch of green to form the barrier between him and the sea. It was like a wall between the world of men and the ocean.

There was a time when, at this distance, almost a block and a long stretch of sandy beach away, the ocean might have felt too far for him to get a grip on it.

Not now, though. It was right there, near as life, as though he could reach out and take hold of every molecule from here to the shores of West Africa, ready to deliver it to a place of his choosing.

Ambulances, police cars, and fire trucks still cluttered the parking lot. Mansion-like houses stood on either side of the public park, and in the distance he could see tall condo towers rising into the sky. People were all around him, like an ocean he had to cross in order to reach the real ocean, the salt spray in the air so near, yet so far.

But even they weren't enough to separate Scott from the feel of the sea.

He parked the government sedan behind a cop car with its lights flashing and stepped out into the warm air. He could taste the salt in the breeze, strong and tangy, and he closed his eyes for a few seconds to really drink it in.

"You the FBI guy?" someone asked, and Scott opened his eyes to see a middle-aged man approaching cautiously, hand outstretched. "You're him, aren't you?"

"Scott Byerly," he said, extending his own to the local cop, who was sweating through a long-sleeved shirt and a thin suit jacket. Scott flipped his ID, more out of habit than because he thought the guy needed to see it. "I heard you had a meta incident."

"Name's Rafferty," the cop said, pumping his hand. "You got here awfully fast."

"I was in Orlando already," Scott said, looking past Rafferty toward the beachfront, where a few cops were milling around up on the boardwalk. The ocean was right up there, he could practically touch it … "Doing cleanup on that thing that went down in Central Florida a couple months ago."

"Oh, you mean that cult compound or whatever?" Rafferty asked with the sort of practiced disinterest that told Scott the detective knew all about it and was just fishing. "Didn't one of your old friends bust that one open?"

"Reed? Yeah," Scott said. "It's still a real mess, though. All these people had been prisoners for years and years in an isolated society of their own. Trying to get them reintroduced to ours is … uh, well …"

"Yeah," Rafferty said, nodding for Scott to follow him. "Our department got a captivity case once. Little boy imprisoned by a kidnapper for six months. I wouldn't want to be the psychologist who had to pick up the pieces of that one."

"I expect it's going to be a long road for most of them," Scott said as they ascended the wooden steps. The boardwalk groaned almost imperceptibly under all the weight upon it; Scott doubted anyone but he could have heard it.

"Figure at this point it'd be more of a job for social workers than an FBI Task Force head," Rafferty said, still fishing. His dark hair was thinning, but he'd grown it out long on top. The sea breeze caught it and pulled it back hard, revealing a sharp widow's peak.

"It would have been," Scott said with the ghost of a

smile, "if my task force was made up of anyone other than me."

Rafferty took that in quick. "You were recruiting."

"Trying to, anyway," Scott said. He kept smiling. "It didn't really pay off." Of course, he hadn't really wanted it to, which might have had something to do with the outcome.

"You covering the whole country right now? By your lonesome?"

"When I'm not task force-ing on the manhunt for Sienna Nealon." He held back his look of thin amusement; it was getting harder and harder to send the other elements of the task force in the wrong direction without having Andrew Phillips sniff him out.

Rafferty grunted. "How much time are you really putting in on that task force investigation?"

"Why, all that I can spare, of course," Scott said, almost mockingly. Rafferty had probably picked up on it. Local cops were always the ones that came at him with questions like this. Some of his fellow members of the Bureau had asked as well, politely enough, but he'd been slightly more circumspect with them. "We are talking about one of the FBI's Ten Most Wanted, after all. Catching her is a vital duty." He restrained his own laughter, because he'd perfectly parroted Phillips on that one.

"Uh huh." Yeah, Rafferty got it. "I'm not sure I'd want to find her, either." He cast his eyes down the shore. "I'm not even sure I want to find these two."

"Two, huh?" Scott looked with him.

The beach was more or less clear at this point, though there were still cops out there taking witness statements, and a forensics scene set up right in the middle of the shore. They hadn't done a chalk outline, since there was sand everywhere, but they'd clearly highlighted where the victim had gone down before the paramedics had rushed him to the hospital.

"Yeah, two," Rafferty said. "Male and female, both Caucasian, late teens, early twenties—"

"Female has strawberry blond hair," Scott took up from memory, "male has dark hair, slicked back with shaved sides—"

"She's tattooed on both arms, and at the small of her back," Rafferty went on, "he's got one on the right shoulder—"

"That matches hers, right?"

"Yes." Rafferty did not look amused. "You've been watching these two?"

"They've been working their way down the coast," Scott said, sighing. "I kept chomping to go after them, but—"

"Task force." Rafferty knew.

"You know how the priorities run," Scott said. "I guess things finally got too public to ignore."

"At least our vic's not dead," Rafferty said. "Sounded like the boy—"

"Elliot."

"—Elliot came back and revived him," Rafferty said. Didn't read from a notebook or anything, just kept the facts in his head. "How would he do that?"

"He's an aeolus," Scott said, leaning both palms against the wood railing of the boardwalk. The sea salt spritzed lightly on his face as he summoned a little taste closer.

"Controls wind, right? Like your buddy—"

"Reed? Yeah." Scott glanced at Rafferty. "I'm not sure we're buddies anymore, though."

"You have a falling out?"

"Not really," Scott said. "Just not sure where we stand. The girl—woman—female suspect—"

"She's the one who put our victim down."

"Her name's June Randall."

"I know."

"From Westerville, Ohio. Outside Columbus."

"I've been watching her, too." Rafferty looked jaded as hell, like he was struggling to keep from blowing up. "How long has your brass been holding you back from going after these two?"

"About two months."

"Damn," Rafferty breathed. "How many—"

"Eight people have ended up in the hospital," Scott said. "No one dead, fortunately. All that's down to June, it sounds like. She loses her temper pretty easy. But it's all petty crime, so—"

"So it takes a back seat to your Most Wanted fugitive. I get it," Rafferty said grudgingly.

"Do you?" Scott asked, then whispered, "I don't."

"So you're going to go after them now, right?" Rafferty asked. "Before something worse happens? Because I would bet this girl is working up to worse."

"Finally, yes."

"Good." Rafferty settled into a lean next to him. "What do you need from me?"

"What do you have that'll do me any good at finding them?" Scott asked.

"They've been heading south until now," Rafferty said. "Their last hit was, what, two weeks ago—"

"North of Daytona, yeah."

"That's a hundred miles north. I think they've been cooling their heels around here since then."

"Probably," Scott agreed. He looked out at the beach. "Can't imagine why …"

"Heh," Rafferty said, "if they've been holding out for two weeks, they're probably about dry of cash, right?"

"Likely. They're pretty petty in their thieving. Make off with a few bucks, burn through it, rinse and repeat as needed."

"So you think they're gonna hit—" Rafferty's radio beeped, along with those of a bunch of other cops. "We have a Code 24 in progress, the convenience store at the corner of—"

"That's a robbery," Rafferty said.

"And there we go," Scott breathed, taking it in.

"Predictable sort, aren't they?" Rafferty said, motioning Scott toward the boardwalk stairs. "That's only ten minutes from here. Less if we floor it."

"Lead the way," Scott said as they both headed for their cars. The boardwalk was a swarm of activity now, cops on the move, leaving the scene of one crime and on their way to the next.

4.

June

"I want some nachos," June said, filling up the plastic, crinkling container with the bagged chips. That done, she tossed the lid off the condiment bar for the wrapped burgers the gas station sold and took a handful of jalapenos, sprinkling them on the chips. Then she drowned the entire mass in hot, synthetic cheese.

"Please, take whatever you want," the clerk behind the counter said. His name tag said "Steve." He looked like a Steve, blushing hard, red hair, all teary-eyed. "Just don't—"

"Hurt you?" June dabbed a chip in the cheese, scooped a couple jalapenos back on as they started to fall out of the plastic tray, and balanced the whole thing delicately until she crammed the entire tortilla chip in her mouth. She chewed and strode toward the counter where Steve was standing, his hands up. June made a face, then spat the nacho, cheese and jalapeno mixture right in Steve's face. He blanched in surprise, then teared up further as a jalapeno slid down his cheek. "These are stale!"

"I'm sorry," Steve whimpered.

"Come on," Ell said, hiding behind the shelves at the front of the store. He was peering out at the cops who were establishing a perimeter around the gas station even now. "Let's just go."

"I'm not done shopping yet," June said, turning on her heel and leaving Steve sputtering, dabbing at his face with his sleeve. She dropped the stale nachos right there on the floor, yellow cheese product splattering on the white tile, browned by age and foot traffic. They'd already cleaned out the register, a couple hundred rolled up in Ell's pocket, making a lump.

"The cops are here, June," Ell said, still ducking behind the display, peeking up. He was always expecting to get shot down in a hail of bullets, the chicken.

"Yeah, and?" She took a Twix bar off the shelf and made a production of studying it. Like she cared about the caloric information. She was young and a meta; her metabolism burned fast.

"And they could—"

"Shoot us?" June asked, ripping open the Twix with a crinkle. "And hit poor Steve? Or—" she looked down at the twentysomething woman standing by the drink cooler at the end of her aisle. "What's your name?"

The woman stood there, shaking, her eyes closed. She actually had to open them up to figure out June was talking to her. "April," she said finally, once it had all clicked into place and she'd decided that answering was smarter than not.

"Yeah, they'd shoot poor April and Steve if they unloaded on us now," June said, a little sullenly. She'd just started talking to Ell again a few minutes before they'd come in here, and now he was practically begging her to freeze him out again. When was he going to learn?

"I don't like this," Ell said, tapping his finger against a can of Pringles with nervous energy. "I don't want—"

"Don't be such a baby, Ell," June said. She moved to the refrigeration units and opened one of the doors to swipe a Coke bottle.

"I'm not a—" Ell started to reply, and then the bell jangled to herald the arrival of someone new, causing both of them to whip their heads around in surprise.

"It's humid out there," the newcomer said. June stared at him in near disbelief. He had sandy blond hair, was tall, and fanned himself by lifting his collar, which was tucked under a nicely appointed suit jacket. "I always thought those people that talked about it not being the heat but the humidity—

well, I thought they were full of it, but—I mean, *damn*. It really is the humidity here."

"Who the hell are y—" Ell started to ask.

But June beat him to it. "I know you," she said, dropping the sweating Coke bottle and pointing at the newcomer. She snapped her fingers once at him as the bottle hit the ground and thumped, carbonation bubbling up silently at the neck. "I've seen you on TV. You're Sienna Nealon's ex."

The man in the door sighed, looking toward the ceiling. "Yeah. It's almost like I'm not even a person on my own. No attributes, just a label—'Sienna Nealon's ex-boyfriend.'

"Ex boy toy, it looks like," June said with a snort. The guy was a meta. But what was his power? Water or something, wasn't it? Pfffft. How dangerous could that be? Especially now that they were off the beach, June wouldn't have minded a little dousing to break the sweat forming in the small of her back.

"June …" Ell said with rising alarm, "… this guy is a cop."

"Of course he's a cop," June said. If she could have shut Ell's mouth for him right now, she would have. "He's in charge of hunting her down, don't you remember? We saw him on that *20/20* feature on her a couple months ago. I think we were in Charlotte at the time."

"Oh, yeah," Ell said softly, like he was recalling it. He glanced nervously from her to the new guy. "What are you doing here, man?" Like he didn't know. June just cringed; he was so cute sometimes, but so dumb sometimes, too. That might have been why he was cute. He was like a puppy that didn't know not to lick the wall socket.

"I'm here because of you, obviously," the FBI guy said. "I'm Scott Byerly. And you must be June and Elliot."

Elliot cringed further. June took it indifferently, forcing a grin. None of this surprised her, but Ell was still just a little too shy about the attention they commanded. "How do you know our names?" Elliot asked.

"It's hard to miss what you've been doing, Elliot," Scott said, favoring him with a knowing smirk. "You've kind of made a mess."

"Good," June said, and grabbed the shelf nearest her and turned it over easily, sending chips and cookies raining to the ground in their individual wrappings. "I like a mess."

"I'm guessing you've never been a janitor," Scott said with that same smug smirk.

June boiled a little. What right did this jackass have to get all up in her business? "I'm guessing by that suit that you haven't, either."

"Excellent point," Scott said, taking her aside in stride. "But it doesn't change the fact that you two are doing a lot of damage in your little crime spree—"

"Ooh, damage," June said, feeling her skin turn hot as he spoke. She reached out and shoved over the next row of shelves, causing Ell to yelp and jump clear as they crashed down, blocking the aisle between her and the FBI guy. "That sounds terrible. I wouldn't want to cause any of that."

Scott stared at her for a second. "Really?" He looked around the store a little theatrically. "Because I wouldn't mind causing a little."

Glass broke behind her and something smacked into the side of June's head as she turned to look. A plastic bottle of Coke ruptured in her hair, exploding in fizz and sugary water all over her like the tide had rolled in on her at the beach. She gasped in surprised and sweet cola shot up her nose and onto her tongue as she turned away quickly. One plastic bottle after another pelted her—in the ass, the back of the left thigh, her hip bone, her arm. They hit hard enough to leave a bruise each time, some of them exploding and others just glancing off and smacking into upturned shelves.

"June!" Ell shouted, and leapt into motion. He thrust his hand at Scott and a small tornado tore at the FBI agent, whipping a dozen bags of chips at the man as he tried to dodge and got stuck in the whirlwind anyway.

"Just get him!" June shouted, trying to get the soda-drenched hair out of her eyes. If she'd been sticky before, this was going to make it so much worse. She threw up a hand, and it belched out a cloud of purple toxin as another bottle struck her in the side of the face and caused her vision to blur from the impact.

"Get me?" Scott shouted over the howl of Ell's vortex. "That's your plan, Ray? Get me?"

"What the hell are you talking about?" June said, another bottle exploding against the back of her head. She shrieked, because it stung like hell, and she reached out, propelling the cloud of toxin she'd just emitted toward this asshole. She kept it concentrated, because her heart was beating in her ears and her fury was overpowering.

This sonofabitch? He deserved to die.

And she sent it right at him, planning to cram it down his throat, knowing that if he breathed it in … she'd get her wish.

5.

Scott

"Uh oh," Scott said. In his view, any mysterious purple cloud was probably best avoided; knowing it came out of the hand of a woman who'd been poisoning the people she'd run across lately made his desire to avoid it even more acute.

The problem was, he was trapped in a bubble of wind created by the other one, Elliot. It whipped against him, his lapels slapping against his chest, collar straining as Scott fought against the little tornado created to keep him stuck in the air.

It was working, unfortunately. Conquering the winds to the sides weren't impossible, but the updraft keeping his feet off the ground? That one was a real pain in the ass.

He continued pounding June with the expulsion of every soft drink in the cabinet. They were streaking out of the coolers across the room now, smacking her all about the back of the head and neck as she covered herself and dodged, probably missing one in three. Scott was ready to start sending the beers next, figuring the cans and glass bottles rupturing on her would probably put a dent in her skull and start her bleeding rather than just piss her off, as he'd seemed to do thus far.

"You don't have to do this, kid!" Scott yelled over the wind whirling around him, trying to get Elliot to see reason. He seemed the more level-headed of them.

Elliot gawked at him, froze, and looked back at June for

reassurance or guidance. "Bae?" he called to her. That was interesting, Scott thought, as he maintained his hovering stasis in the middle of the tornado.

June missed Elliot's look, however; a beer can detonated against the side of her head and she cried out. For Scott's money, she was the target to pick. Elliot couldn't even seem to decide if he wanted to attack without her, which immediately gave Scott a new plan:

Take out of the brains of the operation, and the body would probably stop flailing.

He'd been holding back anyway, trying to keep from making too much of a mess in spite of what he'd said, trying to keep this situation from spiraling completely out of control. Unfortunately, he reflected as the wind beneath him surged and turned him around for the first time, that strategy was not going so well.

Scott had the power to kill them both, of course. He was just hesitant to employ it willy-nilly. He could smash June's skull using a beer can like a massive bullet, but ...

Then they'd be dead. And they were just teens. They hadn't actually killed anyone yet, after all ...

He was trying to find a way to vocalize that thought when he spun around again and found the purple cloud that he'd forgotten about in the midst of his sudden attack of vertigo, now only inches away from his face. "Shit!" Scott shouted, and panicked.

He blew all the bottles and cans in the freezers at once. The Icee machine exploded and frosty syrup came out in a wave of red, blue, green and white. There was only one way he knew to get the hell out of the windstorm, and it wasn't a subtle one.

The purple toxin entered his cocoon of imprisonment just as Scott was forming one of his own composed entirely of liquid. The sink in the backroom blew off and water rushed in to join the symphony of liquid he was directing to come his way. It snaked toward him in a multicolored fusion, a rainbow of liquid, and he cast out all the sugars along the way. It colored the floor as it fell out of his stream in a little rain.

Scott took his last breath a second too late; the toxin flooded in, caught in the whirlwind around him. His ad hoc defense burst through the wind a moment later, warring hard against the direction of the air currents. He resisted its turn even as he coughed, surrounding himself with liquid, the derivative water beneath the soda and Icee combinations responding to his call and dragging the other components and dyes along for the ride.

"What the hell!" June shouted as he surrounded himself with a liquid wall. Her toxin had caught him off guard, and it shouldn't have. That had been a dumb mistake on his part, getting distracted. It burned his lungs, felt like someone had lit a match and caught his bad breath on fire all the way down into his chest. His lips even felt scalded.

Scott couldn't respond, and he might not have even if he could have mustered something. Instead he just concentrated on breaking his way out of the whirlwind around him, riding the water back to solid ground and then lancing out with it as soon as he was free of his prison.

He heard glass shatter and screams fill the air. His eyes were squinted tight, lungs still burning, and he touched the ground a second later as his chariot of water set him down. He hacked and spluttered, feeling like he might cough up everything he'd ever had. That lasted a little while, his metahuman healing warring with the dose of purple toxin he'd been dealt, chest on fire with the pain of trying to cleanse itself from June's poison.

"You okay?" came the rough voice of Rafferty, and Scott forced his teary eyes open. The detective was standing over him, gun drawn, but looking fairly relaxed considering Scott had been engaged in a bout of metahuman combat only moments before.

"I … think so," Scott choked out, looking around. "Where'd they go?"

"Exited in a cloud of that stuff," he said, eyeing a purple, pillowy mass of toxin that had splattered on the floor in a puddle. He offered a hand, which Scott took, helping him to his feet. "I take it things didn't go well." It was not a question.

"If they got away, no," Scott said, breaking into another coughing fit. "Things did not go well." He looked around through squinted, teary eyes. The front windows of the convenience store were all shattered, and a clerk was standing out front, looking shaken, along with a young lady he figured must have been hostage number two, who looked positively catatonic.

"At least there were no fatalities," Rafferty said.

"Did you see their car?" Scott asked, coughing again. He hadn't realized he'd been down that long, trying to expunge that awful stuff from his lungs and his bloodstream. Not that it had been easy; the pain had certainly stretched time.

"They were heading for I-95," Rafferty said. "We have cars in pursuit—"

"Call them off," Scott said, covering his mouth as he coughed again, expelling a bloody mass of sputum. "They're not ready for this unless you're going to just try and pick them off at a distance."

Rafferty's face evinced little criticism of that idea. "We're not authorized," was all he said, though.

"Then pull back," Scott said.

"And what? Let you handle them?" Here Rafferty showed his skepticism. "Because it went so well before."

"I'm not going after them on my own," Scott said, shaking his head. His lungs still felt like he'd breathed in real, genuine fire. *If I wasn't a meta, I'd probably be dead right now,* he thought. "But … I might know someone who could give me a hand …"

6.

"It's this thing I like to do," I said, pulling my robe tightly closed, staring in disbelief at Mr. 5%, who was leering back at me. I was getting the vibe that this guy was thinking I'd gone after him for a reason other than the one I had. A more flattering reason to him, and presumably how he justified his continued existence to the world. "I like to look people in the eyes when I call them stupid. It's good manners, after all. Calling people stupid when you can't even look them in the face just seems rude."

"I'm smarter than you think," 5% said smugly, proving himself wrong in one statement. "I can see what's going on here." He ran a hand down his muscular pectoral partially obscured by his shirt. "You got a good look at me. Now maybe you want a taste of the merchandise. And I can oblige you."

"Oh, lawd," I said. I actually felt nausea. "Aren't you the guy who just insulted his girlfriend for being too fat? And you're out here chasing me?" I was tempted to let my robe spill open, but that would probably just encourage him.

"I could see the hunger in your eyes," he said, supremely confident.

"I was looking at my plate, trust me," I said. "Nothing about you appeals to me. Nothing."

"Come on," Mr. 5% said. "Girl your age … you're not here alone because you want to be." He eased a little closer to me. "You're looking for something." He made a not-subtle motion toward his groin. "I've got something."

"Something that's 5% of what an average man has, I'd guess."

That made him flush. "You're gonna be lonely for a long time, chubby," he said. "And frustrated."

"Better alone than 95% unsatisfied—"

I saw the punch coming a few seconds before it came. He squared off his feet in a way that told me he was breaking off diplomatic contact because he just so flaming pissed at me.

About time. I had been wondering what it was going to take. I'd been insulting the dumb bastard since we met. 5% of his brain indeed.

I leaned in, presenting him a tempting target—my lower jaw. I stuck it out just slightly, enough to entice him to swing for me. I'd had a feeling that a guy who would take out his pathetic inadequacies by verbally abusing his skinny girlfriend in public for being fat, then chase after another woman who wasn't nearly as tiny probably wouldn't have any qualms about hitting a woman for insulting his manhood. Or whatever passed for it.

He swung pretty hard, and he was a muscular guy. I leaned in, bracing my feet and preparing myself. I tucked my hands behind me and clasped my left one at the wrist in order to restrain myself. This was not a traditional battle against a traditional opponent, and loosing myself on him would only result in his death and my unceremoniously fleeing the island.

Mr. 5%'s fist slammed into my jaw with all the strength he could muster. It was a pretty good punch for a human, and I could really tell he'd been working out.

Mostly because when he hit, it broke every single one of his knuckles and caused bones to splinter all the way up his wrist.

He screamed and dropped right on his ass on the pool deck as I stood there, my robe the only thing moved by his vicious assault.

"You even hit like 5% of a man," I said, pulling my robe

ROBERT J. CRANE

back together. Fortunately, I doubted he'd seen anything while he was swinging for the fences at my jaw, being as he was first concerned about belting me one and then concerned about, you know, his busted-up hand.

"What the hellllllll?!" he screamed, rolling around on the pool deck as I headed toward the water's edge and dipped a couple toes in. It was pleasant.

I didn't feel compelled to answer him. He didn't need to know that I'd just used him to test how hard my new and improved jaw really was. I'd crushed it a couple months ago under a ton of weight in Philadelphia, and when it healed back together, it had done so at a consistency that allowed me to crunch drywall easily and even break marble. (I'd tested both these things against the back of my closet in the hotel room—carefully and minimally, because Ms. Gracie didn't want the resort to bill her for extreme damages to the room.)

"What happened here?" One of the pool attendants came racing up, dreadlocks a flyin'.

"I dunno, I think he broke his hand beating on his own chest or something," I said with a shrug. "Maybe he hit the pool deck, I didn't really see."

"You …" Mr. 5% gave me a wretched look, accusing and tearful all at once.

"I … what?" I asked, daring him to say that he'd broken his hand while trying to punch a woman in the jaw. And failing at it. I had a feeling his pride was about to kick in and forbid it.

I watched the emotions dance across his face. "I … hit my own chest," he said finally, holding back the tears.

"You didn't know your own strength," I said sympathetically, "or how diesel you've become with all those lifts. The sad thing is … if you had a little more body fat for cushioning, this might never have happened." Or if he'd possessed 95% less prickishness, I didn't say. Thought it real hard, though, enough that he probably got it.

On second thought … nah. He was nowhere near self-aware enough to pick that up.

I watched the attendant help him up as I wandered off

toward the shore, my robe rubbing against me. I had a one-piece bathing suit beneath, but it didn't exactly cover me modestly. Sometime between when I'd walked out and when I'd taken the punch, I'd decided to drink down by the shore today.

Because why the hell not? It wasn't like I had anything better to do.

I strolled down to the ocean's edge, reflecting on the chaos I'd just caused. I always did this, everywhere I went. Challenged people, pissed people off, and it somehow inevitably trended right toward violence. Maybe because it was the easiest course for me—

Maybe you're just a violent person, Gerry Harmon said in my head.

"I'm not ruling that possibility out," I said, clutching my robe around me as I strolled down the wet sands, toward the isolated end of the beach, far from my fellow vacationers. I dawdled, taking my time, feeling the sand against the pads of my feet.

"I hope there are lots of possibilities you're not ruling out," came a voice from behind me. I hadn't even heard the footsteps on the sand until he was nearly upon me, and when I spun I had a moment of panic because the person I found waiting, just twenty paces away, was Scott Byerly.

The man whom the US Government had set to the task of hunting me down.

7.

Scott

"Nice setting—" Scott barely got out before she came at him, white terrycloth robe flaring in the wind made by her motion. She had him by the lapels a second later, and he reached out instinctively and drew on the ocean standing not ten feet away, dropping it on both of them as though the entirety of a sea had emptied down from above—

· Sienna's eyes flared as the cold water drenched her. She did not let go, however, jerking Scott forward, her movement slowed by the water surrounding them. Her eyes blazed, fire burning out of them, her blond wig removed by the sudden downward pressure of the water that had encased them. She was panicked, he realized, but also furious, and he quickly made a motion—

And the water retreated back to the shore as quickly as it had come. Scott lifted his hands and broke her grip in the way he'd learned from Parks long ago, taking a few defensive steps back as he dried himself with his powers, leaving her dripping, her robe partially open to reveal a one-piece bathing suit beneath. She didn't look quite like how he remembered her, but he didn't think she looked bad. A little wet and a lot irritated, and he did what he could to fix the former while hoping it would take care of the latter.

"I didn't come here looking for a fight," he said as the water streamed out of her robe and hair to his hands where he made a show of discarding it into the sand.

"You're wearing a suit and dress shoes on the beach," Sienna said, that irritation bleeding out as she stood there, looking less and less like a wet cat and more and more like a woman scorned. Which was odd, Scott thought, because he was the scorned one, really. "You can't tell me you're here to party."

"I'm filming an episode of *The Bachelor*," Scott quipped. "I'm sorry, but you're not getting a rose."

"Oh noes," Sienna said, narrowly slitted eyes watching him for signs of deception. "Whatever will I do?"

"Get over it, apparently," Scott said, trying to temper his own annoyance. "I came here because … I need your help."

That did not cause her to get less annoyed. "Bullshit," she said.

"No, really," Scott said, and he coughed. It wasn't a show; he was still gacking up that purple junk, though at least now he wasn't bleeding from the lungs anymore. "I had a clash with a couple of metas this morning who are on a downward spiral power trip—"

"That's my expression." And it was; he'd stolen it from her, though he couldn't recall when.

"Which describes what I'm dealing with here," Scott said, trying to put aside the edge of frustration that threatened to burst out. "We've got a Bonnie and Clyde of metas rolling through Florida right now."

"Nice. Taking care of that sounds like your job," Sienna said, turning her back on him and heading up the beach.

"Actually, hunting you is my job," Scott called after her.

"Way to go on that," she tossed back over her shoulder.

He gritted his teeth and started after her, coming alongside while trying to give her plenty of warning. "I know," he said, "I've been really bad at it. Intentionally, I might add."

"Is that so?" she asked, her robe still dangling open, apparently not so much concerned about it anymore. He looked, unashamedly. It wasn't a stretch for him to imagine why he'd been interested in her, even if he couldn't remember their relationship. "I'm up here," she said crossly, and drew her robe closed.

"You're not *just* up there," he fired back.

"The part you're supposed to talk to is."

"Well, the part of you that's supposed to listen didn't seem to be paying attention, so I figured I'd try a different tack." He started to put a hand on her shoulder to stop her but thought the better of it, grimacing. "Look—"

"How'd you find me?" she asked, keeping up her pace. It wasn't breakneck, or flying, so clearly she didn't intend to lose him … yet. "Anonymous tip?"

"What? No," Scott said. "The guy you were after in New York turned up dead in the US Virgin Islands. I'm not a great investigator, but I can put two and two together."

"It does? Well, if the FBI thing doesn't work out, you've got great career prospects as a remedial math teacher."

"Please," Scott said, gently touching her shoulder and causing her eyes to flare at the touch, "I've been avoiding you. Been keeping them off your trail."

"Why?" Sienna asked, not recoiling away, holding her ground, stiffly.

"Because of everything I put you through last year while I was chasing you."

"You weren't chasing me because you wanted to. You were chasing me because—"

"Because Harmon messed with my head? Maybe. But he had some stuff to work with, so I let him—"

"You didn't let him do anything," Sienna said, sighing. "He's a telepath. People with a hell of a lot less grievance than you got twisted against me by that asshole." She cringed. "You *are* an asshole, and you know it."

"*I* am?" Scott froze, staring at her, slow recognition dawning. "Wait. You didn't … is he … ?" he pointed at her head questioningly, "In there?"

"Unfortunately," Sienna said. "Not by my choice. He tricked me, the bastard."

"Tricked you … into absorbing his soul?" Scott goggled. "How did he do that, exactly?"

"He touched me a bunch of times when I wasn't paying

attention—you know what? People wanting to imprison themselves in my head isn't a fate I'd often considered worth guarding against. So it kind of snuck up on me when he did it, okay? I didn't see it coming."

Scott shook his head. "Fair enough. I don't think I would have, either."

But you're already in here, Scotty. Part of you, at least, Harmon's voice sounded sonorous, suddenly in his head.

"Gyah!" Scott said, spine straightening as every muscle in his back contracted.

Sienna stared at him as though he'd just lost his mind. "What?"

"He talked to me! In my head!" Scott drove his index finger into his temple so hard it stung.

Sienna seemed to think about that for a moment. "Huh. I knew he could read minds in here. I never thought about him being able to reach out to others."

From beyond the grave, yes, Harmon's voice came again, like a distant conversation he could hear on the wind. This time it was slightly less eerie.

"Why are you talking to me, man?" Scott asked, feeling his calm slipping away a little.

Because you betrayed me, Scott.

"You rewired my brain so I would serve you," Scott said.

Yes, but you betrayed me just the same. Like a blender going faulty at the exact moment when you need it to blend a shake.

"I don't believe for a second you make your own shakes," Scott said.

"Are you still talking to him?" Sienna asked. "Because this sounds like a weird conversation. Is this what I sound like to others when I'm talking to the people in my head?"

"Weirder," Scott said.

It's a metaphor, you simpleton, Harmon said.

"Harmon," Sienna said, "stop it, or I will cage you."

Bye, Scott, Harmon said. *We'll talk again soon.*

"I hope not," Scott said.

Sienna frowned. "Were you talking to him? Or hoping I wouldn't cage him?"

"Cage him all you want," Scott said, "please. I didn't

come here to have my brain read through by that bastard."

"He really is a bastard, isn't he?" Sienna nodded, staring off into the distance. "All right ... you want my help. Tell me what you've got, and ... I'll consider it."

8.

Scott showing up on the beach where I'd parked my ass for the last couple months was a bit of shocker, probably only marginally less shocking than Mr. 5%'s entire repertory of comments. It had really caught me off guard, but it was pretty telling that although I stormed away from him, mostly out of a cold and visceral anger from one of our last meetings (the one where he stopped me from keeping my house from burning to the ground), I hadn't immediately flown back to my room to retrieve my crap and vanish.

Yes, the head of the FBI Task Force assigned to hunt me had shown up at the place I was hiding, asked for my help, and I hadn't flown off. In Sienna Nealon world, this would be what I call "dumb."

"There's a couple of bandits working their way down the east coast," Scott said, falling into step beside me as I walked down the beach, my toes sinking slightly into the sand.

"Got a file for me to read?"

"No," he said, frowning. "But I can give you the particulars. Their names are June Randall and Elliot Lefavre—"

"Why haven't I heard about them on the news?" I asked. "You know, if they're tearing their way through the eastern US?"

Scott stopped, amusement lighting his features. "I think we both know that the media has no room in their heart or

37

airing schedule for any other dangerous meta but you right now."

Yep, that sounded right. "Point. Proceed."

"They haven't killed anyone yet," Scott said, a little sweeter and more gently than I would have expected given these were criminals he was pursuing. "I'd like to try and keep it that way."

I stopped, my feet squishing in the soft, wet sand where the tide had recently receded. "These things never go that way. Once someone gets a taste of that power, their ego kicks in. They run roughshod over lesser humans, and let's face it—cops are scared of metas, and rightly so. We're such a mixed bag, you never know what to expect. What are these two, anyway?"

"He's an aeolus," Scott said. "She's a poison type, not sure if it has a name. Creates clouds of toxin that—well, they're nasty. Acidic, and when you breathe it in, the stuff makes it feel like someone doused your lungs in gas and lit a match."

"Lovely," I said. "Why didn't you call Reed about this? He's back on duty. With a crew of his own, no less."

"Reed's good," Scott said, falling in next to me as I started walking again. "But he's not the best. Not at this sort of thing."

"Yeah, but he'd take a more compassionate line on these lawbreakers than I would." I made a face at him. "Come on. I'm the Queen of Mean now that Leona Helmsley is dead. My reputation is finding the bad guys and making them suffer. If you think I'm going to take it easy on a couple of petty crooks aiming to armed-rob their way into infamy …"

"I think you'll take it easy on them, yeah," Scott said, surprising me.

"Like I did for Nadine Griffin?" I asked dryly. "According to you, at least."

His face hardened slightly. "Let's not talk about Nadine."

I studied his face and decided to leave that one alone. "What do you think is going to happen with these two? July and Smelliot or whatever their names are?"

"Clever." He stared out over the ocean and gave it a long bit of thought. "I think if they keep going the way they are … they're going to go out like Bonnie and Clyde, for real. Just roll around a corner one day and find police waiting to mow them down, and nobody's going to mourn them, because let's face it, they're well on their way to earning that fate. When they put their first body in the morgue …"

"That does tend to be a game changer," I said solemnly. How many times had I seen this? Stupid kids with their heads all full of glory because they'd manifested superpowers and nobody could stop them without plugging them in the brain. Surprisingly, drilling someone at a distance wasn't as popular an option as you might think.

Dozens of times, I'd seen some variation of this power-mad spiral. Dozens. And only one of them ever turned out to be a humble, willing-to-take-penance person rather than an angry, confrontational, socially maladjusted miscreant drunk on their own awesomeness.

But the thought lingered—What if this was a trap? A trick on Scott's part to get me somewhere that he could spring a trap of his own on me?

Then you will break out of it, leaving corpses aplenty strewn in your wake, Wolfe said lustily.

Or maybe just fly off, Zack said. *No corpses necessary.*

Boring, Bjorn said.

What was the alternative, though, really? Sitting on this beach for another six months? Failing to put the damned fork down as I ate and drank through my feelings of loneliness, uselessness, and self-pity? Because that was working out so well.

I vote no on that one, Bastian said.

Yes, your ass has gotten fat enough, Eve said.

Seconded, Harmon said. *Thirded, fourthed—all the way up, actually, because your additional square footage allows—*

Asshole! I thought at him, very hard, and also slapped him hard enough mentally to make him cry out in my head. He earned it.

"Okay," I said, putting aside my reservations as I looked

at my ex and imagined all the different ways this idea could go horribly, horribly wrong. Still ... it was better than continuing to do the nothing I'd done these last few months. "I'm in."

9.

June

The hotel was nice, not cheap, which June liked, and pretty far from the beach, which she didn't. She and Ell were laid out on the bed, the deed done again, their bodies entangled. She had her head nestled in the crook of his arm and nuzzled against the faint layer of chest hair that covered his barely-there pecs. She sighed contentedly. "This was nice. It's always nice."

"Yeah," Ell said, sounding preoccupied. He hadn't quite been himself during the act, as though his mind was elsewhere. That wasn't a huge surprise, though, was it? He'd been a little off all day, acting a little outside the usual bounds.

She nuzzled him again, then rested her sweaty hair against his shoulder, closing her eyes. That was all right. Everyone had their off days.

"Why did you do that to that man on the beach?" Ell blurted out.

June's eyes snapped open, and she blinked furiously. She lifted her head off his chest and shot him a fiery gaze as her breath caught in her throat. "This is how you come at me? Right now? After that?"

Ell's eyes widened, then darted left and right as he sat up and leaned against his elbows. "I—I didn't—I mean—"

"No, this is great. Just great," June said, throwing off the sheets and getting out of bed. She let her hair fall over her

41

shoulder in a tangled knot as she headed for the bathroom.

"You didn't need to do that to him," Ell called after her as she sat down heavily on the toilet. He appeared a few seconds later as she flushed and went to wash her hands, staring at herself in the mirror, still nude. "And at the convenience store—"

"You totally wussed out at the convenience store, Elliot," she said, using his full name like a blunt instrument.

He took a staggered step back as though she'd struck him. "I—I was just trying to keep things from getting worse—"

"So you're saying I make things worse?" She pushed past him, not particularly gently, and snatched her tank top tee off the floor, hurriedly pulling it on. She didn't want to be naked right now. Not anymore. It felt too intimate for the moment.

"I'm not saying—"

"Sure you are," she said, throwing it right back at him. "You always say it. Every time we fight. I can see it in your eyes, even when you're not saying it."

"Why are you so angry with people?" Ell asked, throwing his arms wide.

"I'm not angry with people. I'm angry with *stupid* people. There's a difference."

"You almost killed that guy on the beach," Ell said. "In front of his daughter—"

"Oh, who cares about him?" June said, grabbing her panties and working her way into them.

"His daughter, obviously," Ell said.

"Well, she's got to grow up sometime," June said. "The world's not all sunshine and rainbows. My parents died way before I was her age. This is a good lesson for her. She'll probably appreciate him more now."

"If he lives," Ell said. "You might have killed him! And then at the convenience store, you got in a fight with an FBI agent—"

"What should I have done? Let him cuff us and take us away?"

"We should have left before he showed up!" Ell burst out in a fury. "Like I wanted to!"

June just stared at him, her jeans up but unbuttoned. "There we go."

Ell hesitated, his anger fading a little as puzzlement set in. "There we go, what?"

"You said it." June focused on buttoning her pants.

"Said what?"

"Like *you* wanted to," June said, not looking up at him as she tugged her zipper up.

"So?"

"So," June said, "it's just like it always is. Elliot knows best. It's gotta be Elliot's way or it's wrong."

Ell shook his head as if trying to avoid a cloud of toxin. "I'm talking about this time, this *one* time—"

"Oh, it's like this every time," June said. "Don't fool yourself. You think you're so smart, and I'm just some dumb Midwestern girl who stumbled off a farm or something. 'Oh, please, Mr. City Slicker guy, won't you show my rural rube ass how the world works?'" She turned her back on him and slapped her own bottom to illustrate the point. "Which is bullshit, because I know more than you, obviously. Especially in the bedroom."

Ell looked stunned, completely thrown off balance. "I don't—what does that have to do with—I mean, I'm not saying I know more than you or anything—"

"Sure you are. You say it all the time. You say it without saying it, you bring it up all. The. Time."

"I don't—"

"I've lived in the world, okay?" June stared at him angrily. "You didn't just rescue me off some farm when we met—"

"I know that, I was there—"

"I was living my life. I had a life before you. I know what I'm doing."

"I know that. I wasn't saying you didn't—"

"I've had experience. More than you, in fact—"

"Come on, June! You keep bringing that up, like I care you've slept with way more people than me—"

She stopped arguing and favored him with a cold glare. "There it is."

Ell froze, argument gone again, a kind of sick look in his

eyes, like he knew he'd stepped in it again. "There … what … is?"

"I'm so sick of you calling me a slut!" June said, storming past him. She was headed for the door. The volume of their voices had risen to the point where this shout was one among many they'd let off in the last few minutes, and it verged on a scream.

"I didn't call you that!"

"Yes, you did!"

"No, I didn't!"

She reached the door and started to open it, Ell three steps behind her. Her hair was still a mess, her tank top was wrinkled and clinging to her sweaty skin, and she only just slipped on her sandals at the door. "Yes, you fucking did!" she said, throwing the door open to the hotel hallway.

Ell tried to grab the door, and she started to slam it on him. He caught it with a hand and held it open, struggling against her strength. She was stronger than he was, that was just a fact. She could whip his ass in an arm wrestling contest any day. They knew that from experience.

Her hands were slick with sweat, and Elliot yanked the door right out of her grip. It hurt a little, and it shocked her. June's face burned. She was pissed off and humiliated that Elliot—that little shit, he was supposed to be weaker than her, supposed to *know his place*—had just outmatched her.

She hauled off and slapped him right across the cheek, the noise ringing down the hotel hallway.

He staggered back a step, then caught his balance. His face was all bawled up, his hand pressed against his cheek, which had already turned red from the slap.

June stared at him, fire in her eyes, about ready to deliver another, when something about the pitiful way that he looked at her caused her to hesitate.

What the hell had she just done?

"Oh, God," she said, "what did we just do?"

Ell scrambled back from the door, still cradling his cheek, tears already starting to drip down his cheeks. June came back inside and closed the door, but softly, and then chased after him as he retreated from her. He held out a hand to keep her back but she brushed it aside easily and grabbed him in a hug, pulling him close as he writhed. "Oh, God, Ell, I'm so sorry, I'm so sorry. We shouldn't have done that. But you pushed me. You just pushed me and pushed me, and—and I couldn't—I mean, you have to see it—you can't grab the door out of my hand like that when I'm—shhhhhh."

He was sobbing softly now, his shoulders heaving gently against her chest. He said nothing.

"It's okay, it's okay," she said. He'd stopped his half-hearted struggling and was crying quietly, his tears soaking the front of her tank top. "It's just—we let it get out of hand, that's all. It was a mistake—"

"You hit me," he said quietly, in a voice of utter betrayal.

June resisted the urge to lash back, to tell him it was his own damned fault. That wasn't right, was it? They were both to blame. "I'm sorry," she said instead. She had a little bit of trouble getting the words out, but they came. "This place was a mistake."

Ell sniffled. "This … hotel?"

"Florida," she said. "Don't you see? Everything's been wrong since we came here. We shouldn't have gone south, I told you. It's all been wrong since we got here. We need to go north. And then west, once we're out of this—this tiny dick-shaped hellhole."

Ell laughed through his tears on that one. "It … it is kind of shaped like one."

She smiled and lifted his head off her chest. "We need to leave. We need a little money—more than last time—and then we should just go. We didn't argue like this before, when we weren't here—"

Ell hesitated, his eyes searching up and down. He was thinking about Cuba again, probably. She felt the embers of rage start to burn. So help her, if he brought up Cuba, she'd—

Well, she didn't know what she'd do. She was just so sick of hearing it. Why couldn't he see? His idea of going to Cuba was what was killing them, though she didn't want to say it, not now. Who wanted to go to Cuba? Not even the Cubans wanted to be there, which was why they kept getting on rafts that were barely seaworthy and hurling themselves into the damned ocean. You didn't do that if you liked where you were.

"Yeah, okay," Ell said, sniffling again. "But … no one gets hurt this time, okay? You have to promise."

She looked him, afraid to let out a breath of relief. He hadn't mentioned Cuba, and maybe, just maybe, they were finally going to do what she wanted to do. At fucking last. "No one gets killed. I can't promise the hurt thing, because sometimes, in a robbery, people get hurt. But it won't be like the beach," she gave him that little victory, "or the convenience store. We'll be in and out as fast as possible, and no one will get killed, okay?"

His skepticism felt heavy, like a weight. "Okay," he finally said with a nod. "Okay." He looked around, then mopped at his cheeks with his hand, succeeding in doing nothing but smearing the tears that had drained like rivers down them. "Let me get my stuff."

"Shhh, not yet," she said, pulling him close and kissing him. She couldn't just leave it like this. Not after what they'd just done.

"What are you doing?" he asked when they broke from the kiss. He was kinda smiling, like he knew but was fishing for the answer.

She let go of him and sat back on the bed, scooting up so she could lay herself across it suggestively. "I just … hate to leave this nice hotel before we get a chance to make up …" She batted her eyelashes at him in a way that was so far beyond seductive that it immediately elicited a laugh, which was what she was aiming for. "Come here, baby," she said, motioning him to her.

He sat down on the edge of the bed, clearly hesitant to go further—yet. "I—just don't think—"

"Shhh," she said again, rising up to all fours to lean across and kiss him again, long and full of passion, enough that when they parted, he kept his eyes closed for a few seconds. "Don't think," she said. "Just … be with me."

"All right," he said as he opened his eyes. All trace of the sadness that had choked him like a poison was gone, and she pulled him forward, onto the bed with her, as he giggled and laughed, with only a little less enthusiasm than before.

10.

Sienna

Making my way from the beautiful, sunny, island of St. Thomas in the Caribbean to Westerville, Ohio, while one of the FBI's Most Wanted fugitives should have been more difficult than it was. But then, I was not a normal fugitive, and I was traveling in the company of the FBI agent who was supposed to hunt me down.

Traveling with him in my arms. Like a bride.

"This is so ... degrading," Scott muttered, the state of Kentucky below us in all its green, mountainous splendor. It was the middle of the day, and I was keeping to the clouds as much as possible. The weather had obliged, fortunately, the skies overcast and grey from about fifty miles off the Florida coast. I also kept us at an altitude high enough to allow us to stay somewhat invisible to ground observation yet still not gasp for breath.

Yippee.

"Quit your whining," I said. "Think about all the TSA checkpoints and waiting at the gate you'd have had to do if you'd flown commercial. This way, all you have to do is sit there and avoid touching my skin."

He looked me over. "Thanks for changing, by the way. I don't think this would have been made any easier by your robe and, uhh ... whatever beneath."

"It's called a swimsuit, jackass." It just wasn't much of one, admittedly. I hadn't bared my belly, because I'd gotten a little self-conscious of late. If the internet had made fun of me for my non-model shape before, they wouldn't get any kinder after my time in St. Thomas.

"I'm a little mystified why this is the path you wanted to take," he said, nodding at the ground passing thousands of feet below us. "Shouldn't we have gone to Florida and hung out, waiting for the next hit?"

"Maybe," I said. It was a tough call, because in theory these two bandits had just hit a convenience store and maybe had a few bucks to spend. If they followed their pattern, they wouldn't surface again for a little bit, and when they did, it'd almost certainly be because they needed money and were robbing someone to get it. Which, again in theory, left us a little time to do some background investigation.

But if they ended up popping their stupid heads up early, I was going to be super embarrassed, because we wouldn't be in any kind of position to stop them. "How far off are we?" I asked.

"I dunno," Scott said, still sounding a little surly at being carried in this way. Like he had cause to whine; men had carried women like this for centuries. He was heavy enough that I might have felt it if I wasn't using my Wolfe power, but I would have been able to maintain the carry across the entire trip even so.

"Well, you've got the GPS."

"Oh, right." He looked down and thumbed his phone to life. "Good thing I muted these voice warnings. Turns out it's had to recalculate about a thousand times since last I checked because you keep off-roading." He held it up so I could see. The message: "Off route. Recalculating," was emblazoned across the screen again, then again as I apparently skipped over the road it suggested I take around a mountain in favor of just flying over the peak.

"They should make a GPS for me," I said. "Call it, 'As The Sienna Flies.'"

"It would sell one copy."

"It would sell *at least* one copy," I said. "There are almost certainly other flying metas out there, especially at the rate which new ones are cropping up."

Scott's jaw tightened. "You wouldn't know anything about our sudden relative explosion of meta problems, would you?"

"I would know a little about it," I said. "I would know that it's not a natural phenomenon."

He gave me the 'No, Duh' look. "Anything else?"

"I'd blame Edward Cavanagh and his serum for it, but he's so long dead that I don't think he's directly behind it." I paused to think about a rogue possibility. "Though I suppose it's possible he used some of his considerable fortune to gradually drib and drab that meta-making serum out in random spots across our country and possibly others, though it's tougher to tell. Obviously we're seeing a lot more activity, especially in the US, than the six hundred or so supposedly surviving metas should be able to generate on their own. Also, I've met a lot of metas in these last two, three years who were not born to the powers."

Scott nodded. "Yeah. Quite a few people who reached an awfully advanced age before manifesting."

"Exactly." I thought of Jamie Barton, AKA Gravity, in Staten Island, who'd been in her late thirties/early forties before her power had shown up. Or Caden Sims, who had flatly admitted to artificially inducing powers in himself before he'd gotten himself killed by ArcheGrey only a couple months prior. "I suppose I should feel bad for the people in charge of policing that, because hoo, boy, if things continue apace, they are going to be busy, busy, busy." I must have said it a little too gleefully. Scott gave me a very cross look, probably because I was talking about him like he wasn't even there.

"And yet here you are, doing a little policing of it yourself," Scott said when he got his smartass facial expression under control again. "And not for the first time, either."

"I'm sure I don't know what you're talking about."

"I'm sure a Denny's in Pennsylvania that needs a new coat of paint—oh, and a new everything else—would disagree with you."

"First of all, restaurants can't talk, they're inanimate. And second of all … whut? I clearly don't even eat, so, I have no idea what you're talking about." I practically dared him to call me a liar on that one. Though I would have had a hard time denying it, because when I had shed the robe and dressed before we left, I'd found I had to hold my breath to button my new jeans.

Whatever. The weight helped hide my true identity. Yeah. That was a good enough excuse.

Scott wisely remained silent on the subject. "What are you hoping to find out from—"

"From Ohio?" We were on our way to see June's grandmother, who had apparently raised her. "Background, mostly. I want to know who this girl is, what kind of person she was before she got drunk on her own power. Mostly …" I got serious, because this was serious business, "… I want to know if she's the kind of person you save, or that you have put down like a rabid dog."

Scott squirmed a little in my arms. "I brought you in on this in order to make sure we didn't have to put them down."

I shook my head. "Sorry, but you don't get to make that determination."

He raised an eyebrow and sounded vaguely outraged when he said, "But I'm in charge!"

"Not of me," I said politely. "And with all due respect to your position—"

"Which is your way of saying, 'I have no respect for your position.'"

"I have plenty of respect for the position. It's your boss I have no respect for, and you're technically just his mouthpiece or hand or … codpiece, maybe, if you make him look good. Inadequate codpiece if you're making him look inferior."

Scott snorted at that. "I don't think I've ever been pleased to be called an inadequate codpiece, but … here we are."

I chuckled. "So … Phillips is still in charge? Even after Harmon blew out?"

President *Harmon, please.*

"You're such an officious jackass, Gerry."

Scott frowned at my internal/external dialogue. "Yeah, Phillips is still in charge," he said, ignoring my outburst. "And he hasn't changed much."

"He wouldn't have," I said, "Harmon never mentally manipulated him."

Scott stared straight ahead, eyes suddenly unfocused. "Oh, wow. I never thought anyone could be that ... I don't even know how to describe it ... without being brainwashed."

"He's a horrendous shitbag," I said, and Scott snapped around to look at me in surprise. "Well, it does cover it, you have to admit."

"I freely admit it," Scott said with a nod. The phone in his hand beeped. "Speak of the devil."

"I wouldn't answer that up here."

Scott shot me a sly grin. "Because he'll hear the rush of the wind and suss out that I'm being carried across the skies in your arms?"

"No," I said with great amusement, "because cell phone service up here is really spotty."

He pondered that for a second. "Good," he said, and answered the phone. "Hello? Hello ... ? Yes, it's me, I can barely hear you ... the static is terrible ... I don't know if I'm going to be able to ..." He lifted the phone and looked at the screen with a faint grin. "What a shame. I lost him."

"What a shame indeed," I said. We both had another good chuckle as we cruised over the wide, brown Ohio River below as the phone chirped again, recalculating its course for the umpteenth time.

11.

Westerville was a suburb of Columbus, Ohio, one of countless places on the map I'd never been. In truth, I didn't have any real desire to visit there because it wasn't well known for its natural splendor, like, say, Colorado or Arizona, and it didn't have any sort of massive cultural relevance to recommend it, like New York City. But then again, most people probably had the same opinion of Minneapolis, and it was my happy home. Or had been, until I'd had to rabbit.

The GPS guided us to a house in the middle of sprawling suburbia. Houses built in the sixties, seventies and eighties stretched as far as the eye could see when I came down for my landing, in the middle of the day, as fast as I could, Scott holding tightly to me so we could minimize our chance of being seen and photographed together. Probably wouldn't look good for the head of my task force to get photographed, you know, being carried by the subject of his womanhunt.

I hovered in the branches of an old tree, the boughs thick enough to shield us from sight as we both scanned the street for anyone watching. No one was around, the kids presumably in school and adults at work, and the weather was probably a little above fifty; not really the temperature preferred by most.

"I think we're good," Scott said, peering through the branches, looking for motion. Other than a squirrel we'd scared the hell out of when we came down, I hadn't seen any movement at all.

We set down on the lawn and brushed ourselves off. "Not sure TSA wouldn't have been better," Scott said, opening and closing his jaw, probably trying to pop his ears.

"I could give you a quick grope to simulate the experience, if it'd make you feel better," I quipped without thinking that one through. I turned away to avoid his reaction and pulled a twig out of the collar of my blouse.

"Not sure 'better' is the word I'd use to describe the effect of a grope," Scott said under his breath as we walked across the slightly soggy lawn toward the front door. Apparently they'd experienced either some rain or melting snow recently.

I reached out and rang the bell, taking a moment to fix up my hair, but also let it fall over my eyes in a version of the formerly popular Rachel hairdo. It was jet black right now, because I'd brought a wig with me when I'd dropped off my luggage somewhere on the east coast of Florida. Scott noticed my motion and eyed me warily. "What?" I asked.

"It's a good color on you," he said, and I knew he was lying because—hell, I slept with the man for a year and vacuumed up all his memories of our relationship.

I didn't press it, though, and a few seconds later the door opened a crack and an older lady peered out. She wore big glasses, looked to be an inch or two shorter than me, and had that shuffle that seemed to come with advanced age and lessened activity. By looking at her I would have put her in her early seventies. "Yes?" she asked.

"Ms. Randall," Scott said, stepping forward and flipping open his leather FBI ID wallet, "I'm Agent Byerly with the FBI, and this is Agent Nelson," he inclined his head toward me. "We're here to talk to you about your granddaughter."

"Oh, come in," she said, immediately making way for us. The door opened on a long hallway that was covered on both sides with cross-stitched pictures of various things. I saw one of a very blocky, almost pixelated cat. Another, of the state of Ohio with various landmarks stitched in, sort of leapt out at me as I stepped into the house's entryway ahead of Scott.

Grandma Randall shut the door behind us with all her strength, which resulted in the door making the burping sort of noise a Tupperware makes. She clicked the heavy padlock and paced past us, heading down the hall toward a kitchen I could see ahead. To our left sat a formal living room that looked like it hadn't seen use in years, and she stopped halfway down the hall and then shuffled back toward us. "I was going to get you something to drink, but I suppose I should help you find a place to sit, first—"

"We're fine—" Scott started.

"I'm parched, something to drink would be great," I said, drawing a sour look from him. "But really, we can just follow you and talk," I added, to get the conversational aspect of our visit back on track. I knew Scott's worry, and it wasn't that Ms. Randall would run. It was that she'd take forever in the kitchen while we sat in the living room and stared at each other awkwardly.

"All right," she said, and turned around, painfully slowly, to head toward the kitchen again. We passed a couple of doors to bedrooms that were partially pulled to, keeping us from looking around inside. Yet. Either Scott or myself was destined to pull the old, "Can I use your bathroom?" trick, which we would invariably use to snoop around the house for incriminating evidence on June's life before going on the run.

We followed a few steps behind Ms. Randall as she moved toward the kitchen at a glacial pace, trading a look that said we were thinking the same thing: we didn't trust ourselves to get too close for fear we might just run her over.

She finally made it about halfway down the cross-stitch-covered hallway where it split out into the kitchen or continued as a hall into what looked like a bathroom. We veered into the kitchen, where we were treated to a decorating scheme right out of the eighties. Green cabinets, white laminate counters, and a modern fridge—stainless steel, probably replaced in the last decade—setting up a hell of clash in styles. Personally, I was rooting for the eighties to win, mostly because after I left, I would never have to see this gaudy shit ever again.

Ms. Randall hobbled to the fridge and opened it. "I have tea, and Diet Coke, and water, of course … I can put on some coffee …" Her voice echoed out from the depths of the modern fridge as the cooling engine kicked on to replace some of the cold air as she parked herself in the opening.

"Water is fine for me," I said as Scott continued to study the room. There was a long counter that made way for an old, electric stove with heating coils that snaked across the cook top. Cabinets overhung almost every surface. They were built low, obscuring the pass-through into the dining room I could see beyond. It was dark in there, and somewhere off to the right, I suspected, was Ms. Randall's sitting room, because it was clear when I passed it that the formal living room wasn't getting much use. "Can I use your bathroom?" I asked, figuring I'd just cut straight to it while Scott waited for her to finish getting drinks.

Scott, wise to my ruse, shot me another irritated look. You snooze, you lose, bucko.

"Certainly," Ms. Randall warbled, closing the refrigerator door and halting all progress, which caused Scott to sigh, almost inaudibly, at the knowledge that I'd just screwed him over and locked him into talking to her while she fetched drinks. "It's down the hall here," she pointed around the corner back toward where the hallway continued from the entry.

"Thanks," I said, and darted off with a smirk at Scott that caused him to twitch a little. "Remember, I wanted a water." And I disappeared around the corner.

"What was your name again?" I heard Ms. Randall ask as I left.

"Agent Byerly," Scott said in the slightly louder way that people used around those who don't fully comprehend them, as though yelling it at her might make her remember it better.

I escaped back into the dark, cross-stitch-covered walls and was greeted with a picture of a vase filled with flowers, but, you know, cross-stitched. I had to give Ms. Randall credit, though; she'd used different colors of thread to give the flowers some shading, which rendered the whole thing a little blocky but still kind of neat. Not the sort of thing I'd hang on my wall in a million years—not that I had walls at this point—but still. I respected the skill.

I didn't even bother going to the bathroom. I skipped it and went straight for the nearest bedroom door, dipping inside and closing it before I turned on the light. When I flipped the switch, I knew immediately I had the wrong room.

How, you ask?

Why, because of the smell, which was heavy with the scent of cloth and thread, and because there was sewing stuff EVERYWHERE.

An old black Singer sewing machine that looked like it had been through every year of Ms. Randall's life with her sat in the corner, and quilt racks lined with (presumably) her compositions hung on one of the walls. Cross-stitch patterns occupied another table, along with the little blocky pattern thingies that one used when making them. My mother had decided we should take up cross-stitch as a hobby at one point in my early teenage years, figuring it might be a good way to keep me more occupied in my forced incarceration in our home. I hadn't realized she had superior metahuman dexterity at the time, and I still had a hard time believing it now, given exactly how many times she'd pricked her fingers and sworn during the week that she'd attempted that hobby. I'd laughed a lot during that time, and learned a few new swear words that were now part of my regular vocabulary.

Good times.

I gave the room a last glance, and stumbled on the corner she'd evidently dedicated to crochet. Sweet fancy Moses, was there a thread-based hobby this woman didn't have?

Turning out the lights, I opened the door and crept out, down the hall toward the bathroom. I was ready to gamble on the next door being the one, but listened carefully for Scott and Ms. Randall, just to be sure I wasn't missing anything important, like her strangling him.

"Would you like some orange juice?" she asked.

"No," he said, and I could tell by the strain in his voice he was trying to be polite and still succeeding, but barely.

"Tea?"

"Uh … no. Again. I'm fine."

"… I have some Diet Sprite in the garage refrigerator."

Chuckling madly to myself, I kept on down the hall and opened the next door, the one right next to the bathroom. It was so far off the kitchen, I didn't bother to wait before flipping the light.

Bingo.

I found myself in the room of a teenage girl, one replete with posters for girls soccer, a desk in the corner cluttered with old school yearbooks, and a layer of dust that indicated nothing in the place had seen use in quite some time.

There probably wasn't anything seriously incriminating here, but I wanted to give it a good look over, just in case, so I slid open the closet door and moved the clothes on the rack. There weren't many; presumably June had packed most of her crap and taken it with her when she'd cleared out. I made a mental note to ask about the circumstances of her departure, especially since Grandma Randall hadn't asked us yet why we were here, and didn't seem to be in a particular hurry to, either.

There wasn't anything of particular interest in the top of the closet; a couple old shoe boxes filled with notes that looked like they'd been passed back and forth in high school. The content was about what you'd expect: "Oh, Jessie, you're so my BFF." "You're my BFF, too!" scrawled in return. Plainly, they'd lacked cell phones with which to exchange these oh-so-important missives. There were also a couple letters from a guy named Jackson that had red-pen drawn hearts all over them in the same flowery hand that was evident in the other letters. I wondered if she'd gotten these letters back when she and Jackson had done their inevitable and probably drama-laden break-up.

I rifled through the desk and found the usual mishmash of pens, old tape, paperclips and assorted crap. It had all been picked over a while ago, I suspected, either when June left or sometime shortly thereafter, judging by the thin layer of dust on everything. The desk had a pure white, laminate surface and looked like it could be tilted so that someone could draw on it, but based on the fact that there was no sign it had been used thus even before she'd left, I had to guess June wasn't much of a drawer or drafter.

There was a dust shadow in the shape of a square that suggested June probably had a laptop computer she'd taken with her. Not surprising, really. I thumbed through the yearbooks, and it took me a second to realize that the "K.I.T!" scrawled next to a lot of the signatures probably meant, "Keep in touch." Which led me to wonder if she had, because that would make things easier.

If she had a laptop, June probably had a cell phone. That was an avenue we needed to pursue, because with FBI resources behind us, tracking her cell phone down was probably one of the easiest ways to find her. Case over, *et voila.*

On the other hand ... maybe I should hold back on that one, since I didn't necessarily want this case to end just yet.

I stood in the middle of the room, thigh brushing against the bed, and had a thought. When had June manifested her toxic powers? I hadn't found any evidence of a diary, which would have been a hell of a boon because diaries gave insight into how a person thought. If she kept a diary regularly, she probably would have brought it with her, but ... maybe not. And if she'd manifested before she left, it was possible that I could get some keen insight from it. Otherwise I would probably have to go talk to her friends, because what teenage girl shares much of anything with her grandmother, let alone the fact that she's going through an unexpected, superpowered metamorphosis?

Stooping low, I lifted the skirt of the bed to peer beneath it. There wasn't anything down there except a couple soccer balls that were just as dusty as the rest of the room, so I lifted the mattress.

Bonanza! But not the kind I could really use, because it was just a couple of nudie-dude mags. I thumbed through them, just in case she'd hidden a diary in their pages, but alas, all I saw were amply muscled, oiled-up, well-hung men. Drat.

Soft footsteps and a coughing fit from Scott jarred me out of my search just as I was replacing the naughty magazines under the mattress. Wouldn't want to deprive June of her entertainment on the off chance she survived this and the stretch in prison she was looking at for multiple robberies. Those dude mags might come in handy in there.

"Are you quite finished?" Grandma Randall asked from outside the door.

"Almost," I said, adjusting the mattress as she opened the door. I was shameless, because when you're caught snooping, any excuse you use just sounds lame. "Unless you know where she keeps a secret diary."

Scott appeared behind Grandma Randall, eyes narrow with irritation, either at my being caught or at me sticking him with her for the last several minutes. "I don't know how she heard you," he said, by way of apology. "The clatter in the kitchen was crazy."

"I do," I said, staring right at Grandma Randall. She stared right back. "You're a meta, aren't you?"

"For a few centuries longer than you have been, dear," Mrs. Randall said, flinty gaze not betraying a hint of give, "or should I say ... Ms. Nealon."

12.

June

"It's going to be okay," June said, putting her hand on Ell's thigh and squeezing the denim jeans that covered his leg. Sun streamed in through the car windows as they sat there, him trying to work up the resolve to go through with this, and her trying to coax him. It was no use badgering him hard, not now. She'd gotten too close to the edge with him earlier, and there was the faintest hint of guilt and remorse tugging at the back of her mind for how she'd slapped him.

Push him again now, too hard, and he might break, or run, and she didn't want either of those things. However mad he made her during his moments of alternating weakness and willfulness, in almost all the others he made her happy, and she wanted that immensely.

Ell was breathing quickly, sounding like he wasn't all that far from a panic attack, and said, "You promise, right? No one gets hurt? No one gets killed?"

"Scout's honor," June said, holding up her right hand. "We'll do this clean. We just need getaway money, and as long as no one interferes with us … we're golden."

He stopped, his heaving chest slowing. "What's going to happen if someone does … interfere?"

"We'll hurt them only as much as it takes to put them down, get them out of the way," she said. This was what he wanted, this was what she would try to do. "But you're just obsessing about this, and you know most of the time no one

61

even sticks a head up during our robberies. They cower. Because people are cowards." She patted his leg again, then let her hand linger, trying to give him a different kind of motivation. "You need to think about the cool parts of this. We're bank robbers. It's like—like *Heat*—"

"That didn't end well for the robbers …"

"Okay, so … it's like *Pulp Fiction*. Remember, bae?" She leaned in toward him. "We watched that on your iPad. You loved it."

He screwed up his face in concentration. "That heist didn't go so well, either."

June felt her patience start to wane. "Yeah, but it was cool the whole time. And that one didn't go well because they robbed a place where two mob enforcers were eating. I doubt there are any mob enforcers making a deposit here in—" She glanced at the sign of the bank. "What is this town again?"

"Uhm," Ell closed his eyes to think. "Merritt Island, I think it's called."

"Whatever," June pronounced. "I don't think any mob enforcers are going to be making bank deposits in Merritt Island, Florida this afternoon, coincidentally just as we're robbing this place." She rubbed his thigh. "Come on. We can do this. In and out in five minutes." A joke occurred to her, but she withheld it because she wanted to pump him up, not deflate him.

"Okay," Ell said, nodding once. This was as ready as she'd get him.

She got out of the car and he matched her motion on the other side. She straightened her tank top, looking around casually but not too casually. They were wearing sunglasses but no other disguises, because … why bother?

They were metas. The world was their oyster. And the money in this place? It was theirs for the taking.

June led the way, up to the squat, concrete building. It was so bland, so blank, and she threw open the door to the small alcove of a lobby where the ATM stood. She had an idea right there. They needed a pry bar, because they always passed these ATMs that were just filled with cash, but it wasn't like they could claw in with just their hands. A good pry bar, though? They could probably pop it open on their way out, and it'd take thirty seconds with their meta strength and provide a nice little bonus haul to what they'd get out of the bank itself.

As she breezed in the door, June looked around for a guard. None in sight; the bank was pretty open, a nice, wide field of vision from the teller counters to the cubicle desks where the bankers approved or disapproved loans as their hearts desired. She sneered at them, adjusting her sunglasses self-consciously. People played such funny little games with their lives. Sheep. Suckers. June didn't want to be one of those, always on the mercy of other people. Her grandmother had always talked about fitting in, blending in with the normals.

Why in the hell would she want to do that?

"Start the party," June said as Ell took up position beside her, and she nodded to the little island with its deposit slips and chained pens for people to fill out their paperwork before they stood in the line for the bank to acknowledge them.

Ell loosed a massive burst of wind. She could see him strain as he did it, and the tornado hit the little island and uprooted it from where it had been sealed into the bank floor. Wood tore, metal squealed, the wind howled, little pens on chains broke loose from their restrictive holders and went flying in all directions.

June just laughed, because people were already screaming and they hadn't even done anything bad to them. "All right," she shouted, "this is a robbery!" She puffed a purple cloud out of her fingertips and hauled it along. "If you mess with us, he—" she gestured to Ell, "will send you through a glass window, and I will send one of these," she puffed the toxic cloud toward the line of about five people waiting for the tellers, "into your face, where it will burn your skin off." She sneered a little as she said it. Technically, she did have the power to do that, but it would require her summoning up almost all the toxin she had in order to make its consistency strong enough to cause burns.

"I want to see hands in the air," Ell said. His voice was a little shaky, but people started putting hands up, so evidently they didn't hear the shakiness. He kept his palm out, ready to send any heroes straight to their asses to rethink their plans.

June walked up to the counter as a blond lady dressed like a professional, her purse slung over her shoulder and a look of horror on her face, stepped back from where she was taking out money. "You don't mind if I borrow this, do you?" she asked, pointing to the bills the teller had been counting out for the woman.

Judging from the woman's face, she minded quite a bit, but to her credit, she only hesitated a second before saying, "Take it."

"Good choice," June said. "Go stand over there with them." She waved the woman back to the line, and kept the little purple cloud hovering on her shoulder in case she needed it. Not for the first time, she thought it'd be damned cool to have Ell's powers combined with hers. Then she could move the cloud around a lot easier. As it was she, could haul her toxin around with her, but she couldn't make it move nearly as fast as he could. She could still get one in a person's face relatively quickly if they were close, but at a distance? Nope. The cloud crawled toward them. She could run and thrust her hand in their face easier. "Give me the cash," June told the teller. "But no dye packs, and no bills off the bottom of the drawer, okay?"

The teller nodded her understanding. June shifted her attention to the other tellers down the line; there were only two more working today, apparently, which was why they had a nice line formed. She didn't even have to ask, the other tellers sprang into action.

June looked back at Ell to see how he was doing. He was covering the crowd, hand up, his gaze flicking attentively over them and then back to her. He nodded once, as if to let her know he was all right, then got back to the serious business of policing the crowd. She doubted they'd try anything. It was their good luck that there hadn't been a guard—

The thought no sooner sprang to mind than June heard a

click behind her and Ell turned, his wide eyes panicky.

"Don't move," said a male voice tight with tension. June could practically hear him standing there on unsteady legs, and knew what she'd find before she even turned around.

A security guard with a gun leveled at her, his finger on the trigger.

13.

Sienna

Nothing gets your attention quite like being a wanted fugitive traveling under an assumed name only to have someone throw your real one right in your face. My eyes widened, my pulse shot up, and I tried to keep a straight face while deciding whether to lie or just tell the truth to the formerly kindly little old lady standing in front of me.

"You don't seem too concerned about me murdering you horribly right now," I said coolly, and a little more nicely.

"You could try," Grandma Randall said. "I may not look like it, but I could put up a fight."

Scott watched with something bordering on horror. "Listen, Ms. Randall, we're here about your granddaughter."

"Are you?" She looked over at me. "What has she gotten herself into this time?"

I looked at Scott with surprise. He hadn't mentioned anything about a record on this girl; then again, the confused look on his face suggested to me he didn't know anything about it. "She's on the run in Florida," Scott said. "She's … committed a few robberies."

"Oh, goodness," Ms. Randall said, putting a hand on her chest. "Let's go sit in the living room. I've got your water," she said, nodding toward me.

We followed her out, and to her credit, she didn't do that stupid shuffle-step thing this time, which I now realized was pure theater. She walked like a normal person thirty years younger than she looked and seated herself in a chair in front of a window with the drapes open to let light stream in. The walls here too were covered in various thread-based pieces of art from quilts to a massive cross-stitched picture of a meadow complete with blue sky and flowers. Grandma Randall sat there staring straight ahead, shaking her head. "I really did do my best with that girl, but it wasn't easy."

Scott and I took our cue and uneasily sat next to each other in the only other seat in the place—an old couch covered in plastic that squeaked as we sat down. He looked at me, I looked at him; it wasn't a very long couch, and there were crocheted pillows filling either end, so we were stuck a little closer together than either of us would have preferred. "How do you mean?" Scott asked once he'd settled in.

"She had a will of her own," Grandma Randall said, lost in thought. "And she started to manifest around, oh, seventeen. If she was troublesome before that, that only made it worse."

"Did she get in fights?" Scott asked. "Cause trouble at school?"

"More like drinking," Grandma Randall said. "Drugs. Nothing too hard, I don't think, though it's impossible to tell, I suppose. Skipping school, falling grades. And those boys she brought home—when she came home at all." Grandma Randall shuddered. "Classless mutts." She looked at me. "Were you a little hellion as a teenager?"

I tried not to react visibly. "I didn't leave my house until I was seventeen."

She raised an eyebrow. "Hm. So you're making up for lost time now, then?"

I heard Scott suppress a snicker. "Do you have any idea where your granddaughter might be headed? She seems to be going north now, though she was headed south for a while."

"I have no idea, no," she said with a rough shake of the head. "I haven't heard from her since she left. I find it hard to believe she'd come back here, though."

I cocked an eyebrow. "You sound pretty sure of that."

"I remember being a rebellious teenager," Grandma Randall said with a small smile. "When your parents are wrong all the time and you're right, and you'd do anything to reject everything they say. Well, I expect right now she's rejecting me and she's rejecting Ohio and everything else that represents how she was raised. I doubt she'll come back here."

That made a certain amount of sense. "Does June have a cell phone?" I asked.

"She did," Grandma Randall said. "I don't know if she still does. She's not stupid. She might have gotten rid of it if she's on the run."

"Wouldn't she want her friends to be able to reach her?" Scott asked.

"She didn't have many friends," Grandma Randall said. "She had boyfriends, a revolving door of the bastards. And I do mean bastards, for the most part."

I tried to sort out whether that was Grandma's old age talking, or an accurate assessment of June's taste in men. Given that she was now a fugitive, her choices probably weren't entirely sound.

Of course, I was a fugitive, so maybe my choices, in men and everything else, weren't entirely sound, either. No, scratch that. They definitely weren't.

"You're painting quite the vivid picture of your granddaughter, here," Scott said.

"I don't know what you want me to say to that." Grandma Randall shrugged. "I did my best with her, but I was outmatched. June was going to do what June wanted to do, and once she got past the age where I could effectively browbeat her into line … what was I supposed to do? Physically abuse her? Subdue her? Beat her into—"

"We get the point," I said uncomfortably. "And no … that typically doesn't end well."

"She's a grown woman, now," Grandma Randall said, "or as near to it as to make the distinction irrelevant. The law says she is, anyway, and now she's crossed the law. I may not like it, but the consequences are hers. I couldn't do anything about it if I wanted to." She settled back in her seat, looking utterly helpless.

"Do you want to?" I asked.

She looked at me with barely disguised irritation. "She's my granddaughter. Raised like my own daughter. Of course I would want to do something about it. However annoyed I might have been at her intransigence … I don't wish her any ill. I want the best for her."

"Then help us find her," I said.

"What if I'm not sure if you finding her is the best thing for her?" Grandma Randall asked with a sly smile.

I froze. "Who would you prefer to confront her? A local police department that doesn't have a hope of stopping her or her beau without using lethal force? Or someone who could use one of these," I shot a light net at a quilt, binding it into a bundle of blankets, "and a few choice punches to the face to deliver the beating you apparently regret not doling out. Well, I promise I won't spare the rod when it comes to disciplining your kid. But I'll also do everything I can to make sure she doesn't end up dead."

Grandma June just sat there, studying me intently. "All you can doesn't seem to be enough most of the time, dear."

"Look, I don't know what you've heard about me—" I started.

"I know what I've seen of you," Grandma Randall said. "How many people have you killed?"

I shared a look with Scott, in which he basically threw up his hands in surrender, because apparently he didn't have anything to add to this particular conversation. "Hundreds," I said. Why sugarcoat it? I didn't even bother to add a protesting, "But I've been doing better …" If someone was hanging one of those Workplace Accident signs with my name on it, it had been like ninety or a hundred and twenty days since the last time they'd had to flip the numbers to zero on me killing someone.

But of course, most people went their whole lives without killing anyone, so … that probably wasn't much of an endorsement.

"I've lived through quite a few things in my life," Grandma Randall said, getting a far-off look in her eyes. "The Great War. You know what I'm talking about?"

"World War One, sure," Scott jumped in. Sure, now he

had something to contribute, now that we'd moved off talk of me killing people.

"The Great War," Grandma said, like a storyteller of old, acknowledging Scott's contribution with a nod, "was the first one where sending a metahuman onto the battlefield didn't provide much advantage. Between chemical weapons— which were developed by studying my family and our powers—" she held up a hand and a little puff of purple cloud appeared. She rolled it over in her fingers expertly before making the toxin disappear, "—and tanks, machine guns ... our advantages in warfare, which had been so great as to render us as gods up to that point ... were almost nil when you filled the air with enough bullets to snuff even a superhuman being with a few shots."

I'd heard the rumors; human history books weren't exactly repositories of accurate information on meta contributions to the development of mankind, but now that metas were known to the world, some scholars were doing interesting work in trying to map out our own secret history. I'd had second- and third-hand accounts from people I'd personally talked to about how the Great War had done devastating things to the meta psyche, if there was such a thing as a collective thought pool for my people, who were spread out to the four winds.

"It was just devastating," Grandma Randall went on, apparently down the track my own thoughts had been taking. "We were gods. Hidden, of course. Hidden since long before I was born ... but we knew what we were. Knew we could have a place in the world, if we ever chose to step out. Of course there were organizations powerfully motivated by the desire to keep us hidden to protect their own interests but ... I think even they were shocked when that happened, when our own died in such great numbers, and not because their fellows had taken the field against them, but because humans had finally caught up. Their weapons rendered our advantages moot. And their bullets rendered our loved ones ... dead." She blinked, staring at the beige carpet, then up at me. "You ask me which I'd choose, you hunting my girl, or the police? The police with their rifles and pistols and enough to bullets to fill the air and turn her brains to mush … or you, who have killed hundreds of people."

"They pretty much all had it coming," I said, a little weakly. Scott turned his head to give me a *SHUT UP* look. It worked; I clammed up.

"I suppose I'm going to have to trust you to do this," she said, not sounding particularly thrilled about it. "Because what are my alternatives? No human is going to be able to stop my June. They'll have to kill her. But you …" She stared me down. "… You don't have to kill her."

I squirmed a little in my seat. "No. Hopefully not."

"I want your word," she said. "Swear to me you won't kill my granddaughter."

My insides writhed. "I will do everything I can not to—"

"Swear to me." The old lady's eyes blazed, fixed on me like a spotlight.

A ragged breath came from my throat, and I tried to compose myself. I'd faced down murderers, rapists, criminals of all kinds, people with body counts larger than mine, and here I was, intimidated by a little old lady. "No," I said, and shook my hand. "I will give you my promise that I'll do my best not to kill her, but if your granddaughter makes the decision to kill other people, and puts me in a position where I have to choose between her life and an innocent one she's threatening … no way in hell. I will kill her dead and leave her corpse smoking in time with the last pulses of her heart."

Grandma Randall raised her eyebrows. "*But*," I said as Scott adopted a strangled look, like I'd just choked him or something, "like I said … I'll do my best. And my best is going to be a lot better and more likely to bring her in safe and whole than some PD down in Florida that hasn't ever dealt with a meta before and doesn't want any of their brother officers to die at the hands of some asshole passing through with a chip on her shoulder and a yearning to tear up their backyard." I sat back and waited.

Grandma Randall didn't say anything. Not for a long time. She just sat there, silhouetted in her chair, against the window. "I could call the police on you, you know," she said at last.

"And then you'd have no one looking to bring your granddaughter in alive."

"Because I'm chopped liver?" Scott asked.

"Because you're aiding and abetting a federal fugitive right this minute, numbnuts," I said.

"Oh," he said. "Right."

Grandma Randall suddenly seemed to deflate. "You'll give me your word, then?" she said quietly. If her posture said anything, it was that she was about two seconds from sliding out of her chair into a puddle on the floor to cry about everything that had gone horribly wrong in her relationship with her granddaughter.

"I will give you my word that I will do everything within my power—and I have quite a lot of power—to bring in June and her newest wayward bastard boyfriend in alive—"

"I don't really care if you bring *him* in alive."

"Well, I'm going to try anyway," I said. "You have my word."

Grandma Randall nodded, surrender complete. "I don't know for sure that she'll go there now …" She had the slumped shoulders of utter defeat, as though she'd just refought World War One and lost again, "… but she has always wanted to go that … certain theme park in Orlando." She shrugged. "If she's anywhere close to it …"

I tried to imagine June Randall, with her toxic fingers, in the middle of the thousands and thousands of kids at a major theme park attraction. "Thank you for your help," I said in a strangled voice. Scott probably had the same look on his face that I did—thinly veiled panic. That maybe wasn't all that veiled. Without another word, we left Grandma Randall to her contemplations and headed for the door, airborne seconds later without giving a thought to who might see us flying away.

14.

June

"Nobody move," the security guard said as June stood there, back to him, hands in the air. "The cops are on their way, and we're just going to wait here, calmly, until they arrive."

June didn't dare wheel around on him. Could she take a bullet and keep going? Probably. If he hit her in the right spot, everything her grandmother had told her suggested she could go on, maybe even take the gun away from him and beat him senseless with it.

But if he kept firing, and one of those bullets hit somewhere like the heart, or the head …

Her breath caught in her chest. That'd be the end of the line right there, and the prospect filled her with a visceral immediacy, a clenching in her guts that caused her heart to thud like a hammer against nails.

June kept her hands up, and raised them higher. She chanced a look back over her shoulder, albeit slowly. Ell was across the room, and the guard was switching his attention and aim back and forth between the two of them. "Go stand by her," the guard said, jerking his boxy pistol toward June. Ell complied, halting steps carrying him to her at a very slow pace. "Not too close," the guard said when he was about five feet away. "Now … hands on your heads."

She followed his command, with exaggerated slowness, looking sidelong at Ell as she did so. The guard had them now, and there was no way she'd be able to stop him from shooting them. Not in time.

But …

There was one thing they'd discussed, a while back, something Ell could do to possibly stop someone who was holding a gun on them. She tried to catch his eye, but his knees were quivering; in his mind, Ell was already caught. The game was over.

She had to break him out of that.

"You don't have to do this," she said, words sounding across the quiet lobby. She didn't care what the guard said back, she was just trying to get Ell to look at her.

He did, in shock, as though amazed she'd dare speak out with a gun pointed at her back.

"Just keep quiet until the police get here," the guard said, all business.

June kept her head level, but locked her eyes on Ell. She made a very subtle motion of her head toward the guard, while trying to look like she was just standing there, not saying anything, not doing anything. She didn't want to give him reason to fire in case he was jumpy. It would be stupid to die here, in this town, with a gun at her back. Her stomach was clenching, a fear she didn't want to admit to seeping in over that sense of utter recklessness that had been so intoxicating up until now.

No one could hurt her, she'd thought, though she knew, dimly, this was false. It wasn't a thought she liked to harbor, though, and having it driven home to her in this way …

Well, the accompanying emotional stew had more than fear in it. Anger surged out, making her stomach twist even further. She was furious that she'd been surprised like this. It wasn't her fault, though. The guard hadn't been out when they'd come in.

Ell was staring at her, no anger present for him. He was in the grip of fear and fear alone. She tried to mentally project to him—*the gun, go for the gun,* under no illusions that she was communicating mind-to-mind. She just hoped that their time together had given him enough of a basis to make the leap she wanted him to.

He blinked in surprise, recoiled a couple inches as though

slapped on the cheek, and glanced at the guard.

"Hold still," the guard said. "Actually … hands on the back of your heads."

That was a quirk she hadn't expected. So far, June's were just up. If Ell had to put his on his head, though …

Well, that would wreck the plan. So it was now or never.

She looked at him, and nodded once, swiftly. The fear was still gripping him tightly, and he swallowed once, the lump in his throat almost a visual cue. She could practically hear the *GULP!* He blinked a few times, then started to move his hands to his head.

No, she pleaded in her mind, hoping her expression would convey her anger. *We need to get out of here. Now. This is our chance.*

Ell moved agonizingly slowly, hands stretching toward the crown of his head. He remained tense, but as his hands approached his skull—

A whirl of wind so strong June could feel it on the back of her neck blew at the guard's wrist. He cried out in surprise, and she spun to find him with his gun pointed at the window. A crack rang out; then another. He'd fired in his surprise, prepared for them to attack but not prepared for the direction it would come from.

June leapt on him without warning or remorse, pounding him in the jaw, the face, cramming her fingers up his nose and blasting toxin as she slapped the gun out of his hand. The guard snorted and hacked in surprise before the toxin even took hold, wrestling back ineffectually against her.

"Get the gun! Get the gun!" June screamed as Ell appeared in her peripheral vision. He dove for the weapon, clumsily fumbling it but coming up with it at last, clutched in sweaty, shaky palms and pointed at the crowd and bank tellers, still cowed into inaction.

June got up and took the pistol out of Ell's hand before he shot someone with it accidentally. He looked like he was about to rattle apart. "Get the money," she said softly, not daring to look down at the guard. He was gagging, sounded like he was choking to death on his own tongue. There was nothing Ell could do for him now, the poison now fully in his system, blasted directly in via the nose.

Ell stared at him, frozen, as the man spasmed helplessly. Ell looked helpless as well, and June snapped, "Ell!" Then, more gently, "Get the money. Please."

He lurched out of his stupor, moving toward the counter, where the stunned tellers still waited. One of them screamed at his approach, and he spoke to them in soft tones. He still sounded rattled, but like he was controlling it.

June stared down at the guard, white spittle now flecking the corners of his mouth. The gun was steady in her hand, like iron welded to her fingers. She reached out to him, trying to draw any toxin still unabsorbed out to her. A little stream of it came out, a thin thread mixed with saliva and a little blood, and she took it back. She stared down at his unknowing eyes; he was insensate, his body trying to reject the substance she'd so forcefully pushed into his lungs.

Her mouth was dry, her pulse still racing to the hammer's beat. Was he going to die? Would he be the first person she—

"I've got it," Ell said, returning to her. He didn't look at the guard, and she ripped her gaze away from him as soon as Ell spoke. She nodded and they both went for the door, not too fast but not slowly either.

When they burst into the sunshine, June went for the driver's seat on the Pontiac. Ell took notice, even as zombielike as he was, and diverted to the passenger seat. Once in, he threw the money into the back seat as June started the car. The roar of the engine was like a gunshot all over again, and she perfunctorily put the car in reverse. She didn't speak as she gunned it out onto the main road, a strip surrounded by mini malls and chain restaurants that looked faded under the washed-out Florida sunlight.

She pressed down on the pedal as she blended into the flow of traffic coming up to a light. It was green, so she raced through, the engine noise mingling with the sound from the passenger seat.

Ell was crying.

She didn't know quite what to say to that.

He sobbed, hands in his lap, pitiful sounds like she'd

heard from him back in the hotel room. It was an awful noise, his crying, and she ignored it for a few minutes as the rage rose inside her.

Why did he have to get involved, that stupid guard? Why couldn't he …?

How did we miss him? That was Ell's fault—

No. The guard wasn't in the main room when we came in. He must have been on lunch break.

It wasn't anyone's fault but his own, she decided finally, and then spoke. "It's not your fault, Ell. He wasn't there, you saw. He came out when he knew we were robbing the bank. He chose this. He wanted to be the big man. Well …" She didn't finish the thought, which ran along the lines of … *But now he might just end up a dead man instead.*

"We didn't have to do that to him," Ell said, composing himself enough to speak, his voice verging on cracking.

"Yes, we did," she said without hesitation. "Yes. It had to be done."

"No," he said, but she recognized it wasn't so much a refutation of what she'd said as his own poorly expressed wish that he could turn back the clock to a few minutes earlier—and make this whole chain of events play out differently. June felt a little sick, thinking much the same. What if they'd picked a different bank, one where there was no guard? Or one they could have gotten the drop on? Her heart wasn't thudding quite as loudly anymore, but her stomach still felt queasy.

"It's okay," she said, and took hold of Ell by the back of the neck. She stroked his hair at the back of his head, down the back of his neck, rubbing him gently. "It's going to be okay." She pulled him close.

Ell just sobbed, though, like he had earlier. And she held him while he did, whispering soothing words as she took them away from this place.

15.

Sienna

"So … Disney," I said as we soared through the heavens, heading south and sticking to clouds for cover. "She's going to do what generations of athletes have, and go to Disney World."

"What are the odds she goes and doesn't cause trouble?" Scott shouted over the whipping wind.

I shrugged, keeping my ears open for the sound of engines. Occasionally, I needed to watch out for jetliners. "Well, they make trouble everywhere else they go. I wouldn't care to chance the odds in a place like that."

Scott fell silent for a short spell. "Grandma Randall locked you in on that promise, didn't she?"

"She's no pushover, that one," I said, a little darkly. It wasn't like I'd planned to give a half-assed effort to bringing in her baby June alive before, but having that extracted from me the way Grandma Randall had certainly put an emphasis on saving her in a way I might not have focused on otherwise.

"You seemed to take it pretty seriously," Scott observed.

"I don't really enjoy lying," I said. "My mom brainwashed a visceral dislike of it into me through some pretty harsh punishment, so … like Pavlov's dogs, it rings a certain unpleasant bell in my head when I catch myself doing it. I'm certainly not above it, but … yuck."

"So you feel obligated to keep your word."

"As best I can," I said tightly, the tension within me at this annoying state of events bleeding out in my words. The problem with trying to take potentially dangerous criminals alive was that you gave them all sorts of opportunities to cause harm to you and others—and the risk was compounded if they were armed or a metahuman.

"Well," Scott said, "I'll be honest—I was hoping for this to go peacefully all along."

"So was I, dumbass," I snapped back at him. "It's not like I go into these things wondering how I can cause maximum havoc, okay? It's just that when their will to do unlawful shit clashes with my will to make them stop, it usually escalates the situation because, as you mentioned, ego drives a large part of this process, especially with these young and dumb ones."

"I only mentioned the ego thing because you taught it to me," Scott said. "So basically you just referenced back to yourself."

"Whatever," I said, a little too confused to detangle who said what originally. "Can we just talk about our new, burgeoning supervillains walking around a theme park with thousands of people and especially children? Because however nasty June's poison has been for the adults she's come into contact with, I imagine—and I'm no doctor here—that it's bound to be worse on the respiratory systems of the young. Maybe the old, too, I dunno."

"Probably fewer old folks at Disney World."

"This is Florida. It's old folks all the way down here."

"Another thing about this, though," Scott said. "They haven't actually killed anyone."

"Yet," I fired back.

He rolled his eyes, shifting slightly in my bridal carry. "I don't mean to redirect your thunder or anything—"

"I don't do thunder. It's nuclear fire, punching people to death, or eating them like the Lady Dragon I am."

"—but seeing them as murderous threats is getting a little ahead of yourself."

"I think it's just being prepared for the escalation," I said. "Because this is how it happens when you go head to head with the law. Don't be naïve."

"It's hardly a foregone conclusion that—"

"Yes, it is," I said. "This is a battle of wills to them. They reach out their hand, take something that's not theirs. If they get away with it, if no one slaps them back, why would they stop?"

"Because they have human reason and common sense?" Scott asked, dismissing me with a roll of the eyes. "Because they know that sooner or later, they'll get caught?"

"You're thinking about it like an adult," I said. "Like a grownup who's felt the touch of mortality." Probably a few too many times, thanks to his association with me. "They're young. Yes, they could tell you that, of course, logically, intellectually, someday, far in the future, they will die. Because everybody does, basically, and everybody knows that."

"But?"

"But that's not how they *feel*," I said. "When you're young, you're immortal. Death is an abstract concept, so far off that your gut says you're immune to it and your brain doesn't really catch up with the idea until you're years older. They're, what? Nineteen? They're not thinking intellectually about death and the possibility that they're driving up their odds of meeting it head on and losing to its gnashing teeth. Not right now. They're feeling good. They've slapped the system around, beaten *the man*. Maybe they've felt the brush of death, maybe they haven't, but until it gets driven home to them to the point where in their heart they know it's coming, where they wake up in the middle of the night and it's so obvious if they don't stop that they will die, that they feel the fear of it from head to toe, like the cold sweat that they snap awake in ..." I wanted to gesture, but my hands were occupied carrying him. "They won't stop. Because why would they? They're winning. And they won't stop winning until the police come at them hard enough to end this. It won't be gentle, because lives will be at stake in a way they haven't been so far. These two are dangerous. And they're going to provoke a deadly response to that danger."

Scott mulled his reply for almost a minute. "Maybe," he

finally conceded. "But I do have this question … who goes to a theme park when they're on the run? Someone arrogant enough to believe they're untouchable?"

I squirmed a little, remembering a discussion I'd had a couple months back with the souls in my head. "Yeah. Someone who thinks they're unbeatable and for whom death isn't a big concern."

Someone like you, Zack said heavily.

Jah, Eve said, piling on, *what was it you told us? That no one could beat you? That you could only be killed, that they couldn't take anything more from you?*

And I was right, I said, keeping this discussion carefully within the bounds of my head. *But for me … death is an option that's on the table.*

In your head, maybe, Wolfe said. *But just like these kids, you don't feel it breathing down your neck. It doesn't cause you to wake up sweating and afraid in the night.*

Just as well, I hate sweaty bedsheets, I said. *They're gross. Now why don't you all go play with each other or something?*

Oh, not again, Harmon groaned, and I saw Bjorn's leer in my mind's eye. I had to agree with Harmon for once.

"So what do we do?" Scott asked, jarring me back to the real world, the one in which I didn't have to watch the dirty goings on of Eve and Bjorn. They didn't even like each other, which somehow made it so much worse whenever it happened.

"You need to start coordinating a response with the FBI and the Orlando authorities," I said. "Get them involved, let them know we have a threat. Because you and I—or you alone—aren't going to be able to cover this. I've never been to Disney but I imagine it's not a tiny place—"

The ring of Scott's phone interrupted me. He struggled to pull it out of his pocket, and when he got it free he made a face. "Phillips."

"You should take it," I said. "We've been out of contact for a while. It's possible they could have surfaced."

He gave me a look of disgust that told me exactly what he thought of answering the phone, but he did it anyway. "Hello? Yes? Yes, I can hear you a little better now." I angled us lower toward the ground, trying to get us in better cell range. Atlanta was coming up off to our left, so there was surely enough cell service at hand to keep him from dropping the call.

Scott listened, his face like chiseled granite, and then he went slightly grey before he hit the mute button and looked right at me. "You were right. They just struck again. A bank in a town on the Florida coast." He stopped speaking for a moment, and somehow I knew what followed would be the worst of the news thus far. "They took out a security guard."

"Dead?" I asked, the fear that I was about to have to break my new vow to Grandma Randall causing my heart to spike in alarm.

"He's in critical condition," Scott said. "They don't know if he's going to make it."

16.

We were late to the party. I knew it even before we came in for an unobserved landing behind a self-storage place and walked over to the bank. I'd never even heard of Merritt Island, Florida, until today, but I could tell by the time we reached the bank's parking lot it wasn't going to be a place I associated with anything good.

The typical crime scene was already in place when we came strolling up, probably making the cops wonder where we'd come from. They didn't say anything, though, because they were eyeing the crowd of spectators and a couple of press people, which was smaller than you would have seen at a crime scene in a major city. Scott spoke to a sheriff's deputy in a dark green uniform, and he let us into the crime scene, lifting the tape so we could pass under. I glanced back at the press people, but they didn't deign to pay attention to me; just a couple reporters too busy talking to each other to notice that the most famous fugitive in America was crossing into a crime scene right under their nose.

"It's such a pain in the ass that I'm wanted," I muttered meta-low to him, quiet enough that no one but he could hear me. "Makes getting places so much more difficult now. It'd be so much easier if we could just fly everywhere."

"Easier," Scott said tightly, "but not more dignified." Aww, poor baby. He didn't like being carried in my arms like a sulking toddler. "Hopefully no one here has eagle eyes like Grandma Randall," he said, tension in his voice ratcheting up. "Otherwise this is going to get … interesting."

I snorted to myself. We'd stopped off at my luggage and I was wearing my redhead wig, with bangs, that made the shape of my face looked very different, especially given that I was wearing big sunglasses and makeup. I was also way, way more tanned than I'd ever been in my life, so hopefully this wouldn't be a problem. Who looked for a fugitive masquerading as an FBI agent?

Cops, probably. Suspicious bastards. And I say that with love, having basically been one of them.

"I'll just take care to stay in the background," I said. "You be the face of this team." Also, I'd avoid a staredown with any cops, because that could not possibly end well.

"Or next time," Scott said as he hauled the bank door open for me to pass through, "I just don't bring you to crime scenes?"

"Where's the fun in that?" I asked, stepping into the infinitely cooler lobby and straight through the open secondary door into the bank itself.

The place was decked out like you'd expect—wooden teller desk, one of those islands in the middle that had been upended, deposit slips scattered all across the floor. Beyond that were the canvas straps that marked the line to the counter, like a theme park ride with a much more prosaic ending. I shuffled along behind Scott, having changed my usual gait to a very slow stroll, one in which I was a lot more obvious about scanning the room for threats and features of interest.

"Hello?" Scott called out, drawing a plainclothes cop in his direction. The guy looked mid-forties, was wearing an immaculately pressed suit, and greeted us with a smile and a cursory glance. Scott flipped open his badge, and I didn't even bother with my fake one, pretending to look over the shoulder of an evidence technician instead. "Agent Byerly, FBI. This is my associate, Rochelle Nelson."

"Detective Claus, Brevard County Sheriff's office," the man said, extending a hand. He gave Scott a polite shake, gave me a gentle one, and I resisted the urge to crush his pansy grip in mine to show dominance. Because that might give me away.

"We're with the metahuman unit," Scott said, looking around instead of focusing on Detective Claus. "Got anything for us?"

Claus wasn't too impressed by that. "Got two perps that ran. You can have them if you can catch them."

"Gee, thanks," I said, unable to control the overwhelming desire to snark.

Claus smiled. "They headed west out of here, up the road there." He pointed out the door. "That's 520. It leads to Orlando, eventually, but there are faster ways. You know who these perps are?"

"Probably Elliot Lefavre and June Randall," Scott said. "A couple metas who have been working their way down the coast. Looks like they're starting a turn back north now."

"They're the ones who hit that convenience store in Melbourne?" Claus asked. "And did the attack on the beach?"

"Right."

"A little more warning might have been nice," Claus said darkly. "If you knew they were operating in the area."

Scott sighed. "Not my call, but … yeah."

Claus surveyed him pitilessly for a second before loosening up and nodding. "I hear you. Higher ups, am I right?"

"You're not wrong," Scott said, giving only a little ground. "If they were heading west … what do they find if they keep going?"

"We don't know for sure they're headed west," Claus said cautiously. "West is basically the only way to go to get out of here, at least easily. This is a barrier island, so heading east just runs you into the ocean, and if you try and head north, you hit the Kennedy Space Center. If they were looking to run in a hurry, they'll head west, but twenty minutes from here they could pick up I-95 and head north or south, or get on 528 and shave some time off if they wanted to get to Orlando or even Tampa in a hurry."

"We think they might try for Disney," Scott said. "How long would that take them?"

Claus's eyebrow went up fast. "About an hour at a

reasonable speed. Maybe a little longer if they slackass it. You might want to warn the state and the locals that they could be coming. This is the sort of thing they're going to want to have the big guns on standby for."

He meant SWAT, or whatever their local equivalent was, because metas posed a special kind of danger. Also, SWAT teams were starting to get trained on dealing with metas, now that effective tactics and best training practices were starting to spread. "Crap," Scott said.

"All the theme parks and the law enforcement that service them have plans in place for these kind of contingencies," Claus said humorlessly. "But their reaction time will speed up if they have advance warning."

Scott's whole body was screaming tension. "I'll talk to my boss about it."

I could almost see Claus tense up. "There's a lot of kids in those parks, man. Be persuasive." I couldn't blame him.

Scott nodded and shuffled away, already digging for his cell phone. He pulled it out and started to dial, but I caught the hesitation. No way did he really want to talk to Phillips, especially so soon after dealing with him. He'd faked signal loss somewhere over northern Florida just to get the asshole off the line. I could sympathize with that, having once been the sole object of Phillips's attention.

"What's the deal with this?" Claus asked the moment Scott stepped away. I tried not to freeze, staring at him coolly through my glasses, waiting expectantly for him to clarify. "These meta incidents … seems like there are lot more of them happening."

"How would you know?" I asked with a thin smile. "The only thing the media report on is that one giant pain in the ass that hogs the headlines."

Claus smirked. "Yeah. But you know how we locals like to gossip. There was the thing in Orlando a couple months ago. A buddy of mine in San Francisco told me about an incident there last month … I started my career in Nebraska, and one of my old supervisors was telling me …" He shook his head, then waved a hand. "I don't have to tell you this. You either know and you're not allowed to say, or you don't know, in which case ..." He gave me a knowing look, and we both read to the end of the page on that one: *In which case, you're an idiot and why am I wasting my time talking to you?*

"It's not your imagination," I said, trying to keep about as straitlaced as you'd expect from an FBI agent. I debated whether to tell him about the serum, the artificial means by which metahuman incidents seemed to be gaining in number. Why the hell not? I didn't work for the FBI. "There's something new out there," I said. "A drug that unlocks meta powers in normal humans. Someone's circulating it. No idea who."

Claus's eyebrows shot up like they were the dinger on a strength-test hammer game after I took a swing at it, almost touching his hairline. "Holy hell."

"Yep," I said. "All kinds of unholy hell. More and more of it, I'd say."

"Hm," Claus said, falling into silence until his radio beeped at him and started talking.

"We have reports of suspect vehicle on 528 Westbound toward the Orange County line," a dispatcher said under the thin crackle of radio static. "Almost to the St. Johns River."

"They're about to cross into Orlando's county," Claus said, coming to life again after pausing to listen. "About thirty minutes from here."

I swore quietly. Thirty minutes' drive, and we didn't even have a car here. Needless to say, blowing out of here in flight would not do a lot to keep things quiet and on the down low. "Are your guys on them?"

Claus shook his head. "We back off metas, especially when we have an idea of how much damage they can do. We're at 'do not engage' on these two, except with SWAT. Especially given the mayhem they could cause on a crowded highway."

"Thanks for the info," I said, and headed off to collect Scott. "We need to go," I said in a low voice as he paused mid-argument with Phillips. "Gotta get your car."

"It's in Orlando," he said, covering the microphone. "At the airport."

He looked less than thrilled at the prospect. "Give me a

minute."

"This could take all day," I said, nodding at his phone.

"Yeah," he agreed, looking around the mess in the bank. Paper deposit slips were everywhere; Scott had one stuck to the bottom of his shoe like toilet paper, which he took note of and then peeled off, discarding it as an evidence tech scowled at him. He nodded to indicate Claus. "What was that about?"

"The lovebirds are on their way to Orlando," I said. "Confirmed sighting of their getaway vehicle on the freeway headed west."

Scott scowled, keeping his hand pressed over the phone's mic. "And we can't even chase them, really."

I shrugged. "We could. I could bomb their car from above, then swoop down—"

"Real inconspicuous."

"It'd get the job done."

"It'd blow your cover and probably mine." He shook his head. "No. We need to get my car and intercept them."

I nodded toward the door, wondering if Phillips had put him on hold. "We should get moving, then."

He took the phone from his ear, stared at it as though debating whether to throw it or not, and finally just hit the "End" button. I guess he had been put on hold. "Yeah. Let's go."

Scott stopped at the door, throwing a look over his shoulder, and his face bore an expression I wasn't familiar with. "What is it?" I asked.

He kept staring at the damage, the mess, like he was taking stock of it, surveying. "What do you suppose binds these two together?"

"All the common threads, I suppose. Like any of us at that age. Lust. Desire to see the world, spread their wings."

"Such a sweet love story," Scott said with a bitter smile, "to go this way, robbery and assault." He hesitated. "We were never like this, were we?"

I froze. "Like what?" He gave me a patronizing look, one that cut through my desire to sling bullshit and hope the question disappeared into the night. Instead, I took a deep breath and answered as honestly as I could. "A hundred miles an hour into danger and destruction followed by sex and sweat and more danger? Kindasorta. But we kept it on the right side of the law, at least."

"Not quite what I meant," Scott said, looking a little forlorn. And he walked out without making it clear, but I thought I knew.

He wondered if we'd ever been that crazily in love. Because he couldn't remember any of it.

17.

June

June steered the car off the road a little ways after the county line, taking a random exit hoping that it wouldn't lead her to a dead end. She'd been admiring a big power plant cooling tower they were passing when a glance back in the rearview caused her to have a moment of suspicion. Was that a cop car back there?

She couldn't be sure, because she was staring in a rearview and it was way, way back, so she'd gone ahead and hit the next exit, the one that said Exit 31, State Road 520. She took the ramp at high speed and then hung a right, picking the direction at random and flooring it again.

Ell was sitting uselessly next to her, but he sat up at the sudden change in direction. "What is it?"

"Thought I saw a cop car behind us," she said, eyeing the rearview. If it was a cop, he was far up the exit ramp right now, and probably hadn't even been able to see which way she'd turned, thanks to the thick trees pines and palms lining the road.

"What's the plan?" Ell asked, nerves shooting through his already cracking voice. He cleared his throat and sniffled a little.

June just shot him a slow smile. "Why do we need a plan? We'll get away from him, maybe stop for the night." She couldn't see the position of the sun, and their Pontiac was old, its clock display burned out.

"You think they know our car?"

"Probably." She kept a hand on the wheel and massaged the back of his neck again, stroking it slowly. "They probably have for a while; the Parisienne is pretty distinct. But I don't know what you want to do about it. We can't steal another car without being willing to do some harm, because I don't know how to strip an ignition and neither do you." They'd talked about it, but every time they went through it, she kept coming to the same conclusion—if they were going to steal a car and actually get away with it, they'd have to do a carjacking since neither one could start one without keys. And that meant that the person driving the damned thing had to be unable to report it to the cops for a good long while, otherwise they'd be back in the same boat within a few minutes.

Which would be because they either kidnapped the person or killed them. And even she wasn't quite there on that one … yet, anyway. Robbing banks and counting on the cops to keep avoiding them was one thing. Killing people and stealing their cars, hiding the bodies or just flat out doing home invasions and leaving them trapped or dead in their houses … that was gross. Mean beyond what June wanted to do.

She just wanted to have fun, and she needed money to do it. It was so simple. Why did people keep having to get in the way of her and Ell having fun?

"What do we do next?" Ell asked nervously. He was sitting up, tense again, now that his brain was engaged in the work of trying to plan out a next move. "After we find a place for the night, I mean."

June didn't entirely know on that one, but she'd had this thought in her head since they'd first started heading south to Florida, and it wasn't because of damned Cuba. "There's a reason I always wanted to visit Florida …"

"What is it?"

She hesitated. She wanted him to engage on it, and he was still tearful. He should know this anyway, they'd talked about it. "Oh, I dunno. Never mind."

He looked up at her, curiosity punctuating his features.

"What?"

She gave him a knowing look. "You know."

He stared back blankly, once again looking desperately out of place.

Her irritation flowered within, and she sighed like she was admonishing a child. "I've told you this. Like, literally a million times."

Now he just looked trapped, as though she'd somehow become a massive predator who'd trapped him in a corner where he was about to be eaten alive. "I … I don't know …"

She let out another impatient sigh. "Bae, I want to go … to Disney World."

Ell sat up, crooking his neck around to look at her like she was crazy. "What?"

She blushed, cheeks burning. What an ass he was being, acting like she was stupid or something. "I want to go to Disney. I always have."

"Now?" he asked, jaw hanging open slightly.

"Maybe." Now the anger was burning in earnest. "I've told you this, I dunno, more times than I can count. We've talked about it a lot."

He stared off into space. "I don't remember you ever saying—"

"Seriously?"

"I—" he stumbled with the words. "Well … I guess we could … how far away is … ?" He pulled out his phone and started scrolling it as she stared suspiciously. She didn't have one anymore, didn't trust the police not to be tracking her on it. It's why she'd opted for such an old car: no GPS.

"You know what? Never mind," she said, not really meaning it but hurt that he didn't remember. How many times had she told him? "Just forget about it." She clammed up, waiting to see how he'd react to that.

"Are you sure?" He didn't sound very sure.

"Yeah," she said brusquely. "It's fine." It damned sure was not, but she was determined not to let on like it.

"Do you want to go?" He was hesitating madly, as though dangling bait in front of her. "We can go."

This wasn't how she wanted it. She wanted him to

remember, to be excited about it. But that was the problem with Ell; he didn't remember shit. And how could he be excited about it, given he didn't remember them talking about it, her gushing about it ... what a disappointment.

Still ... she wanted to go badly enough that she was willing to let this go. She'd probably freeze him out a little on a normal occasion, but this ... this was special. She'd wanted to go for so long ...

"Yeah," June said. "Let's do it. Let's go to Disney World."

18.

Sienna

"How do we head these crazies off at the pass?" I wondered aloud as we drove out of the Orlando International Airport in Scott's purloined FBI car.

"I don't know," Scott said, at the wheel but also plainly wanting to make a phone call, "but I'm guessing it'll involve coordinating with the people who actually know what they're doing in this regard—local law enforcement and the FBI Special-Agent-in-Charge down here."

"You said Phillips gave you crap over the politics of the situation before," I said, pressing my hand against the warm plastic lining just inside the window. He'd parked in the sun and the car was hot like the inside of my shirt when I went full Gavrikov. Yeouch.

"He's given me nothing but problems since the day I took this job," Scott said. "And half the time, I was brainwashed and under Harmon's control, so he was really just butting heads with his boss's will."

"Hmph," I snorted. "The sad thing is, Harmon didn't even mind control him. He's just naturally that much of an obstructive colon blockage."

"Obstructive—" Scott turned his head to look at me questioningly, and then nodded when he got it. "You can't get shit done."

"Right you are." I thought in silence as he steered us through a few twisty overpasses. "So … why don't you ignore him?"

"Because Phillips is pretty high up in the FBI," Scott said. "If I push too hard, he's going to remove me, and then Sienna Nealon is going to have to contend with a task force commander that's actually working at catching her."

"Yeah, the current one doesn't seem to be doing much," I said dryly. "I mean, I'm sitting right beside him and he still can't find me." I sobered up. "I think you're going to have to at least tip off the local authorities about June and Elliot." I paused. "Or …"

He didn't like the sound of that. "Or what?"

"Or I could," I said. "I'm a dire threat. Put me in play down here and—"

"You could get yourself shot in the head by a remorseless sniper who's tasked with bringing you down, while Elliot and June waltz right past into the Magic Kingdom, which is going to be a lot less magic when she poisons a bunch of children as she robs a hot dog stand or whatever."

"You think they have hot dog stands at Disney?"

Scott stared straight ahead at the road. "Not exactly, I don't think. But I do remember a restaurant in Fantasyland with a Pinocchio theme that had pretty great hot dogs." I just stared at him through dark eyes. Of course he'd been to Disney as a kid, probably multiple times. He must have caught my look, because he got suddenly defensive. "What?"

I should have stolen a few memories of your happy lark of childhood, I wanted to say, but it felt like a contentious thing to bring up, especially given the happy lark times were well over now. After all, he was working for a federal agency almost exclusively to keep me from being brought to justice unjustly. After I'd stolen all his memories of our relationship. There's Sienna snarky, and then there's being an asshole, and this felt over the line.

"Sounds like the happiest place on earth," I said instead. "How do we handle this, though? Seriously. We don't want them boxed in. We want them scared off, not trapped and ready to lash out anywhere near a place where thousands of families come to vacation."

"Well, what would deter them?" Scott asked.

"I don't know—exactly," I said. "It's hard to tell. Will police presence, lurking around the gates make them turn back? I can't imagine Disney would be too sanguine about having cops all over the place at their entry points, lights flashing. But at the same time, if they see nothing waiting for them, in they'll go, because why the hell not? Then maybe you end up with another beach incident, or worse, when someone pisses them off. So it's a line between what the locals will even allow and what will dissuade our fugitives. Cops dissuade me from going places, but I'm sane—"

"So say you, and probably none of the rest of us. Also, you were just in a crime scene swimming with cops."

"Haha, you recruited me to help you, so which of us is crazier? The crazy or the one who asks for help from her?" I paused. "The real question is … are these two actually crazy? Will they see danger and turn back? Or look at it as a challenge?"

"June didn't seem too put off by me as a challenge," Scott said.

"Because you're a pushover, cream puff," I said. "Seriously. I've met marshmallow dips that are made of sterner stuff than you." I wasn't entirely serious. Scott could cause havoc and pain when he intended to, it was just that he intended to a lot less often than yours truly.

"And to think I once drowned a man in a casino lobby for you," Scott said, shaking his head sadly.

I raised an eyebrow. "You remember that?"

"Yeah," he said. "What happened after is a bit blurry, though."

The hot rush of guilt and shame burned my cheeks. Again. I remembered what happened after that, from both his perspective and mine. He'd macked on me back in the hotel room.

"I say you call the locals, ring the alarm bell and get them to post the cops," I said, changing the subject but trying not to seem desperate about it. "And if our dynamic duo decide to make a mess … we stay in close. Because the alternative that Phillips is essentially pitching is to have *no* response ready and just let them come waltzing in … leaving a whole park full of people in the line of fire. Or toxin. In the toxin line." By now I was babbling, my brain still fixed on that stolen memory guilt thing.

"Yeah," Scott said, and nodded once, a resolute look gleaming in his eyes. "I'm not letting innocent people die because Phillips doesn't want to chance this turning ugly." And he hit the search bar on his phone, typing in "Orange County Sheriff," before dialing the number that came up.

19.

June

She and Ell had spent a quiet night in a hotel not too far from Disney's massive compound. Normally when they stayed in a hotel, they'd make love, giggle, laugh, have fun.

There was none of that this time. Ell had gone to bed early, turning out his bedside light to signal that he didn't really want to talk anymore. They'd talked it out about as much as June wanted to, anyway. Ell was sad, and he was going to continue to be sad, especially after they saw the news report briefly saying that a security guard was in critical condition after a bank robbery. No mention of them, June was a little disappointed to see, but that was pretty standard by now. For some reason they couldn't seem to get actual media coverage even if they'd wanted it.

And she did sort of want it. It'd give her a feeling of accomplishment, like she'd done something with her life. More than anything those sorry bitches back in her high school had done by this point.

She'd been excited, though, as Ell had sunk into his sullen silence on his side of the bed. She'd quietly bounced, all thoughts of the robbery and how it had gone wrong banished in her enthusiasm. Sure, she dwelled on it a couple times, let it drag her mood down a little, but ...

How could she stay down?

Because this morning ... they were heading to Disney World.

She drove, because Ell had wordlessly dragged himself to the car, still suffering from the grief hangover he seemed determined to put himself through. She'd had no time for that, though, and burbled happily as she followed his directions to the front gates of the place she'd wanted to visit all her life.

The signs were clear enough that she could have told him to put away his phone after they crossed under the yellow sign that stretched over the road proclaiming "Walt Disney World" in that distinctive script. Cinderella's castle worked into the apex of the arced sign, and it gave her a thrill. She saw the purple overhead lane signs for the Magic Kingdom, and steered the car accordingly.

Just past that overhanging entry sign, she noticed the first cop car. Then, a few seconds later, another. They didn't have their lights flashing, but there they were, like guards at the gates. They didn't do anything, didn't pull anyone over. The cops were out of their cars, just watching, chatting. But there were four or five of them now, in quick succession, and she took notice.

Ell saw it, too. "Wonder if they're always here in force."

"It's a terrorist target," June said with a shrug. The mere sight of cops wasn't going to trample her mood. Not today.

She kept steering on, and glanced in the rearview. The road was now three lanes across, and pretty damned busy. Still, behind her, she saw a steady line of cars following, including—

What the hell?

There was an unmarked police car a few back from her, the profile of the lights on the roof absent, but an antenna still obvious as well as mounted lights on the front dashboard that showed in silhouette. She stared back at the cop car as the traffic slowed, thickening like rush hour in a major city.

What the hell was going on here? Had they picked them up again, here?

Was it luck?

How could they have known they'd come here?

"This has gotta be just a precaution," June said, her

breath catching in her throat. "They were trolling, looking for something else, and—" She didn't want to give voice to her thought, which was that no matter how it had come about …

The cops were on their trail, now. She cursed, low, then louder, an earsplitting scream of profanity causing Ell to shrink away from her in fear. "We should have stolen a different car," she said, in her anger blind to the problems that would have brought about.

"Maybe they haven't seen us," Ell said, looking in his own sideview mirror.

"He's like, three cars back," June said, declaring Ell an idiot by the tone of her reply if not her actual words.

"There aren't really that many cop cars here," Ell said, blushing at her rebuke.

"You're right, sort of," she fumed. There weren't enough that a law-abiding citizen would take much notice of them.

But a wanted fugitive like her, like him?

How could she not notice? How could her heart not skip a couple beats seeing an unmarked car sitting behind her?

"What do we do?" Ell asked, starting to sweat visibly.

"We're in the center lane, surrounded by cars on both side," June said, her own palms feeling slick on the wheel. "I can't turn around yet." Traffic had slowed to a creep, the road widening and splitting for a checkpoint ahead like a big toll booth that stretched across sixteen lanes.

"What do we do, what do we do?" Ell asked, now going full Chicken Little on her, looking around frantically, as though he could find some easy exit.

"Shut up and calm down, you little bitch," she snapped. "This isn't a big deal."

"It's a pretty big deal," Ell said, his voice calming a couple notches. "We're surrounded. They must have known we were coming."

"Why, did you tell them?" June's voice rose almost of its own accord. She was staring hotly at him now; had he made a call while she was sleeping? She kept both hands on the wheel for fear of lashing out at him if she took even one off. "Did you call the police?"

"No!" Ell said, outraged enough that she almost totally believed him. There was still a sliver of doubt, but it was small enough that she shut up, letting her mind race in search of what they needed to do next. "What do we do?" Now he sounded very small.

"We keep going," June decided. "What are they going to do to us?"

Ell went bug-eyed. "Kill us. They'll kill us, June. After what we did yesterday?"

June just shook her head in disgust. "They can't."

"Yes, they can," Ell said. "Boom boom. Two bullets, we both die." He tugged at his collar, sweat already visibly turning his t-shirt damp.

"It's not that easy."

"It's just that easy," he said, breathless, his fear peaking now. He slumped against the window, sweaty and defeated. "How can you not see it?"

"Because I'm not a scaredy chicken-shit," she said, not even bothering to hold back. Stress had her now, panic too, but she wouldn't show it like he did, by giving up. Her panic made her want to lash out, not quit. She would have preferred to leave a pile of dead cops in the road right now than give up on this.

Ell started to speak, but she cut him off before he got a word out. "Don't you dare," she said, strangled. "This is my *dream*."

Ell collapsed back against the window, quiet misery seeping out of him with all the life. "This is turning into a nightmare."

June grabbed at the Pepsi bottle in the center console and heaved it at him. Ell screamed and ducked it by a centimeter. It shattered the passenger window in a spider web of cracks as it came bouncing off. She struck out and hit him in the arm, unable to contain her fury, and he cried out. That didn't make her feel any better, so she struck out at him again, and he squealed in pain, scrambling to try and get hold of the door handle, to open the door and perhaps step out in traffic.

"You suck!" June screamed. "You suck, you suck, you

suck! You're such an asshole! You don't have any spine, any dreams of your own, so you try and shit on mine all the time!"

Ell was crying, unable to even open the door though he fumbled with it, casting pitiful looks back at her. By now her own cheeks were damp with tears of rage, and she kept up the onslaught. "You're such a little wuss! You don't have the guts to do what it takes, even if it means saving your own life, and even when you do, you cry about it like your poor little baby feelings got hurt." Ell finally managed to get hold of the car door handle and threw it open, starting to get out.

"If you get out of this car now," June screamed at him, "I'm driving off without you!" That was an empty threat; the traffic was barely moving.

Ell stared back at her, stooped over, quivering, and she knew in that moment she was about to lose him. Pride and fury were mingled together, though, and she couldn't bring herself to say she was sorry, because in the moment she wasn't sorry for anything she'd done or said; she was only sorry he was such a damned baby.

Before he could answer, the whoop of a siren cut the air from the unmarked cop car, and they both turned, the unspoken danger given form once more. And all the rage, all the anger she'd felt only a moment earlier toward Ell turned in another, more familiar, more manageable direction.

20.

Sienna

I was pretty antsy, standing around not too far from the main gate to Disney. Scott was hobnobbing with the local cops, who'd said they'd done this kind of thing before at times of heightened terror alerts. There was a mobile command center set up about thirty feet behind us, and Scott was anchored by the door talking to the guys who ran it. They'd been really friendly, eager to help, basically valuing doing the job of keeping people safe above playing politics or arguing over jurisdiction. It was beautiful, in a way.

Of course, I was sitting on the outside of the whole thing, because the last thing we needed right now was for me to be recognized for who I was.

I was surprised exactly how many non-palm trees there were in the area. There were actually vast swaths of forest all around the Disney property, including lining the roads all around the parks. Right now I was wishing I was here for my own enjoyment rather than because I was lurking to prevent a dangerous couple of crazy metas from causing havoc, but alas. I'd had my vacation these last few months on St. Thomas, and it was over now.

Which was just as well. I hadn't even eaten anything other than a banana the night before, when I was alone in my hotel room, and I felt surprisingly better for it, though the hunger pangs were working their way through me now. There were donuts set up on a table outside the command center, boxes closed against the bugs, and I was considering hitting one of those up while I waited. The better angels of my nature had allowed me to resist so far, though, and without too much difficulty. It was a such a marked contrast to how I'd felt back on St. Thomas; it was as though temptation was at bay now that I was in the middle of the action again.

You're addicted to the action, Wolfe said. *It satisfies your cravings.*

I ignored him and sighed, wishing I could go talk to the cops instead of standing on the sidelines being introspective. Being antisocial wasn't much fun, but hopefully it would pay dividends in the form of not resulting in a full-on freak-out by the local cops followed by my immediate capture. Because that would be bad. Or worse. I guess it would be taking the situation from bad to worse. Yeah.

Kicking a little stick across the parking lot pavement near where the grass began, I stared into the densely packed woods that started beyond. If shit hit the fan, I could dodge inside, ditch the wig, maybe shed a layer of clothing, and BOOM! Sienna Nealon would be ready for action.

The question I had was … did Sienna Nealon really need to see action here? Or would our criminals just turn around and head down the road, allowing us to confront them somewhere that would put fewer innocent lives at risk? The part of me not jonesing for a hit of violence kinda hoped for the latter, but I'd run across too many pride- and anger-filled metas not to steel myself for the former.

"What's that?" one of the cops in the trailer asked, loud enough I could hear him clearly without straining. "We've got an issue here."

"What kind of issue?" Scott asked, bounding into the trailer.

I lurked outside, shifting a little closer to the woods; I could hear them fairly clearly even at this range. "One of our unmarked cars has eyes on them. They're at the parking booth just outside the Magic Kingdom."

"You make people pay for parking here?" Scott asked. "Really?"

There was no answer to that one. "Sir, the officer is reporting some kind of argument in the car. License plate confirms it's them."

"Tell the officer to stay in his car and not to interfere," Scott said. "Let's not light a fuse on this if we don't have to."

"Understood." There was a pause for a few seconds. "Sir, the officer is requesting backup. He says they're escalating."

"Escalating how?" Scott asked, voice filled with tension. I had a feeling I knew how, having been in a few romance-based arguments in my day. With Scott himself, in fact, though he wouldn't remember them.

"They're yelling. The female suspect has thrown something and cracked the passenger window. Now she's striking the male suspect."

"Their names are June and Elliot, okay? Just call them that."

"Yes, sir. The male sus—err, Elliot—is trying to leave the vehicle. They're still yelling at each other."

"Damn," Scott said. "Give them room. Let them settle this and get the hell out of—"

"They're stuck in traffic, sir," the cop said.

"Stuck in—what?"

"They're backed up at the booths. This time of day, it's probably ten cars deep across twelve or more lanes."

"What the hell?" Scott asked. "Is there any way we can—"

"Sir, the officer has had to turn on his lights."

"The hell he did," Scott said.

"This domestic is escalating, sir, and the officer on the scene had full discretion to—"

"Are you joking?" Scott asked, stomping out the door. "I need a guide to take me there before this gets absolutely out of control—"

"SHOTS FIRED! SHOTS FIRED!" the cop in the trailer shouted. "We have an officer in need of assistance! Other officers reporting a toxic purple cloud in the vicinity of—"

A sick feeling grabbed hold of me and I didn't wait any longer. The cops weren't going to settle this, and who knew what kind of damage could be done by the time Scott managed to get out to this place in his car? While everyone else was panicking and streaming out of the trailer, I ducked into the woods, hid behind a tree, shed my jacket and my wig, and took to the sky, heading in the direction of the purple cloud less than a mile away, hoping that for once I could defuse the situation before it got much, much worse.

21.

June

"This wasn't how it was supposed to be!" June screamed through the cloud of purple toxin. Ell had created a little pocket of clear air around himself, looking just a step below panic. She'd already forgotten about their argument, the more pressing concern of a cop shooting at her forcing June to release a cloud and go to ground. She'd used it to hide for a minute or two as the cop approached, and then she'd snuck behind a car and then bushwhacked him from behind in the chaos of people screaming and fleeing their vehicles.

Now she had him by the throat, tempted to fire a burst of toxin right into his lungs for screwing this up for her. He'd ruined everything, *everything*, and how dare he?

Why was everyone out to ruin everything for her? Couldn't they just let her be for a little while? Let her and Ell have a few moments of joy in the middle of this plague of trouble? Was that really too much to ask?

"June, we have to go," Ell said, looking around, sending the cloud of purple skyward, away from them. People were running, shouting, clutching their kids and carrying them away with nothing but horrorstruck looks cast behind them. "Let's get in one of these abandoned cars and—"

"NO!" she screamed, putting her fist through the passenger window of a nearby car. It shattered, leaving her with a couple pebble-like shards lodged in her hand. It stung a little, and bled a little, too, but she didn't care. She'd accidentally let loose another little cloud of toxin in her anger, and Ell reached out to dispel it.

"We need to leave," Ell said. "You don't honestly think they're going to let us in now, do you?"

She shook with rage. How could this be ruined for her? It should have been so good—a shining, golden day where they could just be, without any of the pressures on their relationship that seemed to infect everything more and more lately. "I don't care," she said, still blind with fury. "I will *make* them let us in. They won't have a choice."

"Y—" Ell started.

"You can't do that," another voice finished for him. A female voice, coming from above. June looked up in surprise to find a woman coming out of the sky, landing only a few feet away from her and Ell. Her dark hair flashed in the morning sun, a little messy like it had been flattened down against its will, and the look of determination on her face shone through even under the uncharacteristic makeup, something June had never seen on the woman, not in any of the innumerable times she'd seen her on TV or in pictures.

"Sienna Nealon," June said, awe cracking its way through her anger.

"The one and only," Sienna said, standing there like a guard, between her and the way to Disney. The way to her dream. "Now ... June ... what do you say we talk about what you're doing ... girl to girl?"

22.

Sienna

June Randall wasn't quite what I expected when I was staring her down, but for that matter, neither was Elliot Lefavre. Grandma Randall had certainly told us that June was willful, but by the way Elliot was cowering a dozen yards away, I got the feeling real quick that June was the brains, heart, and spine of this operation, and Elliot was … maybe a pinky finger. Maybe less than that.

June was suffering a case of being awestruck at the sight of me, so it took a little bit to recover her wits. "What are you doing here?" she asked at last, in a shaky voice.

"I'm here to stop you from taking a series of mistakes into much, much worse territory," I said. "June … you haven't killed anyone so far, okay? And that's good. But this crime spree you're on? You can't possibly think it's going to last. They're not going to let you get away with it forever."

She didn't even blink, just answered back like a snotty teen. "Why not? You got away with yours and they haven't caught you yet."

Ouch. That one hit the mark. "Touché," I said. "But I'm also not committing an ongoing string of crimes that are like a thumb to the eye of the country's law enforcement—"

"What about that New York thing a couple months ago?" June shot back instantly. God, she was a wiseacre. How did Grandma Randall avoid mashing her mouth, as my mom used to threaten when I'd get lippy with her?

"That was a misunderstanding," I lied.

"And that thing where you fought off a bunch of government agents somewhere up north?"

The battle I'd had in South Dakota had gone public? "I … uh … that was against my brother, who was having some issues … and some other friends. Just a squabble. We're all good now. Well, good-ish."

"What about what you did to the president?"

Shit. How was I supposed to even answer that bit of unsourced rumorage? "I don't know what you're talking about," I said unconvincingly.

Somehow, Harmon said, *I don't think she believes you. I'm having trouble believing it, too, and I was there.*

"Dick," I said under my breath, incredibly unhelpfully as I was facing down June. Her expression darkened, and I felt compelled to add, "I was talking to a voice in my head. Not you. Sorry. You're not a dick. Probably."

"I've admired you for a long time," June said, breathing heavily, her feet set, a couple degrees off from the posture people tended to adopt just before a fight. Her tank top strap threatened to fall off her shoulder, the cloth clinging to her thin, athletic build. She was definitely heading toward confrontation, and that was concerning. "But one of the reasons I admire you is that you don't take this sort of crap."

I looked around at all the abandoned cars around me—and a few not abandoned, families panicked and staying inside, as though locked doors and windows would keep them safe in a metahuman showdown. "I don't kill innocent people, June. I don't attack the cops. Yes, I've fought off metas who have attempted to do me—or others—harm, but I don't go looking for fights, okay? And it's not about 'taking crap.' Anyone with our powers could go on a streak of godlike impertinence. It's a tale as old as history, reflected in the thousands of myths that are the only remaining record of our peoples' early days. Flying off the handle at normal folks when things don't go your way or they won't give you what you want is not something I'm known for, all right?" That was mostly true, I thought.

"But you're way more wanted by the law than we are," June said, eyes flashing, a smirk curling the corners of her mouth. "Why would you come here? Why would you want to even get involved in this?"

I took a deep breath. "Because what you're doing is wrong."

She took that like a light punch to the face, head rocking back. "And you're right." She punched back verbally. "I've never even killed anyone."

"Good," I said. "I'm here to make sure you don't."

"You shouldn't be fighting us on this," June said, blinking in a dazed sort of surprise. "You should be with us."

I glanced at her fella, who was watching our whole exchange wide-eyed and fearful. "Three's a crowd."

She smiled lightly. "I guess so." She squared her feet, and I could tell she was about done talking.

"Don't," I said, and she paused. "Don't do this. You don't want this kind of trouble."

"Maybe not," she said, and to her credit, she wasn't shaking. She damned well should have been. "But I haven't been running from trouble, in case you haven't noticed." Her eyes lit up. "I've been running to it."

I cringed, letting out a weary sigh. "The way you're talking, I'm starting to get the feeling that your 'no kills' record is more of an accident than a planned thing."

"Like I said before," she grinned, "I admire that you take no crap."

"You might not admire that so much when this is over." I readied myself, drawing up Eve's light nets.

"You can't expect others to take crap when you're not willing to," June said.

"I'll take a certain amount from you," I said. "For instance … I'll let you leave right now." That caused her to raise an eyebrow. "Get in your car, drive away. No harm needs to come to you this minute."

She gave my offer a few seconds of serious thought, and then she exploded in a cloud of purple so hazy that I couldn't see her anymore. She didn't say anything, just disappeared.

"I guess that's a no, then," I muttered, looking over the hundred cars laid out before me—and she could have been hiding behind any one of them, waiting to take me down.

23.

Great, I thought as a cloud of toxic purple smoke spread out in front of me, dispersing in the midst of the traffic jam I was standing in. I finally got to do my part in this, to face down June Randall, and she decided to play hide and go seek.

Not being a sucker who'd stand around waiting to get hit, I immediately started playing along. I dove for the deck, sliding under the chassis of a giant truck and looking around for feet running between the massive tires. I didn't see anything, but then, my job was slightly clouded by the preponderance of purple smoke still dispersing.

I kept going sideways, figuring I'd slide out behind the truck and use it as cover, maybe reacquire my targets by hunting for them from behind its large frame and heavy engine. That was a safer bet than just standing out in the middle of the road, and not because June had any kind of serious, long-range attack ability. I was pretty sure she didn't, based on case studies I'd read from old files about poison metas.

No, I was worried about her boyfriend, the man with a spine composed of a boiled-to-mush spaghetti noodle.

He had the same power as Reed's, which meant wind could come shooting at me at any time, hampering the hell out of my efforts. I suspected he wasn't as strong as Reed had been even before the serum my brother had been injected with had boosted his powers, but Elliot was still enough of a threat I didn't want to give him a clear shot at me. Only an idiot would do that.

"Why are you hiding?" June shouted across the parking lot between us. "Are you afraid of me?"

I slipped between the bumper of a sedan and a minivan, heading toward the sound of her voice. Footsteps echoed nearby and I drifted that way, keeping low to the ground. I was taking a long, circuitous route toward where I'd heard her, mainly because I wasn't actually after her.

Why waste my time with June? It was pointless to argue with her.

"June?" Elliot called, giving away his position. He hadn't strayed far from where I'd last seen him and was wandering there, as though Sienna Nealon wasn't going to just walk up and slap the hell right out of him. His call came at the worst possible moment, and I swore softly as I shot along, inches from the ground, heading right for him—

June either guessed what I was doing or saw me coming, because she leapt off a nearby car and blotted out the sun with her shadow as she tried to land on my back. I saw her coming at the last minute, though it was a bit of a surprise since she wasn't anywhere near where she'd been when she'd called out to me seconds earlier. Girl moved fast. And stealthily.

I rolled hard and threw myself to the side, and she barely tapped me in the back with a foot as she came down for a landing. Unfortunately for her, my maneuver screwed things up for her; she landed badly, because I jerked her footing from beneath her.

She rolled to her feet a little clumsily, but I was up before her, ready to throw a net. She was damned close, though, and puffed that purple cloud like a skunk once more as my light net disappeared into its depths. She cried out within, but somehow I knew she was gone, my net probably missing her by inches.

I whipped my head around as the sound of a dull roar from wind started up behind me. "How could I forget about you?" I muttered under my breath as a miniature tornado whipped me around in a circle, spinning me like a top toward the cloud of poison.

24.

June

They hadn't been kidding about Sienna Nealon, the people who'd talked about her on TV. She was no pushover, that was for sure. Twice June had needed to blast a wide cloud of toxin to lose her, like a smokescreen she could project to hide in the depths of. It was a trick she'd used on people before, because who wanted to look for her in a cloud of poison?

Unfortunately, it was exhausting to produce, and at this point, June felt like she was running on fumes. She dragged a little more as she ran now, breath coming in ragged gasps as she hunkered behind a nearby car.

This couldn't be the end, could it?

She had Sienna Effing Nealon after her.

Yeah.

This could be the end.

How do I stop her? June wondered. The answer came to her, instantly, and it was breathtakingly simple.

If it worked.

Of course it'll work, June thought, *she came all this way to stop us. It'll work.*

"I'm starting to get cranky," Sienna announced, and the roar of one of Ell's tornados was suddenly blotted out by another sound. June chanced a look and saw Sienna spinning rapidly, bursting out of Ell's little imprisonment attempt. He squawked and leapt aside as Sienna came striding toward him, and that gave June zero time left to work with.

She looked around frantically and found the object of her immediate desire in a car three back. Two parents in the front seat of a big SUV, mom and dad with eyes wide like a full moon, watching everything unfold, frozen in time. And behind them …

June sprinted for the SUV, ripping open the rear door. "Hey, Nealon!" she shouted once she'd done it, sticking her hand into the car.

Sienna stopped only ten feet from Ell, who was already panicking, freaking out, too frozen to run. Sienna stared at her, and her expression hardened instantly. "You sure you want to play it that way?"

June kept her hand leveled inside the car, just over a car seat occupied by a chubby little cherub who had no idea why some stranger's hand was hovering a foot above his face. The little blue cap was dwarfed by his chub cheeks. "I'll do whatever I have to in order to get us out of this."

"That's a big line to cross, June," Sienna said, quiet. "You go over it … there is no coming back."

"Don't make me cross it, then," June said. "You told us we could leave earlier. Just let us go."

"Or what?" Sienna asked. "You'll do something so horrific it'd give a hardened killer nightmares?"

"I don't know anything about what'd give me nightmares," June said, "but if I'm having them out here, where I'm free, instead of inside a prison … I'll take that trade. I'll take that trade seven days a week and twice on Sunday."

Nealon seemed to be thinking it over. "You want to run? Run. Get out of here." She cocked her head, and June realized that the sound of sirens was obnoxiously loud in the distance. "Better hurry."

"Ell," June called, and he shakily started to move, passing Sienna at a run. He moved toward their old car, and June shook her head. "No. Something new. Here at the edge of the lanes." Ell changed trajectory, moving toward the very edge of the impromptu parking lot. He looked into two different abandoned cars before finding a small coupe that was still running. "Over here," he said, and jumped in the driver's seat.

"I think that's my cue," June said, hesitating. She didn't want to pull her hand out of the SUV, because what if Sienna blasted her with something right then. She had that power, right? Yeah. June had seen it.

"Go on, then," Sienna said, and suddenly June realized she looked tense. Almost desperately so, looking around toward the source of the sirens, which were working their way up through the traffic jam behind her.

Of course. She needed to run, too.

"You first," June said, and Sienna rolled her eyes, then rocketed skyward without another word. June watched the heavens for a few seconds after she'd disappeared, and then burst into a run and leapt into the passenger side of Ell's purloined car. "Drive!" she shouted as he bumped along in a U-turn and floored it as they tore past the endless line of parked cars on the other side of the road. "And whatever you do—don't stop."

25.

Scott

It had taken a few minutes to make sure that the cops hadn't closed all the entries to the park. They didn't want that, after all, because then it would trap the two fugitives in a desperate situation, in a place where they were forced to fight their way out. The casualties would be terrible, like when a high speed car chase went off the rails in a busy place. This might actually be worse, because of the concentration of families the target location presented.

"We have a chopper ready to go up," Lieutenant Nunez said, speeding the car along toward the incident. He was one of the officers whom Scott had been interfacing with during the process. He figured Nunez was a pretty good cop and a pretty good guy, but he was probably over fifty and hadn't taken much of this metahuman business to heart in his approach to the job, yet. Old dog, no new tricks.

"Keep the chopper down," Scott said tersely. "The male subject's power is over the wind, and he can easily crash a helo."

Nunez's face fell. "How are we supposed to keep an eye on them for later apprehension, then?"

Scott almost cursed out loud at the frustration on that one. "Traffic cams until we can't keep an eye on them anymore."

"And after that? What if they slip loose?"

"Then they slip loose," Scott said. "For now. This isn't

worth killing over yet, and that's the only easy way to bring them down. I need time—time and space to get a chance to work on these two."

"Up ahead," Nunez said, driving the car at high speed over the shoulder. There were woods to their right, and people were starting to pop their heads out, refugees from the traffic jam who had left their cars when things had gone bad. Scott couldn't blame them. He would have run, too. "I don't see anyone, do you?"

"Not a soul," Scott said. Where was Sienna? Had she run when she heard the sirens? Because if so, maybe the downed fugitives were just hanging out over there, wrapped in a light net or something, waiting to be cuffed and led away. In June's case, she'd need some serum to counteract her powers. Only in his nightmares could Scott imagine letting a woman who could produce toxic clouds walk around with that power in jail.

They skirted the shoulder and rolled to a stop about two hundred feet from the massive line of toll booths that barred entry to the park without paying. Scott eyed them warily, wondering if something would come popping out from between the massed cars, but all seemed silent. He pulled his gun and lifted his hand as he stepped out of the car, taking a running leap and springing atop a Ford Taurus for a better look.

The sunlit Florida day didn't allow for much concealment. Sure, they could be hiding behind one of the cars, but they weren't obviously here, and neither was Sienna. Other cop cars were squealing up now, police officers streaming out. "Search the scene," Scott said, hesitant to let them go into a potential clash with two metas, but also sure that he wouldn't be able to search this entire area himself. "Help the victims," he said, as more families starting streaming out of the woods where they'd taken cover on either side of the road.

"Where's your partner?" Nunez asked as Scott dismounted the Ford's roof, leaving a couple good footprints behind from his meta strength.

"Right here." Sienna angled her way up to them, looking

only slightly disheveled. Her red wig was on right, at least, and the glasses really did change the look of her. "I think they got away."

Nunez raised an eyebrow. "No shit."

Sienna just shrugged, lapsing back to silence. He wouldn't have wanted to know what she was thinking right now, though he suspected whatever it was, it was more toxic than anything June Randall typically came up with. "Any idea where they've gone?" he asked her. Nunez frowned, and Scott said, "Her power is prediction and tracking, okay? She can trace a weak trail sometimes."

Nunez seemed to take that at face value. "That could be useful."

"They took hostages, but left them behind," Sienna said, now freed from having to maintain the illusion she had no clue what had happened here. "Then they ran. Got spooked by something. Something scary." She put a finger on her chin, feigning contemplation. "But also smart. And sexy, I think … ?"

Scott barely kept from burying his face in his hands. "Are they clear of the parks?"

"I think so," Sienna said. "Their old car is over there." She waved toward the abandoned Pontiac that June and Elliot had been driving all this time, trapped in the middle of all that traffic, boxed into the makeshift parking lot. "Their new one is white, a Dodge SUV, tag number …" She concentrated, then rattled something off that Nunez scrambled to write down.

"Damn," Nunez said, "that is slick. I'll get this radioed in right away."

"Make sure when you issue the BOLO you tag it—" Sienna started.

"Yeah, I know," Nunez said. "Do not approach. The metahuman warning." And he headed away from them toward his car.

"Fight didn't go so well?" Scott asked, metahuman low, so that only Sienna could hear him, as soon as Nunez was well out of possible earshot. Of course, he could have been standing right there and would only have heard a very odd sound, but he might have noticed the very slight movement of their mouths.

"She got desperate," Sienna said. "Took a family hostage. I got her clear of it by promising to let them go. Figure we'll confront them again when there's less on the line."

"Yeah," Scott said. "Catch them on some two-lane road somewhere, clear of people."

"Especially now that we've got their license plate again," Sienna said, chewing her lip. "I'd expect them to change cars again. They've gotta know by now that it's how we caught them this time."

"Then they'll be ditching that as soon as it's convenient," Scott said. "How do you figure they'll get a new car?"

Sienna made a face that evinced discomfort. "Brute force. I don't think they know how to properly hotwire a car, and it's not as easy with newer models, so … carjacking, home invasion … something like that. If they're smart, and I'm not sure they are, maybe they'll try and pilfer a set of keys and waltz off with a vehicle hoping that it'll just get added to the background noise and not attributed to them, but … brute force, if I had to guess. So far that's their MO."

"Agreed," Scott said, with more than a little discomfort of his own. He hesitated, then let loose with the question that was on his mind. "Now that you've met them, face to face … what's your assessment?"

Sienna thought about it for a little bit before she answered, and when she did, her words came out halting, like she wasn't sure of anything. "This isn't just a simple ego spiral. Most of the time, those are solo, so it's just one person getting higher and higher on themselves as they go, that sense of invulnerability growing unchecked by another person, by their conscience and doubts."

"But there's two of them," Scott said, "so that's changing the equation?"

"Somehow, yeah, I think," Sienna said. "The love connection … the sense I get, she's the backbone, he's the accomplice. She rolls him like she did Grandma, without even thinking about it. However she has to." She shook her head. "I don't know. This is a mess. I've never quite run across one like this before."

"What do you think they're capable of?" Scott asked. "If we push them."

"Nothing good," she answered promptly. "If they're pushed? I think they'll go as far as they have to in order to stay free." She swallowed visibly. "And given what I just saw from her as she was trying to wriggle out of our grasp ... if she's willing to actually carry through on her threats ... they're going to be a real danger to whoever gets in their way."

26.

June

They drove until they hit freeway, then headed north on Interstate 75. Ell kept his hands on the wheel, eyes nervously shifting to the rearview mirror every few seconds, checking for cops. June knew what he was doing because she was doing the same, studiously watching for any sign of pursuit. Any second, she expected to see light flare in the rearview, a siren issue that stomach-wrenching squeal, but so far they were clear.

And somehow, that didn't make her feel any better.

"Mannnnnnn," Ell said, letting out a sigh that sounded like relief, "I can't believe we got away."

"We haven't, yet."

He looked in the rearview again. "Uh, I think we did. We lost them. Or they never came after us in the first place. We're clear, at least for now." He leaned across the new console that divided them in a way the bench seat in the old Pontiac never had. The seats weren't as plush, either. "Come on. We just beat Sienna Nealon. Fought her and walked away. And I don't know about you, but I'm not even sore. We didn't even get hurt, you know?"

June worked her ankle gently, the one she'd twisted when she'd blown the landing as she was trying to come down on Sienna. "Speak for yourself."

"Well, you're not hurt bad, right?" He spoke with the same nervous energy as always, but instead of despondently hangdog, somehow, now Ell seemed to be experiencing the reverse, a kind of joyful enthusiasm at surviving the encounter at the gates of Disney.

That insensitive *ass*. Didn't he know Sienna Nealon had just crushed her dream?

Of course not. Because Ell only cared about his own feelings, not hers.

"She let us get away," June said, changing the subject before she ended up slapping him down and causing a fight. She didn't have the energy for one right now, anyway. She felt so drawn out, so tired from producing and expelling all that toxin, she might have fallen asleep right there in the seat if she wasn't feeling petrified, sorrowful, and furious all at once. "She'll be back, too. You watch. She's not done with us."

"What's she even doing here?" Ell asked, turning his focus back to driving. He wasn't even doing one mile above the speed limit. Normally she would have chastised him for that, but now? It was probably smart. It'd keep them out of the cops' eyes.

"You heard her." June let her head loll away to look out the passenger-side window. "She came for us."

"Yeah, but she's *wanted*," Ell said. "Like, we're in trouble, but she's really in deep. She's probably the reason you never even see us on the news. How many breaking reports a day do they issue on rumors of where she's gone?"

That was true. June had long since grown bored of watching panel discussions speculating on where exactly Sienna Nealon had gone. It had gotten real bad in the wake of the thing in New York where she'd clashed with Captain Frost and partially wrecked the conference center up there a couple months back, but fortunately had died down some in the intervening time to make room for tireless discussions about the new president, Gondry, and his boring-ass agenda. What a clown. At least Harmon had called the fools out when they crossed him. Gondry was just a snooze.

"You think she'll come back at us again?" Ell asked after a brief silence.

"Probably," June said. "She was more scared of the cops

catching up to her than she was scared of us."

"Aw, man," Ell said. "That's … that sucks."

"Yep," June said, and for the first time since this had all begun, she knew a little of what Ell had felt all along. That crushing weight that something was after them, something ominous, something circling closer and closer, like a shark in calm waters.

And it scared the hell out of her.

27.

Sienna

"We have no idea where they've gone," Nunez said with a shake of his head. "Traffic cams lost them here." He pointed at the map somewhere north of the Disney property. "Not sure if they were aware of their presence, but they turned on a side road, drove for a while, and by the time they came out—and there's like, forty exit points for this section of roads, not all of them even covered by cams—rush hour was in full swing."

"And they picked a common car to steal," I said, nodding along.

"If you could try and give us some insight," Nunez said, fixing me with his gaze. "That might help."

"Sorry," I said, "can't do it if I'm not in a place where they've been recently."

"So you're like a bloodhound?" Nunez said. "But for past activity?"

"Yeah, like that," I lied glibly, staring at the map. "I don't think they're going to stay in the Orlando area."

"We're pulling the camera footage of the confrontation," Nunez said, "but we're having some trouble with it. Someone showed up, but their face is all … I don't even know. The techs are going over it, but whatever it is, it looks like a corrupted file."

"The hell?" Scott muttered. He didn't know about the program that ArcheGrey had crafted to fool facial recognition programs, or how it was now running 24/7 to eliminate me from easy identification anytime I got caught on a grid-connected security camera. Wheeee. I didn't really condone working with borderline psychos like ArcheGrey, but occasionally it did produce certain advantages.

Hear, hear, Wolfe said, proving my point.

A toast to those of us Sienna disdains and scorns, Bjorn agreed. *Long may we be proven useful.*

Even I would drink to that, Harmon said, *causing me to roll my eyes and offend Nunez for no good reason.*

"Well, that's an interesting quirk," I said, "but kind of irrelevant to the matter at hand, which is our two fugitives."

"You don't think someone confronting them is kind of important?" Nunez asked. "This person flew. Like—"

"A bird?" I asked. "A plane? Like—"

"What my colleague means to say," Scott said with his most ingratiating smile, and a warning look at me to back the hell off before I exposed myself, "is that given our small manpower numbers, we try and focus on one thing at a time."

"Huh," Nunez said, shaking his head. "You know your job better than I do," he said, in a tone that clearly indicated he thought we were government idiots. "Anyway … I think these two have probably passed out of our jurisdiction. You don't think they'd be crazy enough to come back, do you?"

"No," I said, thinking it through. "I think they're spooked. They'll run a ways before they raise their heads again."

Scott nodded. "I think you're right. I'd like to be a hundred percent sure, though."

Hell, so would I, I didn't say. But one hundred percent certainty and crazy people on the run were improbable bedfellows. And I would know, being a crazy person on the run myself.

"So … we done here?" Nunez asked.

"I think so," Scott said, blotting at his bleary eyes. "Let us know if you come up with anything else?"

"Will do," Nunez said with utmost professionalism, especially considering he now thought we were morons.

"Let's hit the hotel," Scott said, and I followed him out of the command center.

He waited to speak again until we were in the car. "You got pretty close to the line back there," he said as he started up our borrowed car.

"Sometimes I forget myself."

"Don't do that," Scott said, turning us around in the parking lot, the waning light of day hiding behind the forests that surrounded us. "It won't end in anything good."

"I agree," I said, leaning against the head rest. "I'm just not used to these long days at this point."

"It's late afternoon."

"And I haven't eaten much today." Come on, Scott. I had endless excuses for my crankiness.

"You think they'll head north or south?"

"North," I said. "Trapped animals want space, and south doesn't provide space, running to the end of the peninsula only corners them worse." I paused. "I ever tell you about the time I faced off with a rogue Poseidon down in Key West?"

He looked up, like he was trying to recall. "If you did, it's gone now." He sounded accusing, but at least he didn't look at me.

I searched my own memory, and those of his I was carrying. "I think it happened after we broke up," I said. "But this guy—he had nothing on you. He would have been better off getting a job at a bar watering drinks, but instead he decided to become a confidence man—"

"Seriously?"

"Yeah, even before he manifested, I think. But once he had his powers, he switched it up and started to try and bully his victims once he got caught. Turned kinda ugly, ended in a homicide by drowning several hundred yards from the sea. They couldn't detect any sign the body had been moved, and there was a steady trail of ocean water between the shore and the corpse, so—"

Scott laughed. "Why didn't he just write a confession, sign it, and leave it there for them to find?"

"He was surprisingly tough to track down, given how

idiotically he'd left the scene," I said. "Turns out a witness actually had seen his car there the night of the killing, so we knew what to look for. Local PD pulled him over on one of the bridges, and I had to fly in when he dragged their cruiser into the water."

"Huh," Scott said. "How long did it take to—"

"Not very long. He lacked your finesse, and thanks to you, I knew all his tricks before he pulled any of them."

Scott smiled, but it faded quickly. "How long were we together after …"

I waited for him to finish his sentence. "After what?"

"After Sovereign," he said. "After that last battle over Minneapolis."

"Hummmm," I said, buying time because this was not a subject I was keen to discuss. "Not too long."

"It was after I went to work for my dad?"

"A little after that, yeah."

"How long?" He pushed, but politely.

It still made me squirm. "I don't know off the top of my head—"

"You said months after Sovereign. How much longer was I with you before—"

"It's not a simple—"

"It ought to be," Scott said, and now the politeness was starting to fade. "Something like, 'We were together two months, eight days, six hours'—"

"Thirty-six minutes and twelve seconds? Sorry, I didn't keep track of it like that."

"But it shouldn't be that hard to—" he pressed.

I blew up. "We broke up like three, four times, okay? We'd break up for a night, then get back together. Then break up for five minutes, and get back together. Then we broke up for … ten days? Twelve? I don't even know, because I was working like a dog, and I'd come back from an assignment, and you'd be all, 'I just can't live without you,' and I'd be tired, and exhausted, and heartbroken from the— the damned withdrawals feeling of you being gone, and we'd get right back together again—"

"Withdrawals?" Scott made a scoffing noise. "Like what?

129

I was some kind of drug you couldn't quit?"

"I don't know, man," I said, trying to get him to stop talking about this awful, uncomfortable, horrible period that I wished I could forget as effectively as he had. "It was what it was."

He didn't let that rest for very long. "And what was it?"

I blew air out through my lips in the most exasperated sound possible. "A disaster, probably."

He grabbed the wheel and held it tensely as he steered us toward International Drive, its strip of countless tourist attractions, and our hotel in silence for a short while. I knew it wouldn't last, and it broke loose around the time we were passing a disused water park that proclaimed itself "Wet N' Wild," in faded letters on a loosely hanging sign. "So if it was a disaster in your opinion—"

I blew my stack. "It wasn't just *my* opinion, okay? You told me repeatedly that you wished we could just be done without the pain of separation. That it sucked so bad that we couldn't get our crap together as a couple, but we couldn't seem to get away from each other without some sort of lazy gravity dragging us back together. I was working a lot back then, okay? I'd be out of town for six days out of seven, and on the seventh day I'd drive out to Wisconsin or Iowa or South Dakota or something to check out some stupid, unsubstantiated report of a meta incident that had nothing to do with metas, and I'd come back wired from caffeine but utterly exhausted to a voicemail from you, and I'd be lonely, and you'd be lonely, and we'd both be hurting, so …" I shrugged, so tired of this conversation even though I was the only one that remembered how often we'd had it. It didn't stop it from being genuinely annoying to have to suffer it again, like some kind of hellish reprise of the most dramatically painful relationship I'd ever been in, one that had caused me to not date anyone for years afterward.

He took a turn and pulled us into the parking lot of our hotel, a tower across from the entry to Universal Studios. He was steaming, it was obvious, but he was holding in the choicest of his comments, probably trying to defuse the situation in a way I hadn't been able to just now. That was progress, because before, when we were dating, he was always standing ready to throw that last bit of gasoline on the fire when I was already enraged.

The car thudded into a parking place and he turned to me as he jerked the shifter into park. "What you did—"

"I don't want to talk about this anymore," I said. "This isn't the time, this isn't the place—"

"When is the right time and place?"

"Shortly after I get shot in the head and die, if fate be kind."

He clenched his fist. "What you did to me—"

"I know what I did to you," I said, staring sullenly straight ahead and refusing to look at him. "But rooting through the guts of that right now seems counterproductive."

I doubted that would stop him, and it didn't. He seethed audibly, an actual sound of air hissing between gritted teeth. "This is the reason that Harmon was able to turn me against you so easily."

I rate this as true, Harmon said. *It's always nice to have negative emotion to work with when you're pushing someone. For Scott, it was so easy—he was already a walking mess, sensitive to this because of what happened between him and that thoughtless blond girl that everyone in the country seems so infatuated with.*

Scott's eyes were darting around, and I wondered if he was hearing—"Her name is Kat," he said, confirming my suspicions that Harmon was looping him into our discussion.

Whatever, Harmon said breezily. *Everyone else remembers her name. The least I can do to keep her humble is not do her the favor.*

"He brings up a good point," Scott said, his rage evidently abating slightly. "You had to know that I wouldn't take this well, given what happened between me and Kat, her losing all memory of our relationship in Iowa that time—"

I opened the door and got out of the car, shutting it behind me before he could so much as exclaim in surprise. He hurriedly killed the engine and caught up to me halfway to the lobby door. "Are you serious right now?" he called, only a few paces behind me.

I would have walked faster, but I didn't want to cause a

disturbance by proving I was a meta in the middle of a crowded lobby as I came inside through the automatically sliding doors. "I'm not serious, no. I'm frivolous. Summery, even, though I'm a few months early." I flipped my red wig hair back over a shoulder and headed for the elevator, fingering the card key for my room in anticipation of getting the hell away from this fruitless discussion for a little while. "I understand you're angry—"

"I kinda doubt that, based on your complete and total dismissal of me right now." His face was blood red with rage, his usually dusky skin tone a few shades darker with the fury he was holding in. He probably needed to use his power to lower his blood pressure, but I wasn't about to suggest it.

"If I'm dismissing you, it's because the middle of a manhunt isn't the time to be having this discussion, and the place isn't in the lobby of this swank hotel," I said, crossing to the elevator and clicking the button hurriedly, as though that would speed things up at all. It dinged within a few seconds, which kept me from viciously stabbing the button a few more times.

"When is the time and place, then, Sienna?" he asked once the elevator doors had safely closed and no one could hear him call me by my name. "Because you name it, and I'll be there. In fact, if we'd had this discussion before Harmon got his hooks in me—"

"Nothing would have changed," I said. "The kind of pain you're feeling—the resentment, the legit, 'This person done me wrong,' feeling ... it doesn't just go away, Scott." I looked him right in the eye and opened up my emotions in a way I usually didn't.

It wasn't that usual rage I projected, though a little of that was stirred in.

It was a concoction of heartbreak, from the time I'd lost my first love to unspeakable betrayal. The time my mentor— two of them, actually—had completely ruined me for trust. A thousand occasions when my own mother had locked me up in a metal coffin and kept me there until she was satisfied I'd learned some unknown lesson. That time I found out my first boyfriend, now dead, had been spying on me for someone I had come to hate.

I looked at him with all that, spoke what I did from the heart …

And his expression didn't change a whit. Not one little bit. He was like iron, that anger so clear in his eyes that I couldn't have explained it away any more than I could have stopped the tides from battering the shore. Only he could do that, not me.

The elevator opened as he started to say something, and I dodged out, him following a few seconds later. "If you really want to have this out, let's do it later. Not tonight. Not now. I'd prefer not ever, but … hey, I don't always get what I want."

"Fine," he said, and I knew for damned sure it wasn't, but I'd happily take it for now. "After. But don't think you're going to get away with—"

"Of all the things I think I might get away with—murder, arrogance, being a scofflaw—no, this isn't something I think I'll 'get away with,'" I said, having finally, thankfully, reached my door. I waved the card key over the panel and heard the click of it unlocking, the little green light flashing to let me know I'd done it. "I suspect you'll pursue me to the ends of the earth seeking emotional satisfaction on this."

"You're not wrong," he said darkly, moving to his door, just one down from mine, and opening it. "You're not wrong at all." And he disappeared into the darkness within, and I knew that, nope, in spite of what I might wish, this was not the end of this discussion.

Not nearly.

28.

June

"This wasn't how it was supposed to be," June said into the running shower nozzle. It rained hot, steaming water down on her, boiling her like a lobster under its blazing onslaught, like a sun-stream of heat and liquid scalding her flesh.

She didn't care. Her bare ass was on the shower tub floor, her tail bone protesting at the uncomfortable way she was sitting, steam hanging in the air above her and giving everything that pungent, humid smell. She'd been in here for long minutes, maybe half an hour, but she didn't care. Ell would be fine without her for a while, and she needed this time.

They'd followed Interstate 75 all the way up to Gainesville, Florida, and gotten off at an exit where they saw hotels. They picked one of the big name, mid-range ones and checked in, saying little. What was there to say?

They both knew what was after them now. Was Sienna Nealon going to just give up now that the cops had come after them all and made her run? Doubtful, if she'd actually gone out of her way to come after her and Ell already.

That was the part June couldn't figure out. How did Sienna Nealon know to come after them? Thus far they'd only clashed with—

With that FBI agent. She threw her head back, and hot water ran down her neck and chest, her hair dangling and dribbling down her back. Of course. How could she not have seen it immediately?

They'd beaten him, humiliated him. Of course he would have gone for help. And they were exes, weren't they? So he'd gotten beat, and he'd gone looking for help from her, naturally, because …

Because she was just about the baddest badass he could have picked.

June put her head down again. Of course she would have sided with him. That was one of the things June was having trouble with, and it pissed her off that it bothered her so. Sienna Nealon was like a god—goddess, whatever—and she'd shown up and thrown down against them!

Against her.

It was like a personal insult. A slap to the face, a punch to the gut.

And she'd cost June her dream.

It was probably the single most devastating thing June could ever remember happening to her. Not just the fact that Sienna Nealon had shown up, but that she'd shown up and driven it home, hard, that this wasn't some happy-go-lucky trip. All those good feelings, the love and light she'd felt, those happy moments when she and Ell weren't arguing …

That was all over now. Because of Sienna Nealon.

How could June ignore it, now that this had happened? The cops were after her. Before, she might not have believed they had a chance against her and Ell, but now … trading a kick with Sienna Nealon, and knowing she was being treated with kid gloves …

It had driven it all home in a way nothing else could have.

"Our days are numbered," June muttered under her breath.

Trouble was coming.

A knock at the door sounded and it squeaked as Ell opened it a crack. "Think I'm gonna order a pizza. You want me to get you some?"

She didn't care. How could she eat at a time like this? "No," she said, voice small and lost in the roar of the shower head.

He heard her anyway. "Maybe I'll order extra, just in

case." He closed the door before she could tell him not to bother, and she flashed irritation but ultimately couldn't muster the energy to get up and go after him to complain.

Sienna Nealon was after them.

The cops were on their tail.

Their days were numbered.

She clutched her legs close to her, drawing her knees up to her chest and huddling there, under the steaming spray. Her tears were lost amid the falling drops of water, but she knew they were there. How did you even keep from losing it at a time like this? She had no idea, because she couldn't even—

June stopped, cocking her head, remembering something. She drew a breath, and it wasn't as ragged as it had been a moment earlier.

How did you go on at a time like this?

The same way you went on the rest of the time—you found a new idea and started working on it.

"Sienna Nealon is after us," June breathed, and gave voice again to the thing that was tearing at her, dragging her down. The cops—they weren't the problem. They were half-assing this at best, these local donut eaters, acting like they weren't even really serious about coming after the two of them. Except for maybe that FBI agent, whose ass she and Ell had already kicked.

Sienna Nealon was the problem. She was the one that was gnawing at June's mind, worrying her, harrying her, making her feel vulnerable, scared, like shit.

Like she was going to get bushwhacked at any time.

But that could be a two-way street, couldn't it? June wondered. Sienna Nealon was tough, but … she wasn't invincible.

Was she?

No, she couldn't be. June remembered that much from her grandma. There was no such thing as an invincible meta. Tough ones. Impossibly tough ones, in fact, called Achilles types, but … nobody else was invincible. Sienna Nealon was a succubus, and she had other powers, but … invincibility wasn't one of them. June was sure of that.

So what were you supposed to do to stop a meta? Well, June knew the answer to that, too, from her upbringing, and it caused her to stop sobbing and to finally turn off the shower, because now—now that she had an idea—she finally had the energy to come out and start dealing with things again.

Starting with Sienna Nealon.

29.

Scott

Scott was still steaming the next day when he met her for breakfast. He'd had nothing but time to dwell on the situation, like a man with a nervous compulsion and nothing to do but pick an old scab. And pick he had, until that inflamed little piece of tissue was a screaming, open wound, gushing anger and bitter resentment once more.

If she could only see fit to apologize, maybe we could start getting past it. But she's not sorry.

Not one little bit.

He found her in the hotel dining room already picking at a couple of things on her plate, though she was exhibiting just as little interest in consuming them as she had since they'd started working together. He thought it a little curious—though even with the festering anger that was bubbling beneath the surface, he wouldn't have, in a million years, actually mentioned it—that she had obviously put on a few pounds (okay, more than a few) since last they'd run across each other. Firstly, he wouldn't bring it up because politeness ruled it off bounds, and secondly, because in spite of it, and perhaps even more annoying to him …

He still found her very attractive. Also in spite of the somewhat sour look she wore when he walked in, taking tiny flakes of croissant and trying them experimentally, then pushing the plate away as though they were the least satisfactory thing on the planet.

"No good?" he asked as he pulled out his chair. He knew his manner was stiff, his bearing straighter than usual. Last night's irritations were all too fresh.

"I'm just not that hungry," she said, a little stiffer than usual as well. She hadn't reacted noticeably upon his entry, though he was certain she'd noticed his approach. She straightened up in her seat and put both elbows on the table, causing his mother's voice to sound in his head, reminding him how rude that was. "I came up with an idea last night."

"Oh?" Scott pulled the napkin off his place setting and draped it across his lap, waiting to see what she had to say.

"It's about what June and Elliot need."

"Oh." He tried to disguise his disappointment; he felt sure she would have been thinking about him, maybe finally come to the conclusion she was sorry, genuinely remorseful for what she'd done, but …

Of course not, Harmon's voice sounded in his head. *She's a flawless goddess, at least in her own mind, and the rest of you are mere specks of insignificance. Why would she change the way she thinks when it's clear to her that the rest of you are the problem?*

"You know that asshole in your head?" Scott asked, looking down at his empty plate.

"You're going to have to be more specific."

"The one that can talk to others."

"Oh. Yeah. That asshole."

"He's not doing you any favors right now," Scott said.

Sienna frowned. "Is he talking to you again?"

"Like the devil in my ear," Scott said. "Of course, I'm somewhat used to his devilry, having gotten the worst of it last year, but still …"

"Pipe down, asshole supremo," Sienna said, frowning. "Don't make me lock you up." There was a conversational pause. "No, I don't like to do it, but that doesn't mean I won't. Scott wants you to leave him alone, so screw off, or I'll make you do it."

So long, Scotty, Harmon said. *You're on your own with her. Good luck with that.*

"Because I'll need it?" Scott asked, fingering the edge of his plate. But there was no answer.

"Anyway, I had an idea," Sienna said. "So, we know these two have been staying somewhere on their road trip."

"They could have been sleeping in the car," Scott said, wishing his plate were full for this conversation as his stomach gave off a dull rumble.

"These two? No way. They're not roughing it." Sienna leaned in, pushing aside the Danish pastry that she'd only taken a bite of. "They're staying in hotels. And a defining feature of hotels these days—"

Scott got it instantly. "They don't take cash."

"Most don't," Sienna corrected. "Some do, but they typically require a credit card because they want something to bill you with in case you order room service or trash the place like a rock star."

"How has no one noticed they've been staying at hotels and paying with a credit card?" Scott asked, putting his hand on his head. "This is investigation 101."

"Because you're in charge of the investigation," Sienna said.

"I wasn't until a couple days ago. Why haven't local investigators tumbled to this?"

"Maybe because June and Elliot aren't stirring shit where they're staying," Sienna said. "They're probably not even committing their robberies in the same town. And since this case hasn't gone beyond local until you got on it—"

"No one has done enough backtracing to figure out where they're staying before the robberies," Scott nodded. "Because they think it's instantly been handed off to the feds, but Phillips is just pocketing the damned thing, letting it sit without a soul attending to it."

"Yep. Nice way to starve the investigation of oxygen," she said. "Bad way to catch criminals, though, letting the trail go colder than the dead."

"So they're probably using a credit card—"

"Or multiples."

"—when they check in to hotels at night," Scott said. Suddenly he was a little more awake about possibilities, that bitter nightmare of a sleepless night fading like a distant dream. "We might be able to track them."

"There's a trail, at least," Sienna said cautiously. "They could have fifty cards. They could have stolen some cards. They could have identity thefted some people and be using different ones every night, but …" She shook her head. "The ego on these two? I bet they're not working too hard to cover their tracks, because up 'til now, it hasn't been an issue. You find the card they've used, I bet you find a clear trail to every place they've stayed. Because they're young, and they probably don't have that many credit cards between the two of them."

"You sure? They give applications for those things out on college campuses like after-dinner mints at a fancy restaurant."

"Having never been to college and seldom to fancy restaurants, I'll have to take your word for that. And since June and Elliot are in the same boat as I am in that regard—"

"They probably don't have a lot of credit cards," Scott said. "Point taken. Okay. Well, that should be easy enough to check when I call the office."

Sienna nodded warily. "Didn't Phillips or whoever hired you assign you to do any kind of training on basic FBI stuff?" *Like this?* he could tell she wanted to add.

It didn't sting much because the answer was simple. "Not really," Scott said. "Phillips is a bureaucrat, he doesn't know the investigative end of things from his own rectum."

"That makes it really awkward to poop, I'd guess."

"It was almost like he was more concerned with protecting his little fiefdom within the FBI than making sure we were effective," Scott said with a shrug.

"Knowing Phillips, I'm pretty sure that's exactly what he was doing," Sienna said. "Because in his mind, covering his ass was way more important than sticking his neck out to try and deliver results."

Scott shrugged, and his phone buzzed as he was about to call the office. It was a Florida number, and he answered immediately. "Scott Byerly."

The voice on the other end was intense, professional, and to the point. He was off the phone less than thirty seconds

ROBERT J. CRANE

later, and pushed his own plate back. No time for breakfast this morning. "Come on, we've got to go."

Sienna was up before he even asked. "Got a line on them?"

"Yep," Scott said, turning as she fell beside him. "Sounds like a couple matching our lovebirds just caused a stir in a hotel lobby in Gainesville. Looks like we might just have a direct line to getting that credit card number."

30.

June

She'd planned it out in the shower, with a few details added afterward by Elliot to make sure the plan flowed together. It had elements of risk, but hell, what didn't for them, now?

And besides … it let June get back to doing what she wanted, which was a welcome thing in her mind.

"I'm not signing off on this," she said sniffily, the bill for the previous night's stay right in front of her on the lobby counter, the clerk eyeing her with surprise and a level of wariness on the other side. She was a young one, probably only a couple years older than June, but she had a sense of world-weariness—from working this type of job too long, probably.

"Ma'am, there's no additional charges on there," the clerk said politely. "Signing is just a formality."

"But what's all this?" June asked, not really caring about what she was pointing to—the taxes and ancillary fees at the bottom of the page-long receipt—so much as she wanted to argue.

"Well, the state has certain taxes to cover—"

"It's outrageous," Ell said with his customary reserve. "It adds so much to the bill." It figured Ell would be genuinely pissed off about something they were only supposed to care about in the fiction they were spinning right now.

The clerk just shrugged, looking pained. "I'm sorry. It's the state. We don't have anything to do with th—"

"I want to talk to a manager," June said, not really caring if she did or not. She was enjoying herself, but not enough to simmer and wait while a manager hauled their ass over here, especially if they weren't in the building.

"I can call one if you'd like," the clerk said politely, "but she's going to tell you the same thing I am. This is like sales tax—"

"Sales tax?" Ell almost shouted. "It looks like a hell of a lot more than sales tax!"

"But it's not something we can do anything about," the clerk said. Her name tag read "Marti." June got the feeling this wasn't the first time Marti had been yelled at by a customer. Not even close.

"I want to talk to a manager," June said, raising the volume of her voice and amping up the hostility. She was determined to fake her break before much longer, and she needed to act right to make it look genuine. "Right. Now."

"Yes, ma'am," Marti said, affixing a smile of politeness to her face. She showed no teeth now, but June had noticed them earlier. They stuck out a little too far and looked funny. Marti picked up the phone, started to dial—

June looked at Ell, who nodded, and stuck out a hand, sending a blast of wind that ripped the phone out of the clerk's hand and shattered it against the wall. Marti cried out in surprise, looking just about like Ell had slapped her.

Ell looked a little stunned, too. He'd taken some coaxing to work up to the vitality of this assignment, but he'd finally caved on it. Now, though, he tried to compose himself rapidly, and stuttered out, "Th—that ought to show you!"

Marti didn't reply, too busy staggering back, trying to get away from them. June watched her, and figured the time had come for the coup de grâce, so she pulled out a small cloud of purple toxin and waved it in front of Marti's face.

"You see this?" June asked. "This is poison. You should be familiar with it, because that's what you do here, isn't it? Poison people? Piss them off? Make them mad while you're protesting, 'Oh, we provide a service.' And then lying to them about how much it costs." June sent the cloud toward Marti, halting it a few feet away. "I saw that look on your face. You've had people complain before about this bullshit, which you didn't tell us about before we were signed in and staying, only after, when we were ready to pay. What if we were broke? What if we couldn't afford it?"

"We always tell people about it at check-in," Marti said, back against the wall, staring in open horror at the purple cloud drifting toward her slowly. "I know I covered it with you—"

"YOU LIAR!" June screamed, and hopped the counter, bringing the cloud closer. She'd give herself another few seconds, then she was going to be out of here, give Marti a chance to calm down and call the cops.

"I'm not lying," Marti said, barely keeping it together as the first wafts of purple touched her cheek. "I really did tell you. I'm sorry if you didn't hear it—"

"I'm not paying your damned lying bill," June said. Credit to the girl; she was holding up a lot better than most would, sticking to her guns even now, in the face of threats that would make most people shit their pants. Death staring her down, and Marti was telling it like it was. Good for her.

"Okay, don't," Marti said, eyes open behind those thick glasses. "I can't make you."

"Good," June said, pulling back the cloud. "So we understand each other." She retracted the purple toxin into her hand and hopped back over the counter. "You stop screwing people over, you hear me?" Marti didn't answer, just stared at her. "Come on, Ell," she said, and made for the door. Ell grabbed the bags and followed.

When they were out, the very slight chill of morning air combined with what she'd just done causing June to ripple with goosebumps, Ell said, under his breath, "I think you scared the hell out of her."

"She didn't have anything to be scared of," June said as they hurried to the new car, not bothering to hide their path or steal a new one. "Not that she knew it." She looked right at Ell. "You got the gun?"

Ell tossed their bags in the back of the SUV and patted the small of his back nervously. "Lucky I had it on me when we changed cars at Disney, I guess, otherwise I would have left it behind."

When they were in the car, Ell starting it and putting it in reverse, gently backing out like a grandma—though not hers, Grandma Randall drove fast—she asked him, "Why were you carrying the gun, anyway?" He glanced at her, and she elaborated. "It just doesn't seem like you."

Ell blushed as he took them out onto the main highway. "I don't know. It felt kinda … gangster to have it, so … I did. I liked it." His face darkened further.

June just nodded, slightly impressed, as they headed off down the road. She didn't care where they went, at least for the moment. All that was left to do now was wait.

31.

Sienna

It took us a couple hours to drive from Orlando to Gainesville, an interminably boring drive during which I learned that a) Florida has actual hills, which put it slightly above Iowa in my estimation for interesting terrain, and b) Scott was sitting on a pile of resentment that would have made King Midas's treasure hoard look like an amateur coin collector's first Krugerrand. He did a good job keeping it in during the drive, though. I kept thinking he was going to blow at any minute, spew some vitriol at me like a whale clearing the blowhole after breaching, but he kept it to himself, antsy and squirming the whole way though he was.

When we got to the hotel where the incident had occurred, we found one of those nice, modern places that seemed to have crept up along interstates after the fashionable death of the motel with exterior rooms. I liked hotels, with their interior rooms, better, just for security purposes. Most thieves saw a place where you had to cross a front lobby as something like a moat, and turned back. Anyone could kick down doors in a motel, and probably be gone before the cops showed up or anyone even noticed to call them, depending on how they went about their thieving. A lobby was a nice psychological barrier to crime, even though in practice a hotel was probably just as easy to prey on for a criminal with brains.

This was how I viewed the world. Sometimes I caught

myself, and thought, damn, I was paranoid.

Then I remembered I was a frequent target of criminals looking to show off their badass bona fides, and immersed in the world of catching such scum, and realized that thinking any other way would be stupid.

The front desk clerk seemed to be the sole witness to the incident, and she was being looked after by paramedics when we arrived. She didn't look too badly off, but considering it had been a couple hours since she'd had the hell scared out of her by June and Elliot, and she hadn't gone to the hospital, she was probably made of pretty stern stuff. She looked rattled but not shattered, which put her high in my estimation. I'd met a lot of people that would crumble under a lot less intimidation.

"Marti?" Scott asked, taking in her steel name tag and introducing himself once we'd made it past the perimeter of local cops standing around, waiting to see if the criminals stupidly returned to the scene of the crime. It happens a lot more often than you'd think. "I'm Agent Byerly of the FBI, and I'd like to ask you a few questions."

Marti had the puffy eyes that signaled she'd cried a little bit in the wake of the incident, but that was pretty normal in these circumstances. It would have been a lot weirder if she hadn't had an emotional reaction to being threatened by someone who could conjure a mysterious toxic cloud out of nothing, or a guy who could assault you with empty air. "Sure," she said, and her voice was strong. Her teeth protruded a little from between her lips, but between that and her glasses, she had a kind of cute look, like a little bunny.

"Can you describe the people who attacked you?" Scott asked, sounding like the very model of sensitivity. What a charming gentleman, I would have thought if I hadn't known about the wellspring of rage that he was presently keeping stuffed inside like he was a prized Thanksgiving turkey.

"One was a guy, one was a girl," she said. "She was thin, strawberry blond hair. Freckles. She looked like the trailer trash I went to high school with." Marti's ancillary assessment confirmed for me that she was probably more pissed than scared at this point. Some of that was probably even aimed at herself for not resisting, which was completely normal for a victim in these circumstances. "He was … I dunno. Unremarkable," she said it like it was an insult, "hair with shaved sides, all pointed forward like a rhino horn or something. Average. Pretty normal-looking guy."

"Except for shooting air out of his hands?" I suggested, then shushed myself when Scott sent me a look reminding me that I needed to blend into the background.

Marti barely took notice of me as she replied. "Except for that, yeah. He shot the phone right out of my hands with wind. I've never seen anything like that." Her voice turned hushed, awed. "I mean, I've seen it on TV, but …" She shook her head, eyes fixed in the distance, looking slightly stunned.

"It's different when you see it in real life," Scott said soothingly. "Like a movie jumping off the screen in the theater."

"Yeah," Marti said, nodding along slowly. "Crazy."

"Do you know their names?" Scott asked.

"I know hers," Marti said. "It was on the card, on the receipt. June Randall. I checked them in yesterday," she added, as though that was some pertinent detail.

Scott and I traded a look. "Do you know where they're going?" Scott asked.

"No idea," Marti said, shaking her head. "They didn't say."

"Sir?" A patrolman came walking up to us as a cop car squealed out of the parking lot followed by another. "We just got word of a bank robbery about five minutes away. Sounds like it might be our couple."

I blinked. They'd done this thing, here, in the hotel, some two hours ago. But now they were robbing a bank five minutes away?

Scott frowned. "When did this start?"

"911 call came in two minutes ago," the cop said, hands on his belt, apparently itching to get moving. Another cop car burned rubber out of the parking lot. "It's still ongoing, we think. Caller's inside an office in the bank, hunkered down. Said the male suspect blew a desk over with his hand."

"That'd be them, then," I said, still frowning. What, had they gone out to brunch before robbing the bank?

"Give me the address," Scott said, pulling out his phone to punch it into the GPS.

"You can follow us over there, sir," the cop said as another couple cars queued up, sirens wailing.

"Yeah, why don't I do that," Scot said, and we started toward the car at a run.

"This is weird," I said when we were halfway there. "What's up with the delay?"

"This is a college town." Scott shrugged. "Lots of things to do. They might have gone to see a movie and wanted to knock over a bank after."

"Maybe." That wasn't an unreasonable point. Based on their behavior thus far, June and Elliot weren't exactly megabrains. I stopped just before getting in the car. "I think I should fly over."

Scott's head whipped around. "Are you crazy?" He glanced at the rapidly dwindling number of cops around us. "You think no one's going to notice that?"

"If we wait, they could be gone," I said. "I think the last confrontation scared them. They're probably grabbing cash and getting the hell out of there in a hurry." Something about that didn't sit right with me, either. But …

… they couldn't have actually wanted to run into us again, could they?

No. That was crazy, bordering on suicide. They'd barely gotten away last time, and I'd seen the depth of panic in June's eyes as it hit home for her how close she'd gotten to danger that round. Coming back for another willingly?

That was crazy.

But … maybe not out of the realm of possibility. She damned sure wasn't happy with the pursuit, and she didn't seem too pleased about the cops in general.

"I'm going," I said, looking around. There was a corner of the hotel about fifty yards away, perfect for me to nip around and drop my disguise. I could ditch it on the roof or in someone's backyard as I passed, and be at the bank in less than a minute.

"Don't—" Scott said, but it was too late. I was already running.

This had gone on long enough, and now June and Elliot were acting increasingly unpredictable. It was time to end this, before someone really got hurt.

32.

June

The bank wasn't locked down, because June didn't want it to be. The little crowd of customers was huddled over in the corner against the wall, under a big panel window with the blinds shut. They'd be visible from outside, through the main entry, but no one could see them or anything else past the narrow entry of the lobby. All the shades were down, the first thing she and Ell had done when they'd come in, after pronouncing that this was a robbery, and that everybody needed to be cool if they wanted to walk out alive.

Ell was pacing nervously, behind the counter, getting the tellers to part with the last of the cash. He was getting a pretty good eye for the dye packs and marked bills by this point, and he was quietly instructing the tellers on what not to give him. He was the only one talking in the whole bank; the two tellers were just nodding at his commands, following along meekly, and the customers were mostly quiet, only one of them sobbing profusely.

June rested with her back against the wall, breathing slow and steady. She exchanged a look with Ell, and he forced a smile. He didn't even really know exactly what she was going to do, because she hadn't told him fully what she intended. He had only the barest idea, knew the effect she was aiming for, but she'd flat out lied about the means she was going to use to attain it.

Which was just as well, because he would freak if he'd

known how this was really going to go down.

She felt the tug of the extra weight in the back of her waistband. It didn't give her a feeling of power to have the gun there the way Ell had described. It made her nervous, thinking she might blow off a buttcheek if she shifted the wrong way. She put a hand on it just the same, trying to keep it from rolling around back there in the gap between her jeans and the small of her back.

A thump sounded outside, like someone had just dropped a trash bag from a second story window onto the pavement. It was loud enough that even the normal humans they held hostage looked up in surprise. Ell glanced out the window and screamed, "She's here!" Which was planned, but had just enough hysterical oomph that June knew he wasn't having to act very much. He was genuinely panicked.

He wouldn't have to be for much longer.

June held tight to the gun, hefting it up out of the back of her pants, and turning it so that she faced the entry, gun pointed at the front door. She pulled herself tight against the wall, flat as she could, aided by her skinniness, and just waited, waited for Sienna Nealon to walk in the front door.

33.

Sienna

The bank looked pretty buttoned up as I passed overhead one good time before landing. Someone had gone to the trouble of closing all the shades, probably due to threat of snipers or someone like me just busting through and causing a stir given that they weren't a normal entry point.

I didn't like to enter blind, though, so I ruled out the through-the-window approach once I saw how things looked.

I'd also seen a back door, but ruled that out. It was probably a surer bet, but that was the tack a SWAT team would take, busting in, causing havoc, and letting the bodies hit the floor. Not a bad idea, and certainly safer than going in the front door, but ...

My breath stuck in my lungs, my stomach churning. My promise to Grandma Randall was like a weight around my neck. If I was treating this like any other criminal matter, I'd blow in through the back door and start dropping perps.

But I normally didn't make promises to meta grandmas to bring their only grandbabies in as safely as I could.

If I hadn't been wanted by the lawful authorities of every state, I might have considered different approaches, or started shouting to them inside. Unfortunately, about that time, the shrill noise of police sirens started down the road, and I knew my time to enter the bank without causing this scene to blow up into something so much worse was drawing down quickly.

I'd also seen June and Elliot's SUV parked out back, which hinted at their getaway plans. I thought real hard about blowing the tires to prevent their escape, but that would just box them in. Right now they were trapped in a confined space with a bunch of civilians, and I'd already seen June's ability to blast a cloud of toxin like some poisonous human skunk.

Nothing about this scenario was good. Nothing about it wouldn't be improved by a sniper with an IR scope to look through the shade-covered windows, determine where June was standing, and redistribute her brains all over the nearest wall.

That would have been the safe move. That would have been the smart move.

But that wasn't the promise I'd made to her grandmother.

Sighing again, pushed into action by the sirens drawing closer behind me, I pulled open the front door to the bank and stepped into the cubicle lobby. Elliot was already screaming, freaking out behind the counters at my approach, clearly not ecstatic to see me.

But now I was committed, and I had to hope that maybe—just maybe—I had enough persuasive power to talk them down before this got desperately ugly. Maybe they could be shown reason. Maybe they could see the error of their ways. Maybe the feeling we'd instilled of trouble rumbling down the highway toward them like imminent death at our last meeting would be enough to make them think this through, not do anything stupid.

Drawing another deep breath as Elliot ran out of my immediate sight, I pulled open the door and stepped into the lobby, my hand subtly cocked to toss a net as I looked left to check my blind spot—

The roar of the gun behind me told me I'd picked the wrong direction to look first, and the pain as a bullet splintered through the back of my head and out the front was enough to shove my head forward sharply, as though someone had shoved a drill into the back of my skull. There was high-pitched whine in my ears, and then I felt other impacts pepper my body, pinpricks of pain in my back and side as I faltered, trying to turn around to look—

Wolfe, I said as I fell, twisting and collapsing to the ground in a heap of unresponsive limbs. A gun continued to fire above me, and I dimly felt impacts along my torso and chest.

Wolfe, I said again.

Wolfe!

There was no answer.

My eyesight dimmed, and another flash followed the blooming thunder of a gunshot. This one I felt in my face, but only for a second, and then my sight faded, and I fell into infinite, all-consuming darkness.

34.

The drive to the bank was quicker following in the wake of the cop cars, like a slipstream up the streets of Gainesville, Florida. He kept the pedal down, slowing only when he needed to corner, and barely letting up enough to do that.

It took three turns down sun-washed roads before they pulled into the bank's parking lot. Three cruisers were already set up, cops establishing a perimeter. It was all by the numbers, what was going down here.

Then the shooting started. Scott was out of his car before the others could get clear. The cops were diving for cover behind the hoods of their patrol cars, smart to take cover behind the heavy engine blocks.

The gunshots were loud, blasting away inside the bank, a hard club soundtrack that he didn't like the music to. Sienna was probably already in there, he knew, and waiting for the shooting to stop didn't even occur to him.

He broke into a run for the door, taking note that there were no spider web cracks in the glass, no hint that bullets had come this way at all.

They were all being fired into the bank, then.

Something about that tore at him, and he ripped the door open with a rising level of panic, even before he saw the body lying prostrate, ahead, legs trapped in the lobby door.

It was Sienna, blood pooling out from everywhere—from her chest, from her back, her hair was matted down with it—

And it was pouring out of her face.

157

35.

"Go! Go! Go! Go!" June shouted as they burst out the back door of the bank. They were lucky about the timing; she'd seen the cops pull up out front, but they hadn't started to circle around back yet when she'd started shooting. As it was, she and Ell made it to the car, her on shaky legs, and him on maybe shakier ones. "Just drive!" she screamed before he could yell explosively at her for the part of the plan she hadn't told him about.

The part where she shot the hell out of Sienna Nealon, right in the back of the damned head.

June felt blood sliding down her cheek. One of her shots had come bouncing back at her, but she wasn't sure which one. She was pretty sure it was the last, but the whole chain of events felt fuzzy—scary, even. Like a violent and disturbing nightmare.

Her hands shook as Ell put on the speed and jumped the curb, bumping down onto the road as he made his turn. There were no cops in front of them, nor behind in the mirror as June stared out.

"Ohmig—" Ell started and stopped himself mid run-on. "What did you—what did you—*what did you do?*"

June felt faint, like the blood had all rushed out of her face. It had seemed like such a good idea, such a simple, smart way to get this heavy shit off their backs. Just deal with Sienna Nealon and they'd be home free.

So she'd done it. She'd sat there, waiting until Sienna

walked in, and sure enough, she looked the wrong way, presented the back of her head …

And June had just unloaded on her. Fired the first shot, and then another. She didn't even realize until something struck her in the cheek—that bullet bouncing back, she figured—that she'd had her eyes closed tight for most of it.

"I think I killed her," June said, and made a gulping sound of quiet desperation. She didn't feel exultant, she didn't feel excited, she just felt …

Sick. Like she was about to throw up.

"I think I just killed Sienna Nealon," she said. Then she could hold it back no more, and putting her head between her legs, she vomited all over the floorboard.

36.

Scott

"Sienna!" Scott shouted, knocking the Plexiglas door off its hinges and falling to his knees at her side. Blood was squirting out of her cheek with every pumping of her heart, but her eyes were closed, and—

Shouldn't she be healing? Shouldn't that wound be closing up right now? Like it never even—

"Sienna," Scott said, hands shaking as he fumbled over her, trying to assess the damage. This was triage, after a fashion, the way he'd learned from Glen Parks and Dr. Perugini, way, way back in the Directorate days.

The first thing he needed to do was—

"Stop the bleeding," Scott said, trying to find the most obvious wound. It wasn't easy; she had a finger-sized hole in her forehead that could have been either an entry or exit wound, and the one in her cheek was just spouting red—

Harmon, Scott said, concentrating as hard as he could. *Harmon, are you there? Can you hear me?*

Can't— a faint voice answered back, *—think—dying—* The voice sent panic into his heart, and then went silent.

"He's just messing with me," Scott said under his breath. "He has to be just—"

But the blood flow was slowing, wasn't it?

"No no no no no!" Scott shouted. "Why is it you end up dying with me, Sienna? This doesn't happen when you're hanging out with other people!"

The geyser at her cheek was diminishing to a small fountain of red. Her face was slack, eyes closed, lost in the darkness. He looked around the bank, seeking help, but none was to be found. The customers were clutching at each other or hugging their knees, the horror of what had happened here having stunned them into silence.

That was the net effect of seeing an execution carried out in front of you, Scott figured.

But she wasn't dead—yet.

"What do I do, what do I do?" The words flowed without reason, without stopping, so fast he doubted anyone could understand them. The power of Wolfe was not healing her. She was gravely wounded. He stared at the prominent hole in her forehead, shoving his hand over it to try and staunch the flagging blood flow. He looked around, trying to see—yes, there was an exit wound. Back of the head. Or was that the entry wound? Either way, it was bleeding, and he could see—

"Oh my ..." Scott stared. He had to stop, putting a hand to his face and turning away. She was shot through the head, through and through, with a bullet having passed ...

Right through her brain.

But that was where Harmon, Wolfe and the rest were, right? Did that mean they'd been blown out, like a clog of hair caught in the pipes when a sudden burst of pressure came along?

Were they gone forever?

Scott took a deep breath, then another, then realized he was hyperventilating. He had to get this under control.

"If they're gone, they're gone," he murmured under his breath. "There's nothing I can do about that now. And if they're gone ... if Wolfe's gone ..."

Then Sienna would have to heal herself, with her own meta powers.

But could she do that? With a bullet through the brain, would she be able to heal—to come back from that?

And if she could ... would there be enough left of her to matter?

The squeal of a siren in the parking lot behind him made

Scott turn. He'd forgotten about all of them. They were surely still setting up a perimeter, ready to start negotiating. For all he knew, they had no idea that the robbers had fled. They might have gotten away clean already.

But if the SWAT team came in? They'd bag Sienna Nealon right now, because there was no way she was going to fight back.

"Shit," he whispered.

What was he supposed to do? The first instinct, to get her to a doctor, he overrode quickly. What could a doctor do that she couldn't, with her advanced healing? Even without Wolfe to draw on, Sienna had once grown back her entire arm overnight. What did Dr. Perugini do for her in those situations, when Sienna landed herself in the medical unit for some injury or another?

Mostly nothing. She just sat back and let Sienna heal herself.

But what if she didn't heal herself? What if she was too damaged …?

"I need to get her out of here," Scott whispered. Whatever else might have been going on, this much was certain: no doctor could do enough for her to justify her waking up metacuffed to a hospital bed. Hell, they'd probably use suppressant on her, which would kill her ability to heal.

Which would, in turn, kill her.

That decided it. He sat up, ramrod straight, and gathered her in his arms. He had to get her out of here, to somewhere safe. There was nothing in the world of medicine, in the world of normal humans, that could help her—

Oh.

"Oh," he said as he got to his feet. There was *that*.

One thing at a time. First he had to get her out of here, through a cordon of police cars. Another bumped into the parking lot as he watched through the dull glass, and he closed his eyes. SWAT would be here soon, ready to come crashing in and subdue the bank, pacify things, make sure the bad guys were gone.

He couldn't be here when they came in.

They couldn't be here.

"How far are we from the ocean?" Scott mused as he stood there, Sienna in his arms. Blood was already washing down his suit and dress shirt. He didn't care. It pooled on his shoes, and he didn't care about that, either. How far were they from the ocean?

Entirely too far. But that didn't matter as much anymore, did it? There was water everywhere—in the air, in the pipes, in the convenience store three doors down …

He closed his eyes and concentrated. Took stock of all the water around him, taking care not to accidentally draw out the blood of the people in the bank since he could feel it pulsing through their veins. Before, before the power Harmon had given him, he couldn't feel blood in a human body unless it was flowing out. It wasn't pure enough, wasn't close enough to water for him to hold dominion over it unless it was freely flowing. He couldn't have reached into an unwounded body and touched blood.

Now, though …

He pushed into every wound Sienna had. It wasn't much, but the stoppage would help, at least in the short term. The blood stopped seeping, started crawling back off his shoes, off his shirt, his suit, and flowed back into her as though time was reversing itself, the drips climbing back into her body. The whole pool rose into the air like gravity had quit, pouring back into her.

And in the back of the bank, in both bathrooms and the employee break room, he seized hold of the sinks and blew them up, dragging the water out, pulling it from the toilets. Gallons were disgorged in seconds as he shredded the pipes.

At the convenience store down the street, every single water and pop bottle in the store burst at once, all the liquid blowing out the door and holding behind the fence between the clothing store next door and the fence that separated it from the bank parking lot. For good measure, Scott started to draw every drop of moisture out of the humid air. It probably would have been heavier in summer, but even in spring, Gainesville's air held plenty of water in its molecules.

It took a lot of effort, but he marshaled those forces to

him—the water and soda just waiting past the fence, the moisture from the air outside, pulled in through the doors so that the air outside rippled like a mirage just outside the doors. And the hundreds of gallons of water that were hovering now behind him, just waiting in the air. He ignored the muttered crosstalk from the hostages in the bank, amazed and terrified.

"On three," he said to Sienna. "One. Two. Three—"

He blasted the doors open with the water he'd collected, and it burst out in flood of biblical proportions. He took care to make a perfect car-shaped hole within the wall of water he sent out, and it crawled over his vehicle and washed on, dragging officers and police cars out of the parking lots as they were hit by another wall of soda and water from behind and channeled, screaming and spluttering, out into the road.

Scott took care to make sure no one drowned; that no one's head went under the water and soda for more than a few seconds. But he washed them out on one side of the road with a fury, cars and all, sending them out in a blockage, creating a little moat with no visible edges to halt traffic as he burst out of the broken doors and hurried Sienna to his car.

In the shining daylight he could see her wounds so much more clearly. The plugs where he'd stopped the bleeding were like angry red dots on her face, in her clothing, against her skin. He shoved her into the passenger side door and slid across the hood and into his own seat. Jamming the car into reverse before he'd even finished starting it, he was tearing out of the parking lot seconds later, turning left to avoid the massive wall of liquid he was holding up to his right, cops and their cars imprisoned within it, struggling to the surface for breath.

He let it all go when he was a few hundred yards away, and the wall of fluid burst like someone had broken the invisible dam holding it back. He saw it in the rearview but ignored it and the chaos that it caused in its wake.

Scott had one purpose, and one purpose only—to get Sienna out of here. To get her somewhere safe.

To get her well.

He dialed his cell phone as he drove. "Pick up, pick up,"

he muttered as it rang, as though uttering a prayer.

And on the third ring, it was answered.

"Hey, it's me," he said before they'd even had a chance to finish saying hello. "I need your help."

37.

June

Ell drove and June just stared out the window as they headed down the interstate, trees passing in a blur. They kept going north, Gainesville feeling far behind them even though they were only passing the last Gainesville exit now. The car reeked of her sick, sitting in the floorboard in a whitish puddle that shuddered every time Ell changed lanes roughly. They hadn't said anything since she'd thrown up, because what the hell was there to say?

She'd killed Sienna Nealon.

Done what no one else could do.

And for some reason … it felt like she'd been hit with the worst damned fever she'd ever caught. Not that she caught fevers anymore. That was non-meta stuff. Or kids' stuff, for metas who hadn't manifested yet.

"What the hell do we do now?" Ell asked, voice shaky. He was barely holding it together, but he was driving eighty-five in a construction zone where the signs warned sixty was the speed limit.

"Just keep going," June said, her own voice shaking. "Get us to Valdosta in Georgia, maybe we can stop there for a while. Change cars or something."

"Hell, June," Ell said, thumping his skull back against the headrest, hard. "Bae …" he said softly. "You really did it, didn't you?"

"Yep," she said in quiet horror. Well, there was no taking

it back now. Felt like she'd crossed a line. But she'd been pushed there, hadn't she? Like pride had demanded it.

Pride had demanded she kill the most powerful meta with a bullet to the back of the head.

June bent forward and threw up again, her already empty stomach protesting that there was nothing left to give, waves of stinking bile causing Ell to crack his window and gag himself.

When she was done, they fell back into silence. That carried them ten miles, and June's brain was working about as well as a dull pencil, just scratching the thoughts out slowly.

I killed Sienna Nealon.
Shouldn't that be …
Shouldn't I be …
Isn't that …
… Good?

But the wave of nausea came at her again, and she only just kept herself from retching once more. No, it didn't feel good.

It didn't feel any good at all.

38.

Scott

He drove out of town until he found one of those cheap motels, the kind that looked like it hadn't been touched since the seventies. Tumbling-down red shingles marked the triangular roof in the center of the wide building, where the lobby sat between two wings of rooms that stretched out in either direction like arms from the body. Three of the doors were open on the right side of the building, maid carts sitting out to suggest they were being serviced. A spattering of cars were in the parking lot, and the sign declared that they both had vacancies and that the room rate was $49.99 per night.

Scott pulled in and checked in, leaving Sienna alone in the car for a few minutes, his mind on holding the blood in her body so it didn't spill out in every direction. The clerk was friendly, helpful, and entirely responsible for carrying on both sides of the conversation. Scott didn't say much of anything unless required, handing over his ID when asked, paying in his father's company credit card and not caring, signing his father's name with careful aplomb—his dad wouldn't care anyway, if he even noticed. He always covered Scott's expenses when asked. And even when not, because he still hoped his son would join him in the family business.

Scott pulled the car around to his room, and got out, opening the red door and propping it with a small block of water he summoned out of the bathroom sink. No one was around, but he would have barely cared if they were. Only the keenest observer would have noticed what he was about to do, anyway.

Sienna opened the passenger door and stepped out, faltering a little as she stood. Her eyes were firmly closed, her head lolled just slightly, as though she'd woken out of a long sleep in the car and decided to crawl into bed in the hotel without fully waking. It was the best he could do, controlling her by the blood in her veins. She lurched forward, awkward steps carrying her over the threshold under what looked like her own power.

Scott strained. This was pushing even his limits. If she'd been conscious or struggling, there was no way he could have maintained this flimsy hold over her blood without disastrous results.

He walked her over to the bed and let her collapse, his own breath coming now in long, heavy breaths from the exertion. He dissolved the block in front of the room door and it swung closed of its own volition, slamming noise echoing in the still room.

"Okay," Scott said, standing there, checking the plugs he'd made of her blood, trying to keep it all together. The flesh was starting to knit itself together in her body, and even in her brain, but slowly. Painfully slowly.

Dangerously slowly.

She said nothing. She did not stir. She simply lay there, on the dirty bedspread, unmoving, eyes closed. A simple twitch came a few seconds later, the most life she'd exhibited since he'd whisked away from the bank.

"Are you in there?" he asked, standing sentinel over her. "Sienna?"

She still did not answer. And as he stood in the darkness, his loud breathing and her soft his only company, he wondered if she ever would again.

39.

Sienna

"I'm leaving the agency," Scott said, looking me right in the eye as he said it, his face carrying that morose, "I'm worried what you're going to say but this is really bogging down my mind, man," look that he had when he had overthought something.

For my part, I just stared back at him, for a full second, trying to decide how best to react to this particular stunner that wasn't all that stunning.

"Oh, for the sake of ..." Gerry Harmon said, looking around the scenery. We were in my old room at the agency, before I'd quit, before it'd been reduced to rubble in an earthquake, and before it had been, uh ... toxified and shattered by me being imprisoned in my own body ...

"You really have a dramatic life," Harmon said again, looking around. The scene seemed to have been paused, Scott staring into my eyes with hope and fear and—hell, who knew what else was going on in his mind?

"You know," Harmon said in severe annoyance. "This is *his* memory we're in."

Oh. That explained it.

"How long ago was this?" Harmon asked.

"Why are you asking questions you know the answer to, telepath?" I fired back.

"My telepathy isn't working at the moment," Harmon replied snottily. "Someone got herself shot in the back of the head like a moron. Mind reading requires a mind to read *from*, you know."

"Then why are you still able to do it?" I jibed, realizing that I kind of insulted myself with that one, since he was nominally using my brain as a base of operations.

Harmon made a loud, guttural noise to express his displeasure. "Part of me wishes I wasn't able to, because it's really quite dull reading what you're thinking all the time. I used to spend my days with the brightest of the bright, the most capable and engaged minds. The front row, if you will, focused on policy and solving the great problems of the day—"

"Sounds pretty boring," I said, stepping out of my place in Scott's memory, leaving him and his puppy dog eyes frozen in time.

Harmon shot me an irritated look, pretty much the only kind he seemed capable of, at least recently. "So you're going to leave it off like this? Without playing through the rest of what happened?"

"Aww, did I leave you on the cliff? Poor baby." I looked around my old room. It felt homey in a way I hadn't experienced in a while, and a sudden tug of sadness overcame me. I didn't have this home anymore and I didn't have my old house anymore—

Hell, I didn't belong anywhere anymore.

"Of course, I know how this ends," Harmon said, plainly trying to conceal his obvious interest in watching things play out. "But … you're a terrible conversationalist and I'd rather watch this trainwreck unfold with my own eyes than try and kill time until you die with conversation."

I blinked at that. "Until I die …?"

He stared back at me, dark eyes bereft of their usual amusement. "Yes."

"I don't understand."

"You got shot in the head. Do I need to draw you a map?"

"But I'm not dead."

"Very perceptive."

"I'm a meta," I said. "I'll heal."

"You know what an anagram for meta is? Meat." He still didn't smile. "You know what the common thread between us and the humans is? We all become meat, eventually. We all rot, eventually. No one lives forever, Sienna. Not me, plainly. And certainly not you. You always said you'd either live to see everyone you care about die around you or you'd go out quickly and violently." He looked around the room, as though searching for something. "It appears to have been the latter."

"I heal pretty fast."

"You heal fast with Wolfe," he said. "By yourself ... you do all right. But I question your ability to fix a giant hole through the middle of your brain. Traumatic brain injury, or, if you prefer—a gaping hole in your head?" He poked a finger at the side of his skull to illustrate. "Why do you think it's just you and me in here right now?"

"Wolfe?" I asked quietly. "Gavrikov? Zack? Eve? Bastian? Hell, *Bjorn*?

Harmon smiled tightly. "Should I sing 'Just the Two of Us'? Or have you gotten the point?"

"I bet your voice is atonal and awful, and somehow you'd probably make that song sound terribly smug. I don't want to chance it."

"Have it your way, then," Harmon shrugged. "Still, doesn't change things. You are dying."

"I can heal."

"Bet you'll still be singing that song at the moment of your death," he said, plopping down on my bed. It didn't move under his weight, the bedspread stayed perfectly still, like he wasn't there at all. "It won't sound smug, though. More ... scared, I think."

"Why do you think I'm dying?" I asked.

"Because the bullet, when it passed through your brain, tore out parts that you won't easily be able to heal on your own," Harmon said. The lights flickered around us. "Connections that allow your body to heal, allow the normal toxins we produce to be purged. That allow you to speak to your guests." He tapped his own head again. "In short ... that bullet hit vital systems, the ones that allow you to walk and talk and breathe and be a general pain in the ass. Without them …" He patted the bed. "You won't move. You won't wake up. You'll slowly drown in the poisons your body produces, strangling the last of your fleeting and frankly never-all-that-impressive brain activity. And I get to watch it all happen and accompany you into the abyss." He made that sour face again. "Fortune smiles, and it is a razor-toothed wolf with claws bent on dragging us out of this world screaming."

"That doesn't sound much like fortune," I said, my breath catching in my lungs.

"It is what it is," Harmon said with a grim smile. "And what it is … is death. Even you can't stop that, Sienna." The lights flickered once more. "And it is coming … soon."

40.

Scott

The beating of her heart was slowing down, hour by hour, and all Scott could do was sit there, not even holding her hand, as the time wound down. The room stank of rot, of a fetid body slowly slipping toward death. It probably smelled in here before they even arrived—he couldn't recall now—but Sienna's slide, her breathing running shallow—all of it conspired to make the room reek of an end coming, and not a pleasant one at that.

His phone started to buzz and he answered it without thinking, hoping he knew who it would be.

It wasn't.

"Where the hell are you?" Andrew Phillips barked in that rough, emotionless tone he projected without effort.

"Out," Scott said, yanking the phone away from his ear and flipping through the settings to make sure the GPS was disabled, the way he'd left it. It was. "Why?"

"I just got a report from a crime scene in Gainesville, Florida," Phillips said tightly. "They say Sienna Nealon showed up where those two idiot kids were robbing a bank. Witnesses indicate a struggle of some kind. Nealon got shot. You were there. You took her out of there."

"That sounds far-fetched," Scott said, mind wanting to race but hobbling dully instead, replies coming at half-speed. How was he so tired? All he'd done was sit here.

"The local police report getting hit and entrapped in a

wave of water and soda."

"Weird."

"You assaulted local officers."

"That's a strong charge," Scott said. "I hope you've got some proof."

"You're aiding and abetting a known fugitive."

"Oh, get over yourself," Scott said, shaking his head. "You know she's innocent, that Harmon trumped up all that bullshit. You've seen the evidence—she got attacked in Eden Prairie. She defended herself against a mob of people she put in jail who were attacking her, and to the unaffiliated observer it looks an awful lot like she was trying to save her own life against people our government let out of jail."

"I'm sure I don't know what you're talking about," Phillips said. He was just dull and neutral enough that he was almost convincing. "We have a finding. We have warrants. You have a job to do. Bring her in."

"I don't know where she is," Scott said, pointedly not looking at her. "And I kinda doubt you have security footage of any kind to back up what you just accused me of."

"Just because we can't see her face on the footage doesn't mean we can't come after you with warrants," Phillips said. "We have witness statements. You want to be careful which side you choose right now—"

"I'm on the side of justice, you jackass," Scott said. "Just because you want to deny what happened in Eden Prairie because it's politically convenient to keep your wagon hitched to Harmon's party, don't expect me to lie and close my eyes and pretend I don't see evil."

"She's a murderer."

"So were you," Scott said. He went on into the stark silence. "Don't you remember? You were going to have Guy Friday kill her when she was comatose in the medical unit at the agency."

"She was a clear and present danger to the safety of—"

"Just like those meta prisoners from the Cube were a danger to her?"

Phillips did not evince any emotion in his reply. "You can't honestly think this is going to turn out well for you."

Scott snickered. "Why? You can't prove I've done anything wrong. That bank was dark, your surveillance footage is borked, I doubt you can scrape together a witness outside the bank who saw anything, and even if you could, civil service laws are going to make it a real hell for you to fire me or even tar me with a bad recommendation for my next employer. So ... what are you going to do? Good luck making your case in court, your impotent whinings aren't going to get me to come in or whatever you're wanting me to do ... hell, there are federal employees under indictment still working, so ... what? Whatcha gonna do, Andy?" His expression hardened. "I'll tell you what you're going to do. You're going to fuck right off, that's what."

"I—"

Scott hung up. "Yeah, I don't care," he said, and for the fiftieth time in the last two hours, he took up the edge of the ragged white bedsheet and placed it against Sienna's wrist, using it to insulate himself from her skin as he took her pulse. He counted the beats ...

They were still slowing.

She was still dying.

The phone started to buzz again, but this time he looked at the caller and when he saw it was Phillips, he did not answer. He thumbed the switch to keep it from rattling against the bedside table and leaned in, embracing the silence, counting the minutes and hoping the help he had called for would not come too late to save her life.

41.

Sienna

"Are you going to tell me what happened here?" Harmon asked with breathless impatience. "Or do I have to die of boredom before I die of your brain damage?"

I looked around the frozen scene, Scott stuck in place where I'd left him. This was his memory, but I had this one as well, from my side of things. I stepped out of myself for a moment and looked through his eyes.

God, I looked ragged. Thin, even. Not that it would take much compared to how I was now.

"I dunno. A few months after we beat Sovereign, I guess." I was puzzling over it; time had almost lost all meaning at that point in my life.

"Yes," Harmon said, "when the rats were already abandoning the sinking ship."

He wasn't wrong, though he was being a bit crass. Kat and Janus had left first, signaling their desire to move on. Zollers had gone next.

And, of course, Scott.

"You look really energized here," Harmon said with blossoming sarcasm. "Is this during the period when you were running yourself ragged trying to protect the earth after you'd saved it?"

"It was the period when I would have happily murdered your Secretaries of State and Homeland Security," I said, looking at the dark circles under my eyes. I probably didn't have those now, so recently off my beach vacation, though the spare tire around my waist maybe made up for them. My stomach rumbled as if to underscore the point. "You know, because they offered my agency's help to all these skittish world and local law enforcement agencies, when everybody seemed to think there was a dangerous meta hiding under every bed."

Harmon chuckled. "That was a foreign policy coup, you know. 'Hey, everybody, there's this race of humans that have superpowers, and you probably don't have any, but just in case, here's our expert to help you.'" His shoulders moved up and down in silent appreciation of a joke I didn't find funny at all. "Thanks, by the way."

"Were you actively trying to break me then or was I just another cog in your machine?"

"A cog," he said with a shrug of utter indifference. "You hadn't become a liability yet, so why not use you like an asset until depleted?"

"I dunno, human decency?" I stared at him, and got nothing in response. "Sorry. Forgot who I was talking to." He favored me with a ghost of a smarmy smile, and I started the scene into motion.

"I'm leaving the agency," Scott said again, probably because I was wearing a really dumbstruck look. I'd been blindsided by this one, because …

Well, because I took it personally, but didn't have the emotional energy to express my hurt.

"Okay," I said, staring at him through bleary eyes. Seeing myself from outside during this moment, I could almost see the wheels spinning in my head, trying to gain traction and come to grips with this.

My boyfriend—my love—was leaving me.

"I just need to move on," Scott said, glazing right over how I felt to excise his own feelings. "Sticking in this—it's not good for me. I don't think it's good for us, either. We hardly see each other. When I'm not on assignment, you are—"

"Okay," I said, fatigue showing in my face, as I still tried to push past those burgeoning hurt feelings to put this together.

"—so if I go to work for my dad, I'll be here in town," Scott went on. "That way, when you come back, at least I'll be here. One less messy schedule to coordinate, you know?"

I just stood there, blinking.

"This is some high quality fare," Harmon pronounced, and the scene paused again as I looked at my own face, scrunched up, squinting, so dazed I didn't even have the ability to wear my emotions on it. Unless confusion was the sole emotion I had been feeling, and I didn't rule that out. "It almost beats this manhunt of yours wherein you try and catch the World's Stupidest Couple, bandits so dumb that they call each other "bae" unironically … and you manage to get shot in the back of the head by them."

"You want to talk about that again?"

"No," Harmon said sullenly. "By all means, let's resume watching your idiocy of the past rather than hash through the idiocy of the present. This is probably more interesting, in any case."

"It's so nice to know you care," I said.

"I don't," Harmon snapped, sounding like a child about to have a tantrum. "But this situation is intolerable. If I'd known this was how it was going to be I'd have let you kill me on that iceberg without bothering to transfer my memories and consciousness into your body."

My brain felt slow, like I was adopting the sensation of the me in the memory. "Is that what you call a soul drain? Sounds less agonizing than what it actually is, I guess."

"Don't pretend you don't enjoy it," Harmon said, walking in a tight circle. The world around me seemed darker at the edges, as though the corners of the room were having the light siphoned out of them. "And yes, I call it that. Because that's what it is. Stop your drain too soon, all you get is memories. Consciousness, though … that's the real prize. That's where you get your rush, when you absorb someone all the way."

I shrugged. "To be honest, it feels good all the way through, but yeah, I guess it's like a bonus or a sense of completion or—uhm, something less appropriate—when I absorb someone fully. You're not a prize, though. Worse than anything I ever got out of a cereal box."

"Hmph," Harmon said. "So … how does this end?" He nodded at the other me, the one still trying to concentrate on what Scott had been saying, the me that was frozen in emotional purgatory, without much emotion to expurgate.

"You know how it ends," I said. "He leaves the agency."

"Yes, I know," Harmon said impatiently. "But entertain me and explain it, will you? For heaven's sake, you're just so dull."

Time resumed, and I stared at Scott, wavering as the emotional punch hit home. "You're … leaving …?"

"*So* dull," Harmon said again.

"It'll be better for us," Scott said, that weight on him now gone. He'd been so worried about what I was going to say that now that he'd gotten it off his chest, he felt … excited. It was evident in his face.

"Not working together is going to be better for us?" That was the best response I could come up with.

"In the long term," Scott said, sounding a little more defensive, "yeah. It gives us more time to spend together because we won't both be running to hell and gone all the time."

"No," I agreed, "I'll be doing all the running to hell and back."

"Well, Reed will, too," Scott said.

I rubbed my fingers along my face, feeling the tension in my scalp tissue as I did so. Man, I was a wreck in those days. "For now," I said. How long was this before Reed and I had that falling out over my sheer viciousness? Couldn't have been more than a couple years. It all felt like a blur, like the darkness encroaching on the memory around me was chewing at the edges of my ability to put events into sequence.

"I don't think this is a big deal," Scott said.

That broke through my facade of fatigue. "Oh, well, if *you* don't think so, then I guess we're okay." I sounded snottier now than I remembered being at the time.

"She's got her teeth out," Harmon said.

"There's nothing to be mad about," Scott said, backpedaling a little.

"I like how you're telling me how to feel," I said. "Please, go on."

"Uhhhhm …"

"It's nice to see that even before you scooped his brains out and I bent him like a pretzel, he was still an idiot," Harmon said. "Honestly, I worried after he started to fail at the job I set him to that maybe it was something I had done—but no. He was always a moron. Such a relief."

I withheld my own commentary, the only rebuttal to which I could think of was something lame, like, "Yeah, but he was my moron." Instead, the scene kept playing as Scott got frustrated and finally responded.

"I don't know what you want from me, Sienna. I don't want to do this job anymore. And it has nothing to do with you."

"Well, I'm your boss," I said snarkily, "so I doubt it has *nothing* to do with me."

"Aren't you sick of the fight?" he asked, the air seeming to deflate out of him. "First we tried to prevent genocide—"

"With some notable success, given we're still here."

"—and then we had to go to war with Sovereign—"

"Also successful, in that it ended with him in a lot of tiny, dragon-shredded pieces."

"—now we chase down criminals," he said, sighing wearily. "When does it end?"

"I dunno," I said. "When do you think crime will be over? Just round to the nearest decade."

"Is this really what you want to do with your life?" he asked, probably not meaning to be disdainful but hitting the mark fully anyways.

"Yeah," I said.

"Really?" he asked. "When you were growing up, this is how you imagined you'd spend your days—"

"Well, no," I said, "because I honestly thought I'd probably spend my days continuing to train and getting locked in a metal box when I pissed off my mom, but once I was free to leave my house … yeah. This is what I wanted to do." I swallowed heavily. "It's what I'm *supposed* to do. It's my mission."

"Nice to have a purpose in your life," Scott said, staring almost blankly. "How much of this has to do with guilt for all those people Wolfe killed?"

"Some," I said. "I don't know. I haven't assigned percentages. It's my obligation. My job."

"I don't want it to be mine," Scott said, shaking his head. "You want it to be your beat, more power to you. All I see is the two of us riding this plane to the ground—"

"Is that a metaphor? Because we did actually ride to the ground once—"

"But not on a plane. We fell out of the plane, remember?"

"Oh, yeah," I said. "I get all these flying and plane-related things confused sometimes." I put my hands back on my face. They were cold and felt good against my temples. "All right. Okay. You don't want to do this anymore. Fine." I looked up at him with a near-blank stare. "What are you going to do?"

"Join the family business," he said, and I started chuckling right away. "What? It's an honorable profession—"

"So's being a geisha, but I don't see you grabbing a kimono and that plaster face paint."

"Low blow."

"What? I can't hit you for doing that thing you swore you never wanted to do?" I folded my arms in front of me. "Scott … you were the guy who was jazzed to get an offer to become an M-Squad trainee when I was still trying to figure out how cars worked. Life changed you? The war changed you? Fine. That's fine. You're a big boy, and I can't tell you what to do with your life. If you want to go work for your dad … rock on." That wasn't at all how I felt, and he could see it in my face, hear it in my voice. "Just don't expect me to be super excited because you realized that my line of work isn't for you. Because to me … it just feels like another way we're different. Another thing, among many, that we don't have in common."

"I would have assumed you had lots in common,"

Harmon said. "Monster truck shows, for instance. Professional wrestling, for another."

"You really are quite the elitist jackass, aren't you?"

"We still have lots in common," Scott said, putting his hands on my shoulders. It felt condescending, so I shrugged out of them. "We do. We're in love—"

"Scott, we don't see each other."

"But this will help—"

"Whatever," I said, finally collapsing on the bed myself. "I don't want to talk about it anymore." I closed my eyes.

"Do you want me to stay?" he asked, shuffling back and forth on tentative feet, hands in his pockets.

"Not really," I said, and rolled over so he couldn't see my face. "Not right now."

"Okay," he said, stung. "Okay, I'll … I'll call you tomorrow."

"Perfect," I said, and opened my eyes to look out the window.

"You want the lights on or off?" He was poised at the door.

"I don't really care."

He clicked them off. "Good night, Sienna."

I didn't say anything. I wanted to feel something, wanted to have something swirling inside other than obvious, stinging pain, but I was just too tired. Symbolically, I would have loved to stay awake all night, worrying about our future together, something which had seemed so assured only a week earlier.

Instead I fell asleep within two minutes, completely exhausted, as Gerry Harmon and I watched my past self sink into oblivion, unable to even muster up the energy to cry.

42.

June

"There's a cop behind us," Ell said as they rattled up I-75 in that puke-smelling SUV, half-gagging as they went. They should have been used to the smell by now, shouldn't they?

June wasn't. It was rank and gross and just made her want to throw up again. The panic flowing from Ell in the driver's seat helped center her, though, turning her attention to her rearview. "I don't see 'em."

"A few cars back, directly behind us," Ell said, sticking up his head to look. "Florida Highway Patrol."

June turned all the way around in her seat to give a look. She peered past a sedan, then a Dodge minivan, then a mid-sized SUV that looked like a Ford Explorer, and then past that—

"Oh," she said. Sure enough, there he was. It was actually the Ford. Hard to tell in the afternoon sun, but the Explorer was multicolored. She did a double take. It wasn't coincidence that he was right behind them, was it?

"They've got our car description," Ell said, running fingers through his hair, which had dried after the sweat and stress of the bank job, forming almost a helmet-looking mess on the front of his head. "He's probably following us."

June swallowed hard. "What are we going to do about it?"

Ell got that wide-eyed, panicked look. "I dunno. What can we do?"

June thought about it a second. "You could blow him off the road. If he's after us, it'll take care of him. If he's not … he won't know what hit him."

Ell just stared at her. "That could kill him, June."

"Probably not, though," she said, adjusting the spaghetti strap of her tank top. It felt itchy. "I don't know." She put her face in her hands. "I just—I don't know what to do anymore. Do what you want. Let him follow us if you don't care what happens."

She only had her head down for a minute before she heard it, the crash of a car, squeal of tires, someone honking. She looked up and saw the police cruiser veering off the road at high speed. Its front wheel hit the shoulder and it spun, slamming sideways into a tree where a copse began about twenty feet off the freeway.

"Hell, you did it," June said, not really believing he'd done it.

"Yep," Ell said, sounding stricken. "Hopefully … that's the end of that for a while."

"Yeah, let's h—" But June didn't even get the words out before she saw blue lights flashing somewhere behind them, farther back than the first car had been. And she knew right then that no, this wasn't anywhere close to over.

43.

Scott

Her pulse was barely there now, and no matter how Scott held those plugs of blood in, a little watery ooze kept trying to creep its way out from Sienna's unhealed wounds. It should have surprised him how slowly her body was healing, but he felt too sick to dwell on it much. It was obvious, now.

She was dying.

At the rate she was going, she wouldn't even last the night.

44.

Sienna

"If you don't stop complaining, I'm going to sit here in silence while I die so that I can at least have some damned peace," I said as Harmon wrapped up a whinefest about this latest memory I'd started. "I'm sorry my life has been so dreadful that you can't possibly stand it one more second, but unfortunately, I can't speed up this dying thing, so either watch or get lost, will you?"

"Why couldn't I have been stuck in the dying parts of your brain, safely out of reach, with the others?" Harmon asked, glancing over at the frozen Scott, this one from a few months after that initial memory where he'd quit the agency. "On the other hand, they're probably having an orgy right now, and I'm not sure which would be worse." He let out a long sigh. "Why is this happening to me?"

"I ask myself the same question," I said, "but the only answer I'm coming up with is that I've already died and this is my well-earned hell."

"Why, that would make me the devil, wouldn't it?"

"You said it, not me, but I don't disagree." I tugged on my hair, enjoying the pull against my scalp. If I could still feel this, I probably wasn't dead, was I? Though things were getting steadily darker around us.

"You've felt something similar to this before, haven't you?" Harmon asked. "Death, I mean."

"Well, I didn't think you meant carnival games."

187

"The time that the yokel family imprisoned you in your own body," Harmon said. "Was it like this?"

"Don't you know, mind-reader?"

He made a soft sighing noise. "No. You're so brain-damaged I can't read you or anyone else, remember?"

"No, it wasn't like this," I said. "There I was surrounded by avatars of the people I felt guilty about getting killed. I met a weird version of my dad, too, and he helped me fight against the—whatever the hell was happening there. It was a dream state, not a chance to rewind and revisit my dying relationship with Scott." I stared at the awkward, paused scene of he and I, again in my little room, teed up for another verbal brawl. "Why do you think I'm reliving this, specifically?"

"Because your own memories are too damaged to inhabit?" Harmon shrugged. "Because it's a specific focus of your guilt that was stirred up in the last twenty-four hours? These are all just random guesses. I may know how people think, but that's a soft sense. The physiology of the brain, the science of it ... that's more the territory of someone like Cassidy."

"Hm," I said. "If I'm that brain damaged, why do I remember my life? Shouldn't I have forgotten ... I dunno ... my name, my address, that time my mom threw a slinky at my knuckles because I mouthed off about her ass being fat?" I shook my head. "Looking back, that was some bad karma. I'm paying for that one now."

Harmon just rolled his eyes. "Again ... I don't know the science. All I know is that you're dying, and I can't reach the outside world."

"Great," I said. "Just great." I looked back at the vision of myself squared off with Scott.

"So what's this week's episode about?" Harmon asked with an air of disinterest.

"Hummmm," I said, trying to recall. "There were so many." I set the scene in motion.

"I don't know what you want from me," I said, sighing in plain exasperation.

"I want you," Scott said, as though it were both simple

and obvious. "I want to see you, Sienna. More than I do."

"And yet I'm not here very often," I said. "Work, Scott. You remember? That thing you used to do with me? The ragged feeling it gives you when you travel six days out of seven trying to investigate everything under the sun? It's not like I'm skipping out on you to hang out in Aspen or something. I'm not hitting the slopes with the stars while you freeze in MSP, okay?"

"Well, I know that," he said, again speaking in the obvious tone. "I'm just saying that … we never see each other."

"Never's a strong word."

"You've been gone for two weeks. Before that, a week, so I saw you for one night and you were out again."

"See? Far cry from never."

"Sienna … we can't live like this," Scott said, blinking a little. "There's no future in this."

"Oh, that's cute," Harmon said, freezing the memory. "He thinks he has a future with you."

"He always was the optimist in the relationship," I said, and then my other self resumed speaking to Scott: "I can't even see past the end of tomorrow anymore. Talking about the future is just ridiculous."

"You should quit this stupid job," Scott said. "You don't need it. The government is going to continue to jerk you around for as long as they can. And what is it going to get you? You're not making nearly as much as we were when we were with the Directorate—"

"But I have the added bonus of my boss not trying to kill my boyfriend, so there's that."

"Man, I blew the call on that one," I said, stopping before Scott could make his reply. I glanced at Harmon. "Although, I guess, technically, you weren't trying to kill him so much as bend him to your will."

"Not until later. And I wasn't technically your boss, either," Harmon said. "Boss's boss's boss? Something like that? I forget how many layers there were between us."

"This is not a good career, Sienna," Scott said. "There's no future in this."

I looked at him in weary annoyance. "In my career ... or with you if I keep my career? Because I think maybe you're mixing the two together."

"Both, I would say," Scott threw his hands wide. "I know you're going to see this as a threat, but it's not. Keep your job if that's what you want, but ... how are you going to have time for a family, or a future life if—"

"Maybe I don't want those things," the other me said sullenly.

"For now. What about—"

"What about never?" I asked. "I'm a succubus, Scott. The contortions we have to do in order to be intimate? I get that you're willing to undergo the kink now, but I bet you get tired of it in a few years, that whole no flesh-to-flesh contact thing. And the idea about having a family? Yeah, I don't think I'm on board with that."

"Because you're worried about becoming your mom?" he asked.

He said it gently but I snapped anyway. "Because I don't know what I'm doing half the time, and being exhausted to the point of partial brain death before I even go into parenthood doesn't fill me with confidence that I'm going to be a great parent, no. I'm not ready. I'm twenty years old, okay? I can't even legally become an alcoholic yet. I'm sorry if I'm blurry on what my future entails. This is my time to work, to do the thing—the task—that's set in front of me. You didn't want to do what I did, and that's fine—" It really, really wasn't, it felt personally insulting, and I definitely conveyed that with my word choice and tone, "—but trying to push me in the direction of your dreams is not going to go well, because I'm not ready."

"*When* will you be ready?" Scott asked.

"Maybe never," I said. "Scott, we're at loggerheads. This is what I was trying to tell you before—we want different things."

"I want you," Scott said.

"No, you want me plus a future, and me is not sure me even wants the future you envision." I shook my tongue after committing that grammatical destruction. Mom would have flicked my ear for it.

"Is it so outrageous that I want you and everything the future with you could hold?" he asked, sounding like a puppy I'd beaten a few good times.

"Not outrageous, just not … probable right now," I finished, a little lamely. "You want X, I want Y. Doesn't make us bad people, it just means we want different things. Maybe things that aren't compatible."

He lowered his head, staring at the floor as though it provided answers. "You can't want to do this—this job—forever."

"I don't know," I said. "Maybe not. But … maybe so."

"But—"

"There's no buts," I said. "And no help, you saw to that." The whole sentence bled my resentment at him. Things had gotten so much more difficult since he and the others had left me and Reed to do all the work ourselves.

"Not fair."

"No, it's not," I said. "Because you swore you wanted to do this job a few years ago. But that changed. And I get that it changed. But now you're trying your hardest to squeeze me into changing in the direction you went. Well … I don't want to work for your dad. I don't want leave this job. Not now, and maybe never. I get that it doesn't fit your vision of the future, but you just have to accept that if you're with me, I'm a person who has her own agenda. And if ours aren't compatible, then … maybe we just have to admit that and move on."

"You held it together pretty well there," Harmon said, scrutinizing my face as though critically assessing a piece of art.

"I certainly didn't feel like holding it together at that point," I said, looking at my own face. It was a mask of sheer fatigue and drawn emotion. I remembered how I felt in that moment, though, and it was one where I channeled my excess emotion into my next mission, resulting in a murderer getting punched so hard in the face that he spent a week in the hospital even with his meta-healing before I put him in the Cube.

"How did you feel?" Harmon asked, with something akin to sympathy.

"You're no Zollers," I said sadly, shaking my head.

"Well, I'm all you've got, sweetheart."

I sighed. "You know how I felt—"

"I don't, remember? No telepathy right now. I can't look back in your memories and see."

"Okay, well, I felt terrible. Got it?"

"Saying you felt terrible is like saying grape juice is kind of sweet. Technically accurate, but a poor description that leaves out the texture—"

"Grape juice has a texture?"

"Silky. A little tart. Full-bodied—"

"I think you've been drinking fermented grape juice."

"Shh. It hits the tongue with a bracing edge of flavor, and when you sniff it—"

"You have given this way too much thought."

"—it's inviting. It wants to be sipped, slowly—"

"What do they make whiskey out of? Because this sounds more like whiskey."

"Wheat. And you're missing the point. Whatever your poison—"

"I doubt grape juice is a poison, unless you're a demon and it really is the blood of—"

"—you're describing it without feeling, without life. How did you feel about Scott in that moment?"

"Or you're diabetic. Pretty sure grape juice has high sugar content." Harmon was just looking at me now, one eyebrow raised. "How did I feel? Very little. Dead inside. Tired all the time. Uhhh …"

"Keep going. It's never the first thing you think of that really captures it."

"You sure? Because when I met you, I thought, 'asshole,' and I think, even after all this time, that totally nails it." He waited expectantly. "Fine. How did I feel? Like I lacked control over my life in that moment. Like Scott and I were two trains on two separate tracks that were diverging—except we kind of crashed first—"

Harmon looked at me blankly. "I was clearly asking too

much of you on this description thing."

"Look, I'm doing my best."

"No, no, you wouldn't ask a snail to fly or a lion to eat a salad. It's fine. You're beyond your capability when it comes to metaphor."

I made a low growling sound at him. "Metaphor? You want a metaphor? You make me feel like I've shoved my head into a vise."

"That's a simile."

I barely held in a louder growl, trying to keep myself from becoming a really angry lioness and ripping his imaginary face off. "How did I feel? I felt as though I were going to explode from the heart out. Like I was spinning out of control on an icy road, and the dark night was closing in around me, trees whipping in circles as I spun closer to my death. You happy now? Get it?"

He gave a small nod of concession. "Better."

I looked at the little scene, me and Scott, Scott and I … "I don't know what I could have done differently at that point."

"Quit your job?"

"Wasn't ready yet," I said.

"Make a clean break?"

"Probably," I said. "That would have … probably been a good idea." I sent the memory forward, skipping the next part, where we argued and talked, argued and talked, until the sun was coming up and I was so bleary-eyed I had to lay down. Scott curled up next to me, our anger spent but no passion rekindled—because I didn't have anything left.

"I don't want to fight anymore," the other me said, wearily.

"Neither do I," Scott said. "I didn't want to fight at all, but … we seem to do it—"

"Every time we get together," I answered for him. In response, he put a hand over my belly and pulled me closer, spooning me tightly as we fell into silence.

"So adorable," Harmon said, looking at the two of us wearily cuddling. "hard to believe you two kids didn't make it."

"Cuteness is hardly the best metric for determining the success of a couple."

"Yes, well," he said, "I suppose if you don't hurry up and die soon, I'll get to ride this little tour all the way to the end and see for myself."

Something about that made my shoulders just slump. "I suppose you will," I said, not really very excited about seeing that one again for myself.

45.

June

The howl of the siren behind her felt like the last damned straw June could handle today. "Blow him off the road, Ell," she said, holding her hands over her ears. "Get him like the other one and let's get out of here before any more come after us."

Ell was silent for a moment, and then an ungodly roar of wind swept in behind them, loud enough that June could hear it through her cupped hands. The police cruiser and another car both spun out as Ell stepped on the gas, speeding them down the highway. He looked pale and stricken, but kept his hands on the wheel as the sirens faded behind them.

June didn't dare look back. She didn't want to see what had become of the cop car. She was afraid she might get sick in her seat again.

"This is getting so out of control," Ell said. "It's just— we're swerving all over now, like that cop. And they're gonna keep coming after us."

"Yeah," June said, frozen in her seat. "I know." The faint sound of the siren was dimming at last.

No, wait … it was getting closer? Louder?

"Oh, no …" Ell said.

There they were, two more cop cars, shooting down the opposite side of the interstate toward them. They zipped past and slowed, other drivers avoiding them, as they came to a dirt U-turn and hung it, coming out onto the highway behind June and Ell.

"They're never going to stop coming," Ell said softly.

"We'll make 'em," June said with weary assurance. "We have to make 'em. They can't—there's not an infinite supply of them, and up til now we've run them off just fine. They've never come after us until now—"

Ell just looked over at her like he was dead, and croaked: "We never killed Sienna Nealon before."

"Or anyone," she finished for him, all instinct to strike back drained with that thought. Maybe this really was it.

The end of the road.

"Just drive," she said, hanging her head, and Ell stomped the gas.

"What are we going to do?" he asked, glancing forward and backward, trying to keep as much an eye on the cars ahead as he did the cops catching up on them. "They'll set up a roadblock, June."

"They'll back up traffic for miles if they do it on the interstate," she said. "But ... we'll get off anyway. Double back, maybe." She nodded at a green exit sign ahead. "There. You can get off there, and we'll figure out where to go next."

"But what about the two behind us?" He almost whined. "I don't think I've got much of anything left to blow them away with." He looked at her plaintively. "I'm tired, June."

She looked at him. It was probably true; he was sweating and pale, looked like he'd been for a ten-mile run after spending a month on the couch.

Ugh. He was so damned weak sometimes. "Just keep driving," she said.

"But they're catching us."

"Let 'em try," June said, keeping an eye on the rearview.

Sure enough, the two cop cars were closing. They were the new ones, the SUVs, the Fords. They were three cars back, and then people peeled away, changing lanes to give the police a clear avenue. Probably relieved they weren't the ones the officers were after.

Pretty soon they were a car length away from the back bumper, and June was ready, window down.

"When I tell you to, change lanes and go for that exit, you hear me?" June kept her eyes focused on the rearview, and her hand hung lightly out the window. "And hold your breath."

Ell nodded once. He'd been with her long enough to know what she intended.

The cloud of purple blew out so dense and tight it might have been shot out of the tailpipe of a backfiring car. It hung low over the road as she'd meant it to, puffing and settling just behind them, completely encompassing the two cop cars.

"Now," she said, and Ell swerved, leaving the purple cloud behind as he weaved through the right lane and onto the exit ramp. June watched the cop cars go by, covered in the purple toxin. She honed in on them, centered it, wouldn't let it move one direction or another save for that it stayed on them, with them at its middle, as she and Ell drifted down the exit ramp and took a turn.

Once they were out of sight, she let the cloud go, unable to keep it together anymore. "You think they got a breath of it?" Ell asked nervously.

"Probably not," she said as he sped them up a road, fumbling with his phone to reset the navigation. "They knew what they were going into chasing us. I bet they set their cars to recirculate air." She didn't add the, "I hope," that she felt surprised to be thinking. It was weird, wasn't it? To want them to be okay, to be alive when she'd just killed someone this very morning?

She almost started retching again thinking about it.

"Where do we go?" Ell asked, still fumbling with his phone, one hand on the wheel, ninety miles an hour down a back road.

June settled back, strangely comfortable with the danger she saw in his actions. If he flipped the car, if they crashed and died … it'd all be over in its own way, wouldn't it? There was some relief in the thought, the fear and the running all done. She felt tired, too, she realized, but a different kind of exhaustion than came from lack of sleep, or from using her powers too much. "I want to go to the beach again, Ell. Take me to the beach." She rested against the seat, feeling that sense of bone-weariness settle over her. "Please."

Ell sat there with phone in hand for a minute, contemplating, and then he nodded, once. "Okay. The beach." And fiddled with his phone until it said, "Starting route …"

June closed her eyes, not caring what it took to get there. She only wanted to be out of this, away from all this … back to a time when it was simpler, and when the road ahead seemed to stretch to the horizon … without a cop or a concern anywhere on it.

46.

Scott

His phone had stopped ringing after a while. It had been Phillips, whom he'd shunted to the voicemail every time and whose messages he hadn't bothered to check. They were probably full of overheated rhetoric anyway, empty bluster, threats.

The smell of motel room was getting worse. Sienna's skin had a grey, plasticine pallor to it. Her pulse was now down to thirty beats a minute by Scott's count, though the sheet between his fingertips and her wrist might have been muddling his count somewhat.

The phone lit up again, and he looked at it by habit, hoping for one name—not Phillip's—and getting another instead.

He answered. "Reed?"

"Hey Scotty," Reed said on the other end, sounding a lot more lively than the tortured, angry man he'd been when last they'd crossed paths. "I heard you're derelicting your duty."

"It's a little more complicated than that," Scott said, reaching down to take Sienna's pulse again.

"Isn't it always," Reed said breezily. "I got a call from your boss about this Florida situation, that couple running amok all over the place. He wanted to hire my team to run them down. Sounded desperate. I asked if you were looking into it and he got all clammy all the sudden. I think he's about ready to do something stupid."

"He does that," Scott said.

"No shit," Reed said. "I worked for him, too, remember? Longer than you. He's your best buddy when you're doing everything he wants you to, but the minute you have a mind of your own, the knives come out. Perfect guy to work in bureaucracy, but it makes my heart stop beating when I think about him being in charge of the metahuman response task force. Or whatever they call it these days." He paused. "So … what is the deal, man? You're in Florida, aren't you?"

"Yeah."

"So why are you avoiding this particular crisis? Because I told him flat out, we're too booked to even consider helping. My teams are all over the place—Augustus and Taneshia— we just temp hired her, they're up in Pennsylvania, we hired Jamal, his brother—don't know if you know him—and he and Angel are in New England. I got Veronika and Colin doing business out in Cali, and then I'm in Seattle myself—"

"Get to Florida," Scott said. "Now." Into the silence he said, "Drop what you're doing and get down here."

That stopped Reed in his tracks. "Dude. What's up?"

"Phillips didn't tell you because he didn't want to. This couple—I had Sienna with me. She was helping me—"

"What. The. Hell!" Reed's voice sounded like an explosion. "Gyah, this suddenly explains so much! You called—"

"Damned right I did," Scott said. "But … it's bad. Really bad. And I don't know how much good—"

"You should have called us from the beginning." Reed's voice sounded like metal scraping against metal. "What the hell were you thinking? You're a federal agent and she's a wanted felon. This is not just operating in the damned grey, Scott—"

"They shot her in the head, Reed."

That caused a mighty silence at the other end of the line. "What are you telling me?" Reed asked quietly.

"I'm doing everything I can," Scott said. "But she's dying. Her pulse is—"

"Scott …" Reed's voice went strangely calm. "… Are you telling me my sister is about to die?"

"Yeah," Scott said. "If something doesn't change soon … yes, she's going to die. In a matter of hours."

Reed's reply came back strangled. "I'm on my way. It'll take me a few hours to cross the country. Just … she needs to hang on until I get there. You tell her that."

"It may not come to that," Scott said, checking the time on his phone. "I—"

"Yeah, I get it," Reed said. "I'm on my way." And he hung up.

Scott settled back in his chair, and listened to the slow, steady breathing. She'd been taking deeper breaths before. Longer ones. Now her breathing was getting shallow, the breaths raspy. "How long do we have?" he wondered aloud.

No answer was forthcoming, but he knew it would be soon.

47.

Sienna

"Oh, this is an interesting moment," Harmon said, and he wasn't wrong, not by any metric.

I was sitting backstage in a television studio, my palms covered with sweat. Or at least, the past me was. I was watching myself through Scott's eyes, and he was fuming inside. None of it quite came out that way, though, he kept a pretty solid lid on it until he said, "What the hell were you thinking?"

I looked up at him with defined menace. "Clearly, I was thinking … 'Hey! You know what would be great for making me look like a hugely psychotic ass? An interview with the most famous journalist in the world, Gail Roth. Let's go do that!' And now here we are, mission accomplished, so I can go on with my life knowing that I've crashed and burned as hard as I could possibly do that. What a wonderful feeling, and I'm glad—so glad—you're here to support me now, to bask in my reflected glory." I finished my last, heavy dose of snark, and sank back into silence.

Scott lasted about ten seconds. "What the hell were you thinking?"

"You already asked that," I said. "If you're just going to keep asking it over and over—"

"You didn't answer the questions like a normal person, Sienna!" he said. "Yes, you came off like a lunatic, and I'm glad you see that. But—what—were—you—*thinking?*"

I raised my head with malice and menace. "I was thinking I'm tired because we were up until four last night arguing— again. And I was up at six for an interagency conference call, two back-to-back budget meetings, and a peek at what my next six weeks are going to look like, which is going to include sojourns to Brazil, Botswana, and probably Mongolia in addition to a half-dozen domestic trips. So if I didn't answer Gail Roth's questions like a normal human being, maybe it's because I'm being pushed and pulled and ripped at by most of the states in the union and also the State Department on behalf of a dozen countries needing meta assistance—and every hour that I actually spend at home now seems to be half-spent bickering with you." I stood up even though I didn't feel like it. "Do you know how tiresome that is? Like I don't have enough to manage with you getting on my ass about this—this—this utter, epic failure! I don't even know how to describe this other than as the public relations version of an oil spill in the Supercutey Cute Pet Emporium, caused by a drunken pedophile of a captain."

"Well, at least you have some concept of what you've done," he said, walking away in disgust.

"See, now that was an apt metaphor for the Gail Roth disaster," Harmon said. "Do you have any idea how upset the White House Press Secretary was the next day?"

"I don't really care," I said, trying to tune back in to the argument before me. It was a rerun, sure, but still more interesting than new whining from Harmon.

"Let's just get out of here," Scott said, looking weary and disgusted himself. "I can't even imagine what my parents are going to say."

"I can't imagine giving a damn what your parents are going to say at this point," I said hotly. "But then, they've never liked me anyway."

"They don't … dislike you …" he said, rather feebly.

"Bullshit," I said, my tolerance for lies pretty much at the bottom of the tank.

"Look," he said, trying to catch my shoulder as I started past him, "we've just had a rough few months. This is normal—"

"Whatever we are, normal is not it."

"Well, we're metas," he said, "but other than that … yeah, this is normal."

"You think fighting like this—all the time—is *normal?*" I felt seeping disgust, mostly at myself but some at him for the months and months of this. "Heaven help the poor woman you're going to marry."

He looked suddenly distant, like I'd hit him in the stomach. "I thought *you* were the woman I was going to marry."

I closed my eyes, drawing a breath and clutching at my forehead, which was throbbing. "Come on, let's just get out of here."

"He has no idea, does he?" Harmon asked as we watched the two of us walking toward the door. The world around us was shrouded in thick darkness, a blanket of black laid over everything else, much tighter than the borders of the dressing room and casting a shadowy tinge to even the lights overhead.

"Well, his last relationship ended in tragic memory loss for the other party," I said, stepping out of the moment again, "so no … he probably had no idea what a proper relationship looked like."

"How did you?" Harmon asked smarmily.

"I guess I don't," I said, "but I don't think my conception of it is that far off, because unless you like arguing, why the hell would you want to do it all the time? We're not talking about two people who can get angry and hold no grudge. The sort of fights we were having stumbled right up to the edge and then leapt off. We said unforgivable things to each other, things—you know what, never mind."

"No, go on," Harmon said. "I've heard a few of these 'unforgivable things.' They sounded to me like devastatingly accurate assessments of each others' flaws."

"That's what made them so damned hurtful," I said. "If they were lies, they wouldn't have stung like hell."

The darkness swept in and then faded, replacing the scene of backstage at the interview with my bedroom again. The corners were dark, the bedside lamp unable to penetrate the gloom around the place. "I really am going to die, aren't I?"

"From a bullet, no less," Harmon said, shaking his head almost sadly now. Annoyance I could see, but sadness? Yeesh. "Do you know what your problem is?"

"I would almost be willing to pay you not to tell me at this point."

"Well, I don't need money, so who gives a damn how much you have to offer?" He drew a steady breath. "You accused me once of being too arrogant."

"I … don't remember saying that," I said.

"It went like this … 'If you're so smart … why do I keep beating you'?"

"Oh. Well. Yeah, I suppose I said it like that."

"So here's my corollary," Harmon said. "If you're so damned invincible … why did you walk into that bank and get shot in the back of the head like an idiot?"

"I was not thinking in terms of—"

"Wrong."

"I didn't believe that June and Elliot were that far gone—"

"Ehhhhhhhhn," he made a buzzer noise. "Wrong again. Care to take another stab at it, or do you want to see what my telepathy would tell you?"

"I don't have any duct tape with which to stop you at this point."

"You've been a goddess for so long in your own mind," Harmon said, "you don't even realize how far you've drifted from … here." He nodded at the me that was staring, frozen, at Scott. "What were your dreams?"

"What … then? Here?"

"Before Sovereign," Harmon said.

I laughed. "Before Sovereign, I was a kid. Eighteen. I didn't know what I wanted."

"Oh, but you did," he said. "You want me to tell you? Because it was a very simple thing you wanted, a universal desire."

"Sure, why n—"

"You wanted to be *normal*." He touched me on the hand,

and it didn't burn, his smug smile replaced with one that was … almost disarming. Like the Gerry Harmon who campaigned for every vote, not the one lording it over me in one on one conversation. "You wanted to be … touchable." He ran his fingers over my wrist, and it didn't burn for once, the touch of another human being. "You wanted the same things everyone else did, with a few … modifications. Wolfe did a number on you, pushed you with guilt to want to protect, to defend … to make up for lives lost while you hid. But overall, outside of that … you wanted to be normal. Live, love … be fulfilled."

I had a vague memory of feeling exactly that way, once upon a time. "So … ?"

"So what are your dreams now?" he asked. "Run and hide so that you can survive until another case comes along? So you can take another hit of that sweet feeling you get from solving a problem? I mean, you're a federal fugitive and you're still chasing your drug of choice—relevance in the metahuman criminal justice scene. You don't have hope of a relationship, even a dysfunctional one like this," he gestured to Scott. "You're surviving, day to day, eating and drinking in an attempt to numb the pain while you wait for something bad to happen so you can go be a hero again."

"Well, what else is there?" I asked. "Family life is just as out of reach as it was then, and I'm not convinced I want … any of that—"

"Yes, your mother issues are impressive, but let's leave off those worries," Harmon said.

"I really miss Zollers right now."

"And that's another thing," Harmon said. "Your friends know you didn't do what you're accused of. But you're avoiding them anyway."

"Because aiding a fugitive is—"

"A crime, yes, I think we've established that. But … you've never shied away from committing crimes before. And simply calling them wouldn't be a crime. You could even tell them to report it to the authorities, and you could still have a conversation."

"Well, it's not that easy—"

"It's that easy," he said. "If you didn't want to talk to them that way, why not dreamwalk to them? No evidence of a cell phone call, and you have unlimited minutes. Beats email, talk and text messages."

I didn't know quite what to say to that.

"Do you know why you don't want to talk to anyone?"

"Will you stop with the rhetorical questions? I couldn't pay you or threaten you to shut up, we've already established—"

"Your arrogance is like a poison," he said. "It's coursing through your veins. Has been for years. I pushed you to the brink when you worked for the government, and I saw the effects starting, even at a distance. You walked into a house in England and got your foot blown off."

"It was a bomb—"

"You got in a fight in Los Angeles with a mad bomber and were electrocuted."

"Well, there was some water involved in that, too, it's not like I could have totally anticipated—"

"You're reckless," he said, "and your power has led you to believe you're somehow invincible. You're tough, no doubt, but ... I think we can see by this ... you're not invincible. You never were. And furthermore ... you knew you never were."

"You're kind of all over the place on this. Mind getting to your thesis?"

"This is my thesis," Harmon said. "You've got a death wish. You're tired of being the guardian to this world. Tired of feeling like you're better than everyone and cut off from everyone at the same time. It's not going to get any better, and so you keep walking into death traps because ... you don't have anything worth really living for. It was bad before you went on the run, but now? You're holding onto your so-called job that you don't actually have anymore like a drowning man holds to a life preserver. And when that's gone ..." He snapped his fingers; the sound was surprisingly loud in the empty, darkened room. "Your whole life these last few years is like a cry for help. Even when you got friends back ... it wasn't enough. Even when you tried to stave things off by having boyfriends or one-night stands … none of it held the darkness at bay." He threw his arms wide, indicating the shadows growing long around us with both hands. "Beating me didn't fulfill you; stopping conspiracies and saving lives doesn't do it. You owed—what, two hundred and fifty-something lives after Wolfe? You have to have saved millions by now. When will it ever be enough?"

"I don't know."

"The answer is *never*. It will *never* be enough. Because in your life … it's all you have left. And in your heart … you know it. Which is why you push your supposed invincibility to the limits. You take terrible, pointless risks, because a part of you hopes that you will die … because that will finally, finally let you off the hook."

I felt surprisingly sick, and I wondered if the sensation came from my real body. "Let me off the hook for what?"

"For wanting it over. For being tired of the fight. It's like the hammering waves of an endless ocean—and no one is coming to rescue you from your life."

That was a fair point, and it hit closer to home than I wanted to admit. "Yeah, but … then, what do I do? Just … drift beneath the surface?"

"As surprising as it may sound, I'm not advocating that," Harmon said. "I'm just saying I understand it. The feeling that things are never going to get better, that the surface will always be stormy, and that the only peace you'll find is in the depths below."

"Am I a fool for holding out that faint hope that things will get better?" I asked. I didn't really believe they would, but it was the hope I clung to at night, when I was trying to get to sleep in my empty hotel bed back in St. Thomas.

"Yes," he said, but with a surprising amount of chagrin. "I didn't design this trap I've put you in with the idea that I'd ever be forced into sharing accommodations. Now that we're stuck together, I find myself regretting that I boxed you in so thoroughly. The press is unlikely to admit error now, because they'll look stupid, and their pride and ego rival yours. The government isn't going to back off, because admitting error for them is even a more bitter pill to swallow, especially with that idiot Gondry in charge. The fact that there are still swirling accusations that you masterminded my disappearance is not going to work in your favor with my party, and the opposition is too focused on their own agenda to take up your cause—which is bound to be an unpopular one in any case, absent astounding evidence of your innocence, which I think we both agree would be met, in this apathetic environment, with an overwhelming, 'Meh.'" He shook his head. "No. If there's a light at the end of the tunnel for you … I don't see it. And if it's there, it's probably a train … or so distant as to be pointless."

"When you put it that way," I said, slouching over to the bed and thumping down, "why do I keep going on?" The peace of the depths below that I was slowly drifting toward was starting to sound strangely … inviting.

"It's a strange quirk of yours," Harmon said, shuffling over and joining me, hands on his crisp pants legs, their perfect creases a great illustration of the difference between him—former president, poised, in shape, raised in privilege, brilliant mind—and me—badly fitting jeans, overweight, tired all the time, street fighter, dirty fighter—hell, all kinds of fighter. "I didn't really understand it when we faced off, that persistence that carried you forward in spite of overwhelming losses. You watched every friend you had defect from your side, decry you in public. Anyone sane would have quit at that point, deciding they were too deeply buried to ever get out, but you just kept digging with manic fervor and soon enough you came out in China or something. Impressive turnaround, really, but … it's only gotten you so far. And now … all this mental weight you've been carrying around is your anchor in the deep water."

I had a vision again of swimming in the ocean during a terrible storm. Lightning flashed in the dark night, illuminating the downpour of rain, the black, angry clouds overhead. The waves tossed me about, and no land was in sight.

I was isolated.

I was alone.

I had nothing left to go on for, really.

I looked at Scott and myself, about to get into it again for the last time. "Why do you think I chose the quick and easy route here?"

Harmon stirred, looking up at the spectacle before us. I could have practically quoted every line from this fight, if I'd had to. "Tired people choose the easy way. Why would they want to make it harder on themselves?"

I put my head down, in my hands. "I am tired. So tired. It's like … like a poison, like June's clouds. It creeps in, steals your will to fight, wears you down."

"In a way, that's true," Harmon said. "That's what a toxin does, albeit more quickly—it steals life, a little at a time. It cuts off the flow of oxygen to your cells, and your body starts to die. The mind withers. Hope does the opposite, it's like breath in the lungs, and you … you lack that hope."

"I don't suppose you have any to spare?"

Harmon smiled, but it was thin, almost sad. "I'm stuck in here. Life without the possibility of parole. If you die now, I die, too, but … I find no comfort in that because to my mind … that is simply the end. Meaningless. But if I go on … all I am is a shade. A pale imitation of myself, watching in the corner of your mind with little influence of my own to peddle. You need to understand … for someone like me, someone who has worked the levers of power for as long as I did … the only thing worse than the existence I'm living is no existence at all. There's no joy in you to reflect onto me, no happiness to cling to. You're a being composed almost entirely of sorrow at this point. I've seen enough of your mind to know that it wasn't always so—but it is now. You ask me if I have hope? Well …"

I kept my head in my hands, and a thin tear streaked down my cheek.

"Oddly enough … I do have a small, almost infinitesimally small sliver of it."

I composed myself before raising my head. "Oh?"

"Yes," Harmon said stiffly. "For you see, I am the prisoner of a woman who once beat a conspiracy that should have left her dead. Who once crushed the most powerful metahuman to walk the planet, a woman who somehow—

maddeningly, in fact—keeps defying the impossible odds thrown at her. So, yes, I have hope. A very thin hope. And it is, strangely enough, predicated on the bizarre faith I find myself imbued with, against all evidence of my past, pre-Sienna experience. It's based on the fact that in spite of everything that has happened to you, Sienna, including this very dismal, potentially fatal turn of events …

"Somehow, I believe that if anyone—anyone at all, on the entire damnable planet—could dig their way out of this and somehow triumph? It's you. Nobody else."

I stared at him in wonder as he sat stiffly on the edge of the bed staring straight ahead, as though he'd just said nothing at all.

And I laughed.

Harmon snapped his head around in supreme irritation. "What?"

"I just …" I couldn't stop giggling. "I'm stuck in my own head, dying, with a supervillain who wanted to mind control the entire world … I'm a fugitive wanted for murder after murder I didn't commit … I have basically no chance of overturning that result because of the murders I actually did commit once upon a time … I'm almost certainly clinically depressed … but you just told me you believe in me." I finished chortling and it trailed off into a sad sigh. "That's the best thing anyone's said to me in a while, and I laughed at it." My mirth died. "I'm sorry."

"We react oddly to things," Harmon said, still a bit stiffly. I think he was insulted at my initial burst of laughter. "I once burst out laughing at a State Dinner when I found out through mind reading that a certain South American president was a furry."

"A wha—oh." I took a deep breath and blew it out slowly, staring at the memory before me. The emotion was thick in the air, like a dressing on this salad of suffering. "I don't think I need to see the rest of this. Do you?"

"I don't know what it would prove to you or me," he said. "You were in a dark place when you made this decision, though."

"I know." I looked up at the vision of me and Scott,

locked in perpetual combat to the end. "I thought I was doing him a favor by taking this ... this weight ... but it only helped bog me down. For years. If I could give it back, I would. I don't want to say it was my greatest mistake, because I've probably made bigger ones, but ... it's right up there."

"It's getting very dark now," Harmon said, and I realized he was telling the truth. I couldn't recall ever seeing him so somber before. "I don't think it's going to be very long."

"No," I said, a little sadly. Should I have felt relief to know that my long struggle was about to be over? I didn't even know. And I didn't know how to feel. In my heart was just a great numbness, events moving along without my attention or choice.

"That's my way of saying that if you've got any miracles on hand, it might be a good time to spring one," he said.

"If we really are cut off from Wolfe and his powers ... I think my miracles are kind of at an end," I said, resting my elbows on my thighs as the darkness kept creeping in, millimeter by millimeter. Scott's face was now shrouded in the dark, his mouth frozen open in angry reply.

"Such a shame," Harmon said, with a tinge of amusement. "I was just starting to like you, too."

I laughed again, but it was an empty sound, hollow of joy. "Yeah. You ain't so bad yourself, El Presidente. At least when you're restricted from world-conquering activities."

He chortled a little bit at that, then turned sober. "Shame to get out this way, though. A bullet in the head from some Bonnie Parker wannabe."

"Is it bad that the thing I feel most right now ... even over that weird relief that maybe it's finally over ... is regret that I didn't get a chance to at least finish out that case before I leave?" I asked, almost plaintive.

"Not bad ... it's just you," he said, as the darkness started to settle. "Seriously, though ... last minute reprieve? Final, amazing, out-of-nowhere plan to save your own life?"

"Wolfe?" I called, into the encroaching darkness.

Only silence replied.

"I think I'm all out," I said sadly. Harmon nodded once, then bowed his own head.

There was nothing left to do but wait for death to take us.

48.

Scott

It was close now. Her pulse rate was dropping like some hapless soul Sienna had let go in flight. "She's letting go," he said, trying to figure out what to do. CPR would be difficult to say the least, and Reed was still hours away.

"We're not going to make it," Scott said.

The septic stink, like a hospital gone horribly wrong, filled the motel room. The dark tones as night had covered the place had only lengthened, shadows becoming beasts of darkness that had taken hold in every corner. He hadn't turned on a lamp for fear that moving away from her, shifting his attention for even a second, would mean he missed it when she inevitably crashed, when her heartbeat finally slowed so much that her brain no longer received any of the marginal share of oxygen that her shallow, agonized breaths were delivering.

It was a death rattle, and there was nothing he could do to make her breathe.

"Sienna," Scott said, as though she could hear him, as though there were anything she could do from within to heal herself. "You can't go. Not yet. Not like this …"

He brushed the back of her hand, skin to skin contact, and felt the short burn. He'd touched her too much today, even in the brief, passing moments that he'd made contact. If he so much as held her hand for a few seconds, she'd absorb him, too, dragging him into the lurch of death with her.

He'd thought about it. Thought about seizing her hand and holding it until the end, letting that burning pain run through his skin, letting his soul leave his body in a rush, with a scream. He'd plunge headfirst into her dying body with her, and maybe—

No, it wouldn't do anything. If her body couldn't heal itself with a succubus's high-powered regenerative abilities, even an amplified Poseidon wouldn't add a single second to her life.

She started to choke, a desperate, guttural sound deep in the throat.

"No, no," he said, rising out of the chair he'd pulled to her bedside. "No no no—" His helpless hands shook as he held them over her, unsure of where to direct them.

She barely twitched as she struggled for breath, her body fighting the last fight before it gave up. He stood there, looking down, agonized. "You can't leave. Not—no—"

But there was nothing left to do.

No CPR—as though that would bring her back when her body seemed dead set on giving up the fight.

No defibrillator.

No last ditch effort.

No superhuman healing.

He had done everything he could do to save her …

… And he'd failed.

"I'm sorry, Sienna," he said, taking her hand through the thin bedsheet. "I'm sorry I dragged you into this. I know I should have called Reed, but …"

He hung his head. "I didn't want Reed's help.

"I wanted you."

The admission tugged at him, ripped at his insides. He hadn't wanted to give it voice, this insane desire, the idea that he'd had on that beach in Florida. He could have done the smart thing, hired the people who weren't wanted, weren't hunted, weren't at risk of being shot dead if they found themselves in police sights.

But I wanted you.
Needed you. Needed to know …
About us.

Needed to know ... about things I can't even remember, like whispered voices in an empty room.

She shook, jerking in spasm, but it was already fading in intensity along with the slow decline of her last breaths.

Her last breaths.

The bed rocked with a hard twitch, her meta strength causing it to squeak, to cry in a way that she no longer could. She wasn't breathing now. He couldn't even feel the hint of a pulse through the bedsheet.

I did everything I could for her.

And it still wasn't enough.

Not enough to—

Save her.

Silence reigned in the room. She wasn't stirring, not even so quietly that only a meta could have heard it.

Somewhere in the distance, a car bumped against a curb, but Scott barely noticed it.

His phone buzzed quietly in the darkness, and he ignored it.

Why did any of it matter?

She was dead.

The hammering at the door stirred him, like a shock of cold water poured down his shirt. He froze, for just a second. It couldn't be—

"Scott!" A high voice shouted, followed by the frantic—though restrained—slamming of a palm against the door.

He rose in a frenzy, ripping the chair out of the way in his rush to get to the door.

He tore it open without disengaging the lock, almost ripping it from the hinges—

And there she stood in the Florida moonlight, waxy-pale and tired from the long flight, her supple skin lacking the usual make-up, her blond hair hanging in stringy ringlets, unstyled—

"Kat," he breathed, "she's—" and made it no further before Katrina Forrest shoved past him unceremoniously, into the room and toward the small figure lying still and silent on the bed.

49.

June

They "traded" cars in a small town along the way that she never even caught the name of. They just stopped at a gas station where cars had been parked overnight, maybe an auto service place or something, found one unlocked with the keys behind the shade, and started it right up. It was a seventies car, and June liked it, because she could lean against Ell as he drove with one hand and kept the other wrapped around her shoulder.

It smelled like a steady diet of air fresheners and something else—smokeless tobacco, maybe, long ago used and long ago discarded. It had a kind of sweet scent to it, lingering in spite of a lack of evidence that it had ever been here at all. It reminded June of her grandfather and the way his car smelled, and something about it soothed her.

Night had fallen and they'd found a quiet place to park in a wooded grove. They'd gone back roads the whole way but Ell was tired and June was tired, and so they pulled over and held each other, kissed, her salty tears that she couldn't stop not spoiling the quiet, intimate moment they shared. When they were done she pulled her pants back up and her tank top back down, ignoring the red splotches on the white so as to keep from throwing up the nothing she'd eaten the last few hours.

"We're maybe thirty minutes from Daytona Beach," Ell said. They'd settled back, resting, her head on his chest. They could go. Could start the car and just go. "You want to leave now?"

"No," she said. It was right there, on the horizon, so close it wouldn't take any time at all to get there. And she wanted to see the beach.

But somehow she sensed the danger there, too, and wanted to put it off, at least a little longer. There was peace here, in his arms, peace that might not be waiting for her in Daytona.

"Okay. We'll wait until tomorrow," he said, his chin brushing lightly against the top of her head.

"Mmhmm," she said against his chest as it moved up and down in time with his breaths. She didn't know what was ahead, exactly—trouble, she suspected—but here was like an oasis in the desert of it, and trouble didn't seem to know where they were. If she could have, she might have stayed here, forever.

But the beach called, and she knew this feeling of safety was false, was temporary. Tomorrow they'd set out again, but for now, June was content to lie there with her head on Ell's chest, enjoying the quiet moment with him, trying not to think about when—or if—they'd ever get another.

50.

Scott

"How long has she been down?" Kat asked, shedding her rumpled, long-sleeved blouse in favor of the white tank top she wore beneath it. It was a different look on her, lacking her usual makeup, and was reminiscent of their days together, half a lifetime ago.

"A couple minutes," Scott said, picking himself up from where she'd shoved him aside. "I didn't think you were going to make it."

"You saw my text about the flight delay?" She pushed hair back out of her eyes as she leaned over Sienna, who was unmoving, unbreathing.

"Yeah."

"I convinced the pilot to move his ass," she said. "Being a prima donna celeb has its occasional advantages." She rubbed her hands together. "I can't do this for long without—"

"I know."

"Pull me back if it looks like I'm too far gone—"

"I will." Scott stumbled to her side, ungainly on his legs, as though he'd not used them in forever. "I don't want you getting sucked down the drain with her if she's—" He didn't dare finish the thought.

Kat drew a deep breath, like she was steeling herself for something deeply unpleasant, and then shoved her hands down—

219

She made contact with Sienna's cheeks and pushed her palms flat, skin to skin. "Come on, Sienna," she said. "Come back to us. Just a little bit … just enough to …"

Scott stood there, watching, as breathless as Sienna. There was nothing momentous in Kat's action, no burst of light or sudden movement. Just the two women locked together in a touch, Kat's hands on Sienna's pale, lifeless cheeks.

Then both of them of them jerked at the same time, and Kat started to scream, and all hell seemed to break loose while Scott stood helplessly again, watching.

51.

Sienna

"I see light," Harmon said, looking left to right abruptly.

I raised my head from where I'd hung it, like a refugee prisoner, and glanced around. "Uhmm …"

He wasn't wrong. There was light where darkness had started to consume us. A few moments before, when last I'd looked, the other me and Scott had both been completely swallowed up. Now, I could see our features once more, a faint glow on the horizon.

"Huh," I said as the room started to brighten again, the table lamp seeming to increase in wattage as the scene appeared to change, the shadows shortening all around us. "Do you think … this is it? That … this is the end?"

"No," Harmon said, face screwed up in thought. "I feel … something … again. My power starting to—"

"This is a cozy scene," Bjorn said, the big Norseman suddenly appearing as though I'd snapped my fingers and made a wish for more annoyance in my life.

"I have never been so glad to see you," I said, coming off the bed in a hurry. I almost hugged him, then remembered who he was. "Uh, I mean … you're a dickbag."

"Always the truth," Eve Kappler said in that thick, Germanic accent, suddenly there with us, looking around at the room. "Where are we?"

"Blast from the past," Roberto Bastian said as he leapt into fully-formed existence on the other side of me,

221

surveying the place like a dozen meta ninjas were going to jump out and attack at any time.

"Did I miss movie night?" Zack asked as he appeared. When I stared at him in weak relief, he smiled. "I get the feeling we were circling the drain there?"

"A very astute assessment," Harmon said stiffly, rising to stand with the others.

"Glad to see we dodged that bullet," Wolfe said in that low, gravelly voice of his, slinking out of the darkness behind me.

"Can you—" I started to ask him.

"Working on it," he said, his massive shoulders hunched up, his face all heavy with concentration. "Any idea what chang—"

"I know," Aleksandr Gavrikov said, voice thick with feeling.

And for one of the first times in all the years I'd known him, the Russian was smiling.

"Kat," I whispered, and felt a surprising rush of fond emotion.

52.

Scott

"Unnnnnnnh!" Kat groaned, hands anchored to Sienna's cheeks as she rolled, thrusting her head back as though she were going to roar like a lioness. Her hands were white, the color leeched from them by the darkness of the room and the exertion of her contact with Sienna's skin.

"How are you d—" Scott started to ask and stopped himself when she writhed again, her legs buckling before she caught herself on the edge of the bed. He was counting the seconds, and was up to fifteen, trying to keep steady in spite of the nearly unseen urge to speed up. It was as though the numbers wanted to slip away from him, come out in a rush. "Sixteenseventeeneighteennineteen—"

Kat's legs folded, and this time she hit the bed, landing on Sienna with her elbows but failing to hold herself from collapse. Her hands were still anchored to Sienna's face, though, even as both women heaved and jerked at the intensity of their exchange.

"Twentytwentyonetwentytwotwentythree—" He was counting for thirty, unable to stop speeding forward with it at this point, as though caught headlong in a gravity well and flying into it at unsafe speeds. He watched for anything—the flutter of Sienna's eyes, the widening of them, a shocking gasp of breath, anything to suggest the job was done, that life was restored sufficiently—

In spite of the muscle movement, she showed no signs of

recovery, her power working past death to drag Kat along. But was it doing any good? Was Kat's power to heal working beneath Sienna's own power to drain? Or had Sienna's ability to heal died with her, with the stopping of her heart? If so, the only thing happening now was the death of Kat, who seemed to be holding in a scream, her mouth open wide and head thrown skyward, eyes tightly shut in agony—

He hit thirty and ran right past it without noticing at first, and was almost to thirtyfivethirtysixthirtyseven- before he reached out and slapped Kat's hands, breaking the contact because she couldn't—

Kat tumbled down and he caught her before she slid off the bed head-first, his arm catching her around her chest and holding her there as her legs drooped uselessly. She was lighter than he remembered.

"Did I ... ?" Kat asked through ragged breaths, her eyes clamped tightly shut. Her head bobbed in whatever direction he moved her as he tried to lower her to the ground. He set her back against the bed, her head rolling against the threadbare comforter, as though she might sleep sitting up. "Did it ... did it ..." Her voice was low as a whisper. "Scott ..."

He stared down at Sienna. The wounds were still there, he could feel them, those little plugs of blood. The pulse— he could feel it again, the liquid moving steadily, slowly through her veins ...

"I think—"

Sienna's eyes broke open like a vase cracked in half with sudden violence. She sat up in bed forcefully, drawing a frighteningly loud breath, a panicked breath, almost a screech. She looked left, then right, wide-eyed, and met his, sagging back, thumping into the headboard.

"I think she made it okay," Scott said, leaving Kat to rest against the side of the bed as he stepped up to stand next to Sienna, who was still staring up at him. "Are you—"

"Is Kat okay?" Sienna asked, breaking away from him and looking around again, her eyes settling on the patch of yellow hair that was caught on the bedspread near her feet.

Kat threw a hand up limply. "I'm ... I'm okay, I think.

Lightheaded. Skin kinda burning, like a rash or something …
but …" She let out a breathless sigh. "I'm okay."

"Good," Sienna said, slumping back against the
headboard like she'd just died again. Scott let out a held
breath and found his legs suddenly too weak to bear his
weight. He came crashing down on the floor of the motel,
his tailbone finding the thin carpeting a poor landing place,
but all he muttered was, "Ow," as the two women in the
room with him—the only two he'd ever loved, really—both
turned their heads to stare at his sudden and entirely
unexpected collapse.

53.

Sienna

"Well, that was a kick in the head," I said once I'd composed myself a little, enough to hang my legs over the edge of the bed.

"You think it was bad on your end," Scott said darkly, arms folded, leaning against the wall next to the bedside table, "try sitting there watching someone who's damned near invincible die in front of you."

"I'm sorry," I said to him, and he blinked at me, caught somewhere between surprise and amusement. I tried to make my expression convey what I really meant, but I failed, so I just spoke it aloud. "I'm sorry for everything, Scott. Everything I did to you."

That caused his eyebrows to go high on his long forehead. "Well … okay, then."

"This is really cute," Kat said, still collapsed against the side of the bed. "But what I want to know is … how did you damned near die in the first place?"

"Long story," I said.

"She took a round in the head," Scott said.

"Ouch," Kat said.

"Wait, you didn't know what happened?" I asked.

"No."

"I told her you got hurt," Scott said. "And she hopped on a plane."

That is my Klementina, Gavrikov said. *So sweet. So …*

heartfelt. So ...

I didn't interrupt him like I normally would have. "Thank you, Kat," I said, once he was done getting teary over his sister.

"Just glad I could help," she said, looking at me wanly. She crinkled her nose. "Ugh. Seriously, though ... this place?"

"It's the smell, isn't it?" I asked with a little embarrassment.

"It's the décor, right?" Scott asked.

"It's the exhaustion, and that the bed is soiled," Kat said, looking with great unease at where I was sitting. "I cannot sleep in that. And I'm going to need to sleep. So very soon."

"Oh, yeah, no, I wouldn't expect you to," I said, burning a little in the cheeks. It wasn't like I'd been in great condition to get up and use the toilet while I was dying. I heaved back up to my feet and made a face. "Yeah ... let's get you a different room, maybe, and, uh ... fresh clothes for me?"

"Yeah, I'll ... get your bag from the car," Scott said, nodding once. "And another room for Kat." He nodded a couple times and headed for the door.

"And, uh, Scott?" I asked, causing him to turn back to me. "If the lobby has a vending machine ... ?" I mimed eating something.

"They do have one," he said, thinking it over. "Snickers? Chips?"

"If they have anything healthy," I said, blushing a little, "start with that. If not ... do the best you can?" He nodded and started to leave again. "Thank you," I called after him, and he hesitated, just a second. "For everything."

He nodded again, and turned to leave.

"Hell of a night, huh?" Kat asked, sounding drained as though I'd opened her veins and let her bleed almost every drop out. She looked like she was about to go to sleep right here.

"You said it, sister," I agreed, and she smiled, probably at my most peculiar choice of words, but she did not say anything to dispute them.

54.

June

Sunrise blazed in the windshield and woke them both up from an all-too-fleeting slumber. June didn't feel like resisting it, like trying to squint it away. She'd stared at the black night for most of it, not even realizing she'd drifted off at some point, probably from exhaustion.

"What do you want to do?" Ell asked, shifting against her, his ribs a suddenly uncomfortable pillow.

"Get something to eat, I guess," June said languidly. There was no joy in her movement now, just a strange resignation to getting back on the road. At the end of it was a beach, but no excitement for it now, just a destination to head toward, a box to check. "Then get on with it."

"Okay," Ell said, and he started the car with a sputtering roar. It sounded labored, like the car didn't want to get going, either. She sympathized with it. But it didn't change anything; she felt the call, and it was time to move. Just like the car—start her up, point in the direction, and apply gas until they reached it.

Ell backed them out of the dirt road carefully, long grass brushing the underside of the car, sounding like the chassis might be batting aside a few sticks in the process. It was like a grinding symphony to June, loud and irritating, but she didn't react.

She just held tight to Ell's side, figuring she'd ride right here until they got to Daytona Beach. Then, the next thing would happen, and the next …

And probably, pretty soon, they'd run out of next things. One way or the other. And that bothered her less than she would have thought.

55.

Sienna

A shower with the quiet hum of the water washing over me, and the surprisingly felicitous chatter of my souls now back in my head allowed me a few minutes to recuperate from the ordeal of getting a big, sloppy tongue kiss from death itself.

Also, Scott brought me a package of peanut butter and crackers, which I scarfed in about two seconds. Hey, it was better for me than devouring a Snickers bar.

When I'd finished toweling off and dressing, I walked out to find Scott waiting there, silently, guarding the door, which hung off its hinges. "What happened there?" I asked, wondering if there was a hair dryer available to help me keep from soaking my shirt. Ahh, it didn't matter, I realized. The water just helped me feel alive again.

"Kat broke it on the way in," he said, giving it a quick look. "She barreled right past me to get to you."

"Hmm," I said, tapping my ear to get the water out. That never worked. I did once try boiling it out by turning an entire half of my head into flames, and even that didn't work. Annoying.

"You surprised?" Scott asked.

"That Kat came running? Sorta," I said. "I'm grateful, though."

"You still have friends, Sienna," he said. "Reed's coming, too. Sounded like he was the one dying when I told him."

I didn't know quite how to take that. "How's Kat doing?"

"Probably sleeping," he said. "Got her the room next door. You want to check on her?"

"Might as well," I said as a car bumped by on the highway outside, its lights drifting past slowly in the fading darkness. Sunrise was visible out there, the sky a fiery orange in preparation for the breaking day. I tossed my used towel on the bed, feeling a little bad for the maid who was going to have to clean this up. I felt surprisingly tired given I'd just woken up, but I hadn't really been having a restful sleep. I scooped up my bag and carried it with me, figuring I probably shouldn't leave it in a motel room that couldn't even be properly closed.

When we came into Kat's room, she was pretty out of it, but she looked up as the door clicked shut. "Hey," she said, and waved her cellphone at me. "I was just about to go looking for you guys. Any minute now. Really." She shifted a little in bed, but didn't try to sit up.

"What's going on?" Scott asked.

"Text from Reed," she said, looking like she might die if she tried to stand. "I told him you're okay, and he took it predictably in stride. But he warned me, since he knew I was here … I guess Phillips is still trying to get him to intervene in this situation with those kids that shot you."

I dropped my bag on the floor behind a table and chairs, not quite sure how to feel about that, either. "Oh?"

"I guess they assaulted some cops on the road last night," Kat said, struggling to get up on her elbows. She failed, and didn't try again. I wondered if Scott had carried her over here. "One patrolman in the ICU, another couple in the hospital with respiratory issues."

"But the perps got away?" I asked. That promise I'd made Grandma Randall was nagging at me stupidly, like a hole in my skull or something. Or another one, at least.

"Yeah, but," she said, stopping to take a breath. She was winded. "… I guess they've got access to these kids' Google Maps for their cell phone, so they know their destination and Phillips is moving in a special tactical team to take them out."

Scott stirred. "He's done playing, then. He's issuing a kill order."

"Yeah," Kat said with a heavy breath. "And except for Reed and me ... we have no one else who could get into position to help. And Reed's still over Alabama or Mississippi or something."

I looked out the window, messing with the crappy, seventies-era curtains. "When do you think these kids are going to roll into ... wherever they're going?"

"The destination is Daytona Beach," Kat said. "I don't know when. They don't have a track on them anymore, because I guess they lost it for the night, but Phillips is setting up an ambush for them on the beach. Or near it. I don't know." She lay back, completely spent.

I couldn't blame her. She was exhausted from more than just the use of her powers; I could feel a shadow inside me, hints of her personality, her liveliness, maybe even a couple memories, though I was avoiding looking at them. Not just because I respected Kat's privacy, either, but because I knew the kind of old guys she'd slept with before and I really, really wanted to avoid seeing Janus in the altogether through her eyes.

"That tactical team will bring them down," Scott said, more sedate than I'd heard him on this entire endeavor. Watching me damned near die seemed to have really taken it out of him.

It had taken it out of me, too, but that promise was still nagging in my head, along with something else. "No," I said, shaking my head.

"No what?" Kat said.

"I'm not letting them bushwhack those kids," I said.

"Because turnabout isn't fair play?" Scott asked with a healthy dose of sarcasm. "If they get shot through the heads, I think it's well deserved at this point."

"Maybe," I said. "But I made a promise I'd try to bring them in."

"You tried," Scott said with grinding intensity, "and look what happened."

"Yeah, but I'm not dead," I said.

"But clearly you're hungry for another shot at the prize—

I can't fucking believe this," and he blew up in a way that very much reminded me of how he'd been in those stolen memories. "We move heaven and earth to try and save your life and now you want to just throw it away by—what? Walking in there and getting your head blown off by June and Elliot again? Or worse, the FBI Tac team? Because let me tell you something, they will not just let their scope pass over Sienna Nealon and think, 'Gosh, I'm here for these other two, I better let her go.' You are priority number one for them. They will kill you!" He thudded his fist against the wall, barely slowing it down enough to keep from tearing into it at the last second. "I should have seen it before. You've got a death wish."

"I don't," I said. "I might have before, I don't know. But no, I don't want to die. I got close enough this time, I don't need to see it any closer. This isn't about me wanting to die."

"But you realize why it might look like that to those of us casually watching from the outside?" Kat asked, speaking up before Scott got a chance to interject again.

"I do," I said. "I've been reckless for a while. I … I've been arrogant … a lot. Lost track of how I could still be vulnerable. I think I lost my respect for my life. Lost hope, maybe, too … but … that's not why I want to go after them."

"Why, then?" Scott asked, sounding just as exhausted as everyone else in the room. "Why?"

"Because I know I was dying. I know what that feels like now. And because if someone doesn't stop these kids … they're going to feel it, too."

"Forgive me for saying, 'Let them,'" Scott said.

"I forgive you," I said quietly, "but … it doesn't change the promise I made that girl's grandmother. Maybe she's too far gone, like … like so many others I've met over the years. But I figure … my word is worth one more chance. One more time throwing myself into peril."

"Why, Sienna?" Kat asked, channeling the apoplectic look on Scott's face into a quieter version of his question.

"Because it's my job," I said, my hushed whisper so low I feared it might scrape the floor. "And because no one else is going to do it for them."

"You're right," Scott said, not daring to look at me, anger all over his face. "No one else wants to give a chance to these two because ... who, honestly, wants to die? They ambushed you. They would have killed you. Giving them another chance seems ill-advised, at best. So why do it?"

"Because I'm hoping someday maybe I'll get another chance," I said in a hushed whisper. "And if I let them just die ... shot down in a hail of bullets when I could have stopped it ... I'm afraid I won't really deserve it."

"All right," Scott said after a long few moments of silence. "Let's go to Daytona Beach."

I looked up at him, brushing away the tears in my eyes with my sleeve. "You sure? You've done enough already."

"I brought you into this," Scott said, nodding once, like it was settled. "Let's finish it together."

56.

June

The sun was up, rising high in the cloudless sky, and they cruised down A1A, just a block from the beach. June could see it out the passenger window. For some reason, Ell was still studying the GPS on his phone, as though he didn't know where he was going.

She gently took the phone from him and tossed it lightly into the floorboard. "We don't need that now," she said quietly.

"You have arrived at your destination," the phone said in a robotic tone, muffled where it pressed against the weathered carpeting in the floorboard.

Ell pulled off into a parking lot on his right. It was a construction site, a massive condo tower that stretched ten, fifteen stories up, with glass only partially covering its metal and concrete skeleton, the rest still in varying degrees of completion.

The car came rocking to a gentle stop just outside the construction perimeter fence that divided the parking lot. It was pulled open for cement trucks and work trucks and all manner of other rugged vehicles to pass. The sound of jackhammering reverberated through the car as Ell put it in park.

"Why here?" June asked, looking out the windshield at the half-completed building. It would probably make someone a very lovely place to live when it was done. The view was surely glorious. She looked east, and wondered if the sun was glaring down on the ocean.

"I dunno," he said, "I just picked Daytona Beach and it brought us here."

"Why pull in here, then?" she asked, smiling slightly mischievously. She thought she knew the answer; it was because Ell was a guy who ran on a track, and didn't adapt easily to breaking out of that. She thought of it as a rut, but either way, it made him somewhat predictable.

A couple days ago, that would have raised her ire. She might have argued, loudly, for how he ought to be more spontaneous.

Now? She just didn't have it in her to quibble anymore. It was a source of faint amusement in the face of a fatalistic end that felt like it was drifting ever closer on the horizon, a dark cloud she could sense but not see.

"I just followed the GPS," Ell said almost helplessly, as though he were utterly blind and saw no other way to have done things differently.

June understood that, too. Better than she would have before. "Come on," she said, and brushed his hand as she sat up. "Let's go make our way down to the beach."

57.

Sienna

I flew with Scott in my arms again, toward the sunrise. It would have been a beautiful sight if I wasn't dreading what would come with it.

Daytona Beach was ahead, and not far. Scott had the details supplied by Reed on his cell phone, guiding me to the spot the FBI had marked for June and Elliot's arrival, while he sat silently cradled across me. I felt surprisingly resilient thanks to my rapid recovery; there was no healing like Wolfe and Kat healing.

Grrrr, Wolfe purred.

Not like that, Wolfe, I thought. It would have been nice to have brought Kat along for this, too, but she'd fallen asleep just before Scott had made his fateful decision to accompany me, and we both knew she was far too tapped out to be useful to us in Daytona. If she'd had to use her healing power even a few more seconds, it was likely to result in some kind of memory loss or personality loss. And if she had to use her power again on me, it'd result in death and absorption.

A tragic fate, Harmon said, but slightly less sad and moody than he would have sounded about it a few hours earlier. He might have been coming around a little, I don't know.

"What's this tactical team that Phillips is deploying?" I asked. "Is it like the FBI's Hostage Rescue Team?"

Scott shook his head, looking up from the phone. "It's

one of Phillips's initiatives. I don't think he wanted me to know about it, but my co-workers don't keep secrets any better than anywhere else. It's three squads of six guys each, plus an additional sniper for support on each team. The idea was that the teams would deploy to engage criminal metas using the latest tactics and weapons. Precision snipers for the most extreme threats, close-in tactical work that would include suppressant countermeasures as well as bleeding-edge weapons systems to take down ones that required a closer approach. Hostage situations and whatnot."

"They any good?"

"Should be the best," Scott said warily. "It's an elite team, ex-spec-ops guys who live and breathe this stuff, but trained to deal with the new reality: us."

"Any chance he'll be there?" I asked.

Scott pondered it a second, then realized what I meant. "Phillips? Probably. This is the kind of thing he'd want to spearhead, since it involves minimal peril and maximum positive exposure once they mow June and Elliot down like dogs."

I narrowed my eyes, contemplating that little possibility. "Good." Then I froze, suddenly aware of how that probably sound. "Not good about him mowing them down, I mean. That would be bad—"

"Yeah, I got it."

"I meant—"

"I know what you meant." He studied his phone. "If they're in this area, as predicted, it looks to me like there are condos on either side. Tall towers. Good vantage points for sniping. If they're smart, they'll have the locals close off the avenue of escape by car once they're in by blockading this road—A1A, I guess it is. That'll create a—"

"A kill box," I said, looking at his phone. It was two large condo towers surrounding a third that looked like it was under construction, no more than a foundation whenever the satellite mapping shot had been taken. "Do you suppose this building is done now?"

"Impossible to say from here," Scott said. "If so, it's a nice little mini-city on the shore. Ideally placed for me, but also for snipers. Then the squads will roll up to wherever they are and spray them with weapons fire until the threat is null." He said the last bit with a fair bit of sarcasm.

"They really are a threat, you know," I said.

He looked at me in irritation. "Of course I know that. I carried your insensate body out of that bank in Gainesville, remember? I argued for—"

"I get it," I said. "I just don't want you to forget, since you've decided to come with me in my somewhat insane effort to give them a last chance—"

"Hard to forget the insanity part of this."

"—that I'm not blinkered about this. They get one chance, and then it's no more Miss Nice Sienna. If they come at me hard, I will put them down." I adjusted my flight path a couple degrees to the left, trying to match the bearing on Scott's screen by sight. "I don't necessarily disagree with what these FBI guys are doing. It's not an unreasonable response given what June and Elliot have done so far. A little heavy-handed for my taste, but the government really only has one tool in their toolbox when it comes to someone like June."

"Remove them from the board, as quickly as possible," Scott agreed. "Still, if dumbass Phillips had let me get involved in this earlier—"

"It might have escalated more quickly. Who knows, honestly?" I sighed, though it was lost to the wind as we flew, cool morning air chilling my cheeks. "I don't want these FBI guys hurt. They're just doing their jobs."

"Agreed," Scott said tightly. "I can help with that."

"What do you want to do?"

"Deploy me here," he said, pointing to the ocean. "Just drop me as you pass. Then you'll need to—"

"Yeah, I know," and I nodded. "I've done this kind of thing before."

"You sure? This is a little different than—"

"Trust me," I said. "I led these teams, remember?" I smiled, anticipating the raw challenge of getting in a scrape with a whole bunch of anti-meta SWAT guys. It was a feeling that was heavily mixed anticipation and fear, especially since

I'd so recently felt, most acutely, what having a bullet pass through your skull and brain felt like. "I know the priorities."

"All right, then," Scott said. The towers were ahead, a couple miles away or less. The center was, indeed, still under construction, drawn already to its full height but lacking a full, finished outer surface; it looked skeletal in a few places, steel beams peeking out from beneath partially covered segments of glittering, reflective windows and hard cement walls.

"This is where it ends," he said upon seeing it. I nodded, thinking much the same, and the percussive sound of a gunshot splitting the morning quiet seemed to agree with us.

58.

June

They were walking across the dusty parking lot when the shot rang out, cracking in the sunny morning. They were passing by a concrete truck with its rolling rear cylinder making apocalyptic levels of noise, but the shot was audible even so.

Ell jerked, pushing June aside. She hit the parking lot pavement and rolled, her elbow screaming at her in pain, the worst funny bone hit she'd ever experienced, no humor in it at all.

She rolled, though, instinctively, underneath the frame of the beastly concrete mixer as another shot exploded from above. She reached out and grabbed Ell's hand, jerking him toward her, pulling him beneath the cover of the spinning concrete mixer.

Ell let out a low moan of pain. Blood ran down his jacket. She traced the origin of the wet stickiness as it spread over his t-shirt, and let out a gasp of her own. "Ell," she breathed.

Another shot clanged off the truck above her and June hurriedly reeled Ell in close to her, dragging him as she moved on her back toward the other side of the vehicle. Beyond it lay an entrance to the building under construction, plastic covering the entry whipping lightly in the wind.

"Come on, Ell," she said as she dragged him out from beneath the concrete truck. The shots were coming from the

241

residential tower on the opposite side of the parking lot, high up somewhere beyond June's field of vision. She kept the truck between her and the shooter, drawing Ell into her arms, cradled. "We have to go." She turned and sprinted for the cover of the plastic as the sound of squealing tires came from behind her and two large, black vans with SWAT lettered on their sides pulled up, the backs opening and men in frightening black tactical gear spilling out.

June hurried, rushing into the building, pushing past the plastic to find a construction site with bare concrete floors, elements of drywall hung around it. Construction workers were fleeing out the other side, casting fearful looks at her as another rifle shot came in over the cement truck and hit the floor behind her, shards of concrete stinging all down the back of her legs. June cried out and dodged behind a heavy beam. Where could she go next? Ell was laid across her, and she looked up.

There—a hole in the floor led to the second story, and she jumped as the rustle of the plastic behind her suggested that the men in black were coming. Her legs bore the shock of the landing, the weight of both her and Ell combined, and she stopped, dropping to her knees, a small bit of cover afforded her by a massive steel beam that stretched from floor to ceiling. There was enough drywall up in this part of the building to obscure her view to the other side of the second floor, but the exterior glass windows were not in place, and June had no idea where to go next.

"How you doing, Ell?" she asked, worriedly. That wound on his chest looked bad, the blood spreading out in a steady circle.

"I don't know," he said, over the sound of booted footsteps moving below. She dragged him away from the hole she'd leapt through, making sure someone didn't just shoot up at them.

"You're going to be okay," she said, caught somewhere being hopeful and just flat-out lying.

"I don't think so," Ell said, with a light moan of pain. His face was contorted, and he was crying a little, tears rolling down his cheeks as he whimpered. "I think this is it for us."

242

"Yeah," June said. "Maybe." She settled back on her haunches. "I guess."

"It was ... inevitable," Ell said, touching her tank top with his bloody fingers, soiling it worse than it already was.

"Mmhmm," June said in sad agreement. "It did feel inevitable, didn't it? As inevitable as if we took a lungful of my poison."

Ell looked blank for a second. "That hasn't ever killed anyone yet, June."

She felt a little grey in the face when she answered. "I think it might have killed us, Ell." She looked behind her, as though the steel barrier that watched her back might disappear at any moment. It sure wasn't going to be a help much longer. "I think it just might have ended up killing us in the end."

59.

Sienna

I dropped Scott in the ocean as I overflew the trio of high condos quickly. He disappeared without a splash, the water probably snatching him up quietly and without a whisper, and I honed in on where I needed to be.

Top floor of the condo building directly across the parking lot from the unfinished one. Corner balcony.

A long-barreled rifle was focused across the parking lot, sweeping for a target. I could hear the sniper talking quietly into his comms gear. "Subjects have entered the building."

I landed on his ass so hard that he didn't even have time to give off a surprised cry. I tried to be a little gentle, but tactical gear is tough, and I tried not to think about how I was going to have to render this poor bastard unconscious. Once it was done, I pulled his vest off and put it over myself; it didn't fit as loosely as I might have hoped. I also bent his rifle barrel so that it was unusable, just in case I'd been too gentle in knocking him out, and then stole his comms gear, threading it into my ear so I could listen in on the squad's movements.

"They're on the second floor," a strong, male voice said in my ear as I finished attaching the unit to my belt.

"Moving," another said.

"Damn," I said, taking care not to trip the button that would activate the mic. I had two more snipers to take out before I could come dropping down, anyway. With a sigh I shot into the sky, off to get the next one.

60.

June

"This is it, June," Ell said, as a little trickle of blood spilled out the corner of his mouth.

"No, no, you're—" she started to say, but the sound of boots thundering up down the way stopped her. "Hold on."

She picked him up again, ignoring the strain of his weight, and sought out another hole in the ceiling above. There was one a little ways ahead, a gap that looked like an elevator shaft. It wouldn't be an easy thing to navigate, but she needed to get off this floor, maybe hop up two levels at the same time.

If she ran for it, though, she'd have to leave behind the cover of the steel pillar she'd been hiding behind all this time, exposing her to fire from the same sniper who had already shot Ell.

If she didn't … the SWAT team would be all over her in a few seconds.

The decision came quickly. She might have known all along they were walking into death, but for some reason there was a clarity that came to her now, a desperate instinct to keep trying, even if it would only buy them a few minutes.

There was another tower across the way, and running for that elevator shaft, empty and dark and inviting, would expose her. She'd need to be quick, to run so fast that any watching snipers wouldn't have a chance to peg her one before she was back in the cover of the steel beams. That'd be tough, because the steel beams were spaced in such a way that she'd be exposed for a few seconds between them each time.

"June, I can't—"

"Shhhh," she said, readying him in her arms. He felt so light—surprisingly so, given how tired she was. "You just wait. I've got you."

He made a gurgling noise, but she ignored it, sprinting out of the cover of the beam, lit by the long shadows between the steel pillars that held up the building. She waited for the sound of a shot, for the thundering approach of death, but it did not come.

She passed into the shadow of the next steel pillar, and the next, and still no sound of gunfire broke the quiet.

When she reached the edge of the elevator shaft, she counted her good fortune for only a second before looking up, her bloodstained shoes hanging toe-first over the edge. This was not a simple jump up, especially not with Ell in her arms. She was going to have to leap off the opposite wall …

She jumped and pressed a foot into the hard concrete, bouncing off of it and up like she was in a ninja movie. She landed lightly on the third floor, barely missing some sort of heavy equipment, then turned around and made the same leap twice more.

"That wasn't so bad, was it?" June asked as she stopped on the fifth floor. The sound of boots pounding had softened, now lost several floors below.

Ell was pale as death, as it was surely upon him, and June gulped when he didn't answer, sending baleful eyes toward her.

"Ell, no," she said. "Come on, Ell. Stay with me!"

But he didn't. His eyes rolled one last time, and were still, and the breath left his chest in a last rattle.

And June was left sitting there, on her haunches, on the cold concrete, holding him as he left her alone.

61.

"Sweeping the third floor," came the cold voice over my earpiece.

"Second floor all clear," came another, "moving up."

"None of this sounds good," I muttered to the unconscious sniper at my feet. He was the last of them, stationed on the building opposite the one I'd started on, to the north of where the SWAT teams were sweeping for June and Elliot. I frowned as I looked down on them. Eighteen guys with guns versus Elliot and June. Given half a chance, they'd just plug our two fugitives full of lead and call it a day, high-fives and beers all the way around.

And before I'd met Grandma Randall and gone through my near-death experience … I might have done the same.

"What the hell am I doing?" I muttered under my breath. I spied a command center, a semi-trailer painted all in black set up down the road a couple blocks, with a few cop cars stationed all around it.

Trying to save someone no more virtuous than yourself? Harmon, that paragon of moral virtue, asked.

Trying to save yourself by saving someone else, Wolfe said, and I blinked.

"That surprisingly insightful, Wolfe," I said, nostrils flaring so hard I could feel them swell.

Everybody needs a second chance sometimes, Gavrikov said.

But usually it's better not to give them to people who shoot you,

Bjorn said. *Is bad for business, yes?*

Tactically unsound, Bastian agreed.

I wouldn't go making it a habit, Zack agreed, *especially for some of the particularly angry and irredeemable souls you seem to cross paths with, but ... give 'em a chance. Maybe you'll save a couple lives here.*

"Third floor clear. Moving to fifth floor."

"I'm not going to save anybody sitting up here," I said, lifting up into the air. "If I were a fugitive June and Elliot ... where in that big building would I be?"

62.

June

She heard the boots coming, but there was no point in running now. She couldn't motivate herself to do it, even though a distant part of her mind was screaming for her to get up, to run, to grab Ell if she needed to, to keep hauling ass up the elevator shaft a double jump at a time.

But her bare legs lay against the cold, rough concrete and stayed there, unmoving, her cutoff jeans soaked in blood and Ell's unmoving body draped across her lap. She cradled him, taking care not to let his head fall back. She held him close to her chest, the way she'd leaned against him as they drove, remembering the feel of his breathing against her.

He wouldn't be breathing anymore now.

They were coming, and she held tight to him, waiting. Maybe they were a floor down, maybe two, but they were coming, and soon.

The thump of shoes behind her caused June to look up with surprise—

And start to scream, before a hand descended over her mouth and squelched it.

Sienna Nealon was standing there in front of her, dark hair hanging loose around her shoulders, inscrutable look on her face until her eyes dropped down to take in Ell, lying there, lifeless—

"Damn," she said, looking him over. She touched his arm, felt for a pulse, and came up wanting only a second later.

"You scared the shit out of me," June said, blurting it out without thinking things through. She'd shot this woman in the head, hadn't she?

"That's one of my lesser-known powers, being a metahuman laxative," Sienna said, clasping her on the shoulder, but not too rough. "We need to get out of here."

June didn't flinch at the touch; it was a lot lighter than she would have expected. Her mind backpedaled, though. "Why?"

"Because these guys with the guns? They're going to kill you, June," she said.

June just stared at her. "Why do you care?"

Sienna took a visible breath, like she was trying to keep patience with a wayward child. "Because I told your grandmother I'd try to save your damned life. Now come on—"

The squeak of boots further down the floor gave way to the rattling of shots—loud, echoing in the interior of the building, like they were played over a theater speaker, booming between the steel beams and through the guts of the tower.

Sienna scooped her up and yanked her along; bullets whizzed past and out through the opening behind them where Nealon had entered. Sienna dragged her, instead, deeper into the building and behind an interior post that cracked with the shots, spitting a little spray of concrete dust over June as she was pulled behind it.

"That's not good, either," Sienna said, taking a knee and looking to her right.

June stared at her, wondering what she was talking about.

Then she heard them. More boots, clapping their way up stairs to their right.

They couldn't go forward, because a team was already waiting.

They couldn't go left, because if they stepped out, the team would shred them with fire.

They couldn't go backward, because the wall behind them was solid concrete, a pillar probably designed to hold the building up in the event of a hurricane.

And now they couldn't go to the right because they were seconds from being cut off by another team.

"I knew the end was coming," June said as the footsteps from two directions drew closer … and closer …

63.

Sienna

"Dammit, Debbie Downer," I said, trying to have sympathy for the gal because I knew what it was like to lose a boyfriend, but at the same time deal with people trying to murder you, "this is not the freaking end, okay?"

Before she could answer, I kept low and dragged her with me toward the stairs where a SWAT team was hustling their butts off to ascend in hopes of putting a shit ton of bullets into her and her now-dead beau. We were concealed by a half wall, but if the team already on our floor and advancing on us figured out we were skedaddling, that sure as hell wouldn't stop the bullets they sent our way.

The stairs were about twenty feet away, a solid concrete set that weren't covered over by any kind of carpet or padding yet, which meant I could hear even the muffled footsteps of the SWAT team trying desperately to advance without making noise. I hoped there were only six of them coming up, but the numbers were about to be irrelevant.

"Okay, stay here," I said to June, letting loose of her, probably about five seconds before I would have started to drain her soul.

"What?" She was dazed, plainly, her eyes still as big as when I'd surprised the hell out of her by flying in behind her.

"Stay here, and if those guys come around the corner, do your skunk thing and disappear in a puff of toxin, okay?"

She blinked at me. "But … if you're right there … won't

it hit you?"

I looked at her flatly. "Don't get all concerned with my life now," I said in a hushed whisper. "I'm not going to be right here. Back in a flash."

Before she had a chance to question what I was going to do, I leapt over the edge of the staircase, which helpfully had no railing, and zoomed downward.

Six guys in tactical gear were waiting below, guns raised, but fortunately not quite at the right arc to catch me as I descended. They moved fast, one of them, the farthest from me, swinging his weapon around. I pointed a finger at his gun barrel and yelled, "Gavrikov!" without really thinking that one through fully.

I shot a quick burst of superheated air, aimed as precisely as I could. With my reflexes in top form, my dexterity well-tuned, and a total lack of movement from recoil, I'd become a pretty good shot with my little fire bursts.

This one, though, was expert. And maybe a little lucky.

It caught his M-16 variant right in the barrel and snuffed as it dove in the narrow breach. A puff of smoke came out a second later as he stroked the trigger.

The rifle blew apart in his hand, drawing a scream from him and panicked looks from his fellows that gave me just enough distraction time to land in their midst.

"Yeehaw!" I yelled, grabbing one guy's MP5 and melting the barrel with a flaming hand. I yanked him hard and ran him into the next nearest of their number and both wobbled, teetering on the edge of a ten foot drop to the stairs below.

Another gun swung in line with me and I yelled, "Eve!" and blasted the guy with a glowing web of light that yanked him backward as his weapon chattered through half the magazine. He was anchored to the wall behind him, weapon secured across his chest, and I spun low, knocking the legs out from beneath the guys who'd been on the edge of falling a second before.

They both went over, flipping in midair and crashing to the stairs below. Grunts of pain told me they weren't dead, but they were out of my way for a second. I fired a couple light nets over the edge to make sure they stayed down there while I wrapped up the last two of them.

I clapped the guy whose rifle I'd blown up across the back of the head; he was stumbling around blindly, a trickle of blood running down his forehead from a nasty superficial wound. I caught him as he stumbled from my blow, wrapping my wrist around his neck and using him as a human shield.

Two guys remained, and they were both at the top of the stairs, aiming down at me. If I hadn't had their buddy for cover, they probably would have had me dead to rights. "It's Nealon!" one of them shouted.

"Bjorn," I said.

Both of them dropped their guns as I hit them with a wave of mental anguish. Their weapons snapped against the bounds of their slings as they went to grasp at their heads, suddenly under psychic assault. It didn't surprise me the government hadn't trained them for this sort of thing, because without Harmon, who the hell would show them what it felt like?

I took the last two out with some well-placed punches, and stitched my human shield to the stairs with a light net, coming back up just in time to see June blink in surprise at my reappearance.

"You stopped them?" she asked.

"Yeah, it's kinda what I do," I said. "Come on. This is our exit."

"What about Ell?" She was still down on all fours, where I'd left her, but she cast a pitiable look over her shoulder, where the body of Elliot Lefavre waited in front of the empty elevator shaft.

I didn't feel like we had time to be delicate. "Come with me or you end up like him."

She stared at me, dully, her eyes red and puffy from that crying she'd done. I regretted my choice of words instantly, because when I'd gone through this ...

Yeah, dying would have been an option to consider.

"I don't know if I want to—" she started to say.

But she didn't have time to finish.

Around the corner where we'd taken cover, six men came

advancing, their guns coming up, drawing a bead on us from forty feet away—not quite point blank but far enough that I couldn't take them out with a light net, a fireball or the Warmind.

And then they started to fire.

64.

Scott

It was unsurprisingly peaceful under the waves, even this close to the shore. Scott remained submerged, in the fetal position and working, from the time when Sienna had dropped him into the loving embrace of the ocean.

Because there was so much to do.

The unfinished building was just like every other high tower on the beach in one regard: it had an elevated pool deck behind it, on a platform fifteen feet above the beach. Scott sent tendrils of water crawling up through the sands, seeping slowly at first, then with greater rapidity, climbing up the sea wall and into the pool. It wasn't finished; he could feel its rough edges, the concrete bottom waiting to be fitted with a liner.

But it worked for his purpose, which was just to hold a couple hundred thousand gallons of water until needed.

From there, while he continued to fill the pool, he sent streams creeping up the steel pillars inside the structure. Along the way, he absorbed a little water left in small puddles by a recent rain, or spilled by careless construction workers. The tendrils of water snaked through the building, feeling, listening, the sonic waves of gunshots absorbed through the water molecules and communicated back to Scott in the sea ...

He moved the water toward the source of the sound, somewhere up on the fifth floor. He couldn't see it, but he imagined it looked a little like waterfalls in reverse running up the side of the building. That thought prompted a smile, which no one could see.

The thrumming sound of the shots increased in intensity as he sent coils of water running in a flat stream around the corner. He couldn't see, exactly, but he let the structure he'd maintained go, let it run and rush over the concrete floor like a burst pipe, and it fed sensory details back to him through the long chain, down to the pool, over the decking, through the sands to where he waited in the ocean …

Boots. Six pairs. Where the gunshots were coming from.

Reaching out, he set his powers to work, the pool emptying, the water flying out and up in a great rush—

65.

Sienna

An epic, Moses-leaves-the-Red-Sea-level flood washed through the fifth floor just as the tactical team opened up on us in earnest. Before I had a chance to yank June down into the cover of the stairwell, before she had a chance to scream, before I had much of a chance to even blink, more water than I'd ever seen on the fifth floor of a building came around the corner and wholly engulfed the SWAT guys.

Then it just stopped, reversed course like we were watching a Blu-ray someone had hit rewind on, and dragged all six of them back around the corner.

"What the hell was that?" June asked, her mouth hanging open.

"My ex," I said, grabbing a handful of the back of her shirt and pulling her after them.

The immense water mass was rolling back out the side of the building now, the tactical guys screaming and shouting and generally freaking out about being caught up in what looked like a writhing, sentient mass of water. I dragged June over to the edge and we looked out together, down five stories to the pool deck below, where the tactical team was keeping their heads above water, barely, by the grace of Scott.

"I ... did not see that coming," June said, staring strangely down at the spectacle before us.

"Watching your enemies get washed away when you're

high in the air on a sunny day isn't a real common thing, so don't get used to it," I said. I took hold of her spaghetti strap and yanked her again, this time pushing her back against the nearest concrete pillar. I watched her carefully; if she so much as twitched purple, I was going to burn her to ashes before she had a chance to poison me.

June just stood there, my hand pressing against her, back against the wall, all the will to fight gone out of her. She looked up at me, as though expecting me to kill her right there. "Go on," she said in a hollow voice.

"I told you I wasn't here to kill you," I said, "but now I need something from you." I put my fingers up, and lit them afire.

"Tell me why I should save your life."

66.

June didn't look like she heard the words, at first. She stared at me with dull eyes, the tears still drying on her cheeks. Her back was against the wall, my hand against her chest, pressing against the tank top, cold steel of a support beam against the back of her neck. "I don't know that you should," June said when she finally composed an answer. "I don't know that I'm worth it."

I pursed my lips, searching June's eyes. "Why do you say that?"

"I've done things," June said. "Things I shouldn't have done. We …" She looked back over at where Ell's body still rested, eyes pointed toward the ceiling above. "Oh, Ell," she said. "This is all my fault. He never wanted to do any of this. Didn't want to … shoot you. Didn't want to rob banks. I convinced him to do it all."

"Team Three, move up." Andrew Phillips's voice sounded distantly in my stolen earpiece, which, I realized, was hanging loose around my knee. I scooped it up and stuffed it back in my ear, then straightened so I could look at June. "And where's our overwatch?"

"Why?" I asked June, trying to keep one ear on Phillips's orders and the other listening for her response, which was bound to be muted at best. June Randall looked like she was ready to hurl herself off the top of this building.

"I just wanted to …" She closed her eyes and screwed up her face. "I grew up in—well, you know. And Grandma—we didn't have it that good … not that that's an excuse … but I just wanted to … I just wanted to … live. In a way I never did." The tears started to flow, and she didn't even bother to sweep them off her cheeks. She just let them go, crying right there in front of me, her back to the pillar, trapped—and somehow, maybe because I had felt that same desperate lack of hope—I knew her running days were done.

67.

I worked to suppress the urge to give a lecture about working for what you wanted instead of robbing banks, as I let her loose. I doubted it was the moment or that it'd be well received. I just kept my stare on her and she bowed her head again and kept talking.

"So … I don't think I'm worth saving. Because I did terrible things. Selfish things. I got the person I loved … killed," her voice cracked in a very genuine way and her shoulders heaved with the exertion of trying and failing to hold in emotion. "I think I'm … pretty well beyond redemption at this point." She stared at her feet, face red and puffy. "I'm … I really am poison."

I watched her for signs of duplicity, but all I could see was the trauma of her own choices and their consequences punching this girl in the face in that nasty way reality had. Anything I said to her at this point would be superfluous. Life had caught up with her, and now she saw all her wrongs reflected back on her, which was something that happened very, very infrequently in my line of work.

"I worry if I'm irredeemable, too," I said, and she looked up in surprise. "If I'm beyond … hope. Poison is maybe a little too literal in my case, but … I've made some pretty toxic choices in my life, ones that have … left my garden pretty salted."

"But you're out here still trying to catch bad guys," she sniffled, then laughed to the point of sobbing again. "And you're more wanted than I am! What's that about? Are you trying to … balance the scales?"

"The good I do doesn't ever erase the bad," I said. "It's not a scale. There will never be balance for the people I've killed who didn't deserve it. But I don't know if redemption is really about that. I think it's about … making it so that whatever sins we're living with, that we've spread in our lives … that they don't poison us fatally. I've met a lot of really bad people in this line of work. And lots of them made similar choices to you and me, but … the difference between them and you is … they never once stopped to reflect, to say, 'Yeah, this is my fault,' and just cut it out moving forward. Most of them didn't even feign remorse, they just flat out wouldn't admit they did it. They were never going to change. They were never going to get better. They would have kept driving, June, kept going for what they wanted."

"I don't want to drive anymore," she said, and I believed her completely; the fatigue in her eyes … I'd felt it myself.

She really was done running.

"You ready to face your consequences?" I asked. "Even if they mean jail time? Because I can't promise you a happy resolution to this. You did terrible things. But … if we can get you in front of the local cops, not this federal death-strike task force, and you surrender to them, make a confession, exhibit real remorse when they try you … you might just walk out of jail someday in the far future. Maybe even while you've still got some life left in you."

"I don't …" She wavered, and a hint of that arrogance flared in her eyes, that all too familiar arrogance. "Why should I have to—"

I wanted to shake her. I wanted to snap open her stupid head, scream directly into her brain until she realized what she'd done, the damage she'd wrought to herself and others. I thought about pressing my fingers to her face, letting her feel the burn of a succubus threatening to rip her soul out of her body, but I wondered what good that would even do.

Instead, I twisted her so she could see Elliot's body. "That's why. And because if you don't face the consequences on the legal side, you're going to face the consequences of a firing squad of guys in black tactical vests that are heading up those stairs right now."

That took all the fire right out of her, and she looked away abruptly, back to a commendable imitation of a ragdoll. "Yeah. Okay. Yeah. I'll—I'll go to jail. I ... I deserve it."

"Good answer," I said, and grabbed hold of her. "Now let's get out of here before they come and kill us both." And with her under my arm like a Thanksgiving turkey, I flew out and up, trying to get out of sight so that I could pull off my next trick without any fatalities.

68.

Scott

He was having a hell of a time keeping the damned SWAT guys from drowning themselves as they flailed in the swimming pool, trying to get free. Every time they'd reach an edge he'd push them back, letting them tread water a little longer. Ultimately he was having to hold them up to keep them from drowning, and hold them back to keep them from getting free and causing more problems …

It was actually damned funny, and Scott was having the most trouble with not bursting out laughing underwater constantly. Not that it would hurt him.

"Scott!" The voice rippled through the water above, and somehow he knew Sienna was there. He rose up out of the inviting surf and found her there, hovering over the surface with June Randall clutched under her arm, tucked in like a football. June looked like she'd either been sunburned or cried her fair share, and based on her limp-as-a-ragdoll bearing, Scott suspected the latter. "She's ready. She needs an escort to take her to the local cops, though."

Scott stared up at Sienna, hovering a few feet above. "You sure about this?"

"Just do it," Sienna said, and dropped June into the water unceremoniously, prompting a squeal from the girl and forcing Scott to catch her on a platform of water before she fell into the surf. With that, Sienna said, to June, "Remember what we talked about."

265

June, eyeing the water column that was holding her dry and out of the surf, looked up and said, "I will."

With a nod, Sienna launched straight up into the sky, and was out of sight in mere seconds, as though she'd never even been there.

"Well, then," Scott said, giving June a cursory look, "let's get you ready, shall we?"

69.

Sienna

It's hard for me to hand off a good plan, because I'm always afraid someone is going to screw it up. In this case, though, marching June Randall through a free-fire zone and into custody was practically guaranteed to end with me being shot through the head again, so delegating to Scott seemed the prudent move.

I watched from up above, hanging out behind a nearby building as he marched her through the parking lot encased in a massive globe of water the size of a van. I couldn't see June all that well within its barriers, but I knew by the shadow she was in there, trapped as Scott walked like a sheriff at high noon across the parking lot of the construction site and out onto A1A.

Local cops were lined up behind their cars, their perimeter established, lights flashing all up and down the street. You could have jumped from the hood of one cruiser to the next for about a mile without any trouble at all. I mean, I wouldn't need to, because I can fly, but if you really wanted to win a game of hot lava, that would have been the place to play.

"I'm a federal agent," Scott called as he got close to the perimeter of local cops, lifting his FBI ID high in the air. "I have the suspect in custody."

I heard one of the cops, a portly guy with a mustache straight out of the seventies, say, "You ever seen anyone get arrested in a big damned ball of water?" His partner shook her head.

"The suspect is surrendering," Scott said, still keeping his hands high in case there was a misunderstanding. "There's no need for any violence." I got a feeling that by the ripple of muttering that went up and down the assemblage of cops, not many people took that instruction immediately to heart. I couldn't really blame them; June had just poisoned two cops and helped wreck a third only yesterday. And that was in addition to a lot of other people that had gotten hurt through her and Elliot's little drive.

Scott started to bring the bubble of water down closer to the ground. "I'm going to let her out to surrender to you—"

"I thought you had her in custody?" that same cop with the mustache asked.

"You don't want the glory of the catch?" Scott asked with a smirk.

"Federal boy turning over a prisoner?" Mustache's partner asked with a snort. "First time for everything, I guess."

He set the bulb of water down on the ground and rolled back the top of the dome, letting it melt away to reveal June standing there, her hands crossed behind her head. She knelt down slowly and the mustached cop came up just as slowly. I saw a pair of heavy duty metacuffs in his hand. Good to see he'd come prepared. His partner came a few steps behind, a syringe of what I assumed to be suppressant in her hand. Even better.

Mustache had her cuffed in a few seconds, and his partner administered the dose of suppressant a few later, without a peep from June. She took it all in stride, and I could almost hear the collective sigh of relief from the assembled police once the drug had a few seconds to sink in.

"What the hell?" a familiar voice said, at last, as Andrew Phillips stepped out of the command trailer just below me. The local PD captain had come out first, but there was Phillips, slightly more rotund than when last I'd seen him, standing on the steps of the trailer and about to wade right in and take charge of the situation.

We couldn't have that now, could we?

I darted down and yanked him up into the air, shoving a hand over his mouth so he couldn't protest. We were a few hundred feet up in the sky a couple seconds later, far enough away from the assembled cops that it wouldn't matter anymore if he screamed, because there was nothing they could do.

70.

June

They cuffed her and drugged her, the pinprick pain of that shot in her arm unpleasant, but not nearly as bad as she remembered from when she got them as a kid.

But then again, she was experiencing bigger pains right now.

"So," the mustached cop that had cuffed her said in a drawling voice, "all that and you just gave up, huh?"

"Yep," she said quietly. She almost didn't want to say anything at all.

"Got anything to say about it?" his female partner asked. She was an older lady, probably in her forties. She had eyes like a bird, watching everything.

June thought about it. She'd heard what Sienna said. About redemption. About being so far gone that maybe it wasn't possible to come back. Something about that brought to mind that guy on the beach, the one with the daughter, the one who had yelled at June. His face had turned blue, and he'd choked right there. Had he made it? She hadn't wondered until now if he'd lived. She thought so, mostly thanks to Ell blowing the toxin out of his lungs, but ...

No more running.

No more hiding.

"I'd like to make a full confession," she said, feeling the weight of those cuffs on her wrists. Maybe someday she'd see the end of this. Or maybe she wouldn't. Maybe the thought of Ell dying, or of that man on the beach ... maybe those thoughts would wake her every night for the rest of her life, in whatever hard jail bed she was sleeping.

Right now ... she wasn't really sure she cared. All she knew was that her running days were over, and for some reason, in spite of the uncertainty ... there was something almost reassuring about giving in to the inevitable. It wasn't peace, but she felt like maybe, just maybe, it was as close as she could hope for at this point.

71.

Sienna

"Oh, stop being a pain in the ass," I said to Andrew Phillips as I dropped him off—gently—on the roof of a condo building two miles down Daytona Beach and came in for a landing behind him.

"You just abducted a federal agent," Phillips said, as flat and emotionless as if giving me his coffee order. (He tried that once. It did not result in coffee for him.)

"Add it to the list, then, Andy."

He stared at me blankly and went for his gun. The dumbass had gone with an under-arm carry, and it took him forever to pull it. By the time he cleared the holster and his suit jacket, I had closed on him and had my hand around the barrel. I flared hot and he made a little scream of surprise, letting go of the pistol.

I turned his gun to slag and tossed it behind me. Even if it was useless as a pistol, he could still have conceivably used it as a club had he gotten hold of it, and I didn't need any more head injuries right now. "Okay," I said, "are you done trying to escape for now?"

"No," he said, and tried to bolt past me for a small shack-sized outgrowth on the roof that led downstairs.

I snagged him by the collar and spun him around, right back to where he started. "How about now?"

He whirled around to look at me again like a caged animal, as though he might start pacing behind the invisible line I'd just established as his cage. "What do you want, Nealon? Because this isn't going to help your case, holding me hostage."

"I'm not going to hold you hostage," I said. "Believe me, I have absolutely no use for you."

He didn't relax, which was probably smart. He just watched me, looking for an opening that his bureaucratic ass would be extremely ill-poised to exploit.

"Here's the deal, Andy," I said. "You know I didn't do that crap in Eden Prairie for no reason. My life was at risk. Those metas you clowns turned loose came after me—"

"I don't know what you're talking about," he said, a little too loudly to be convincing.

"That's a lie."

He didn't try to argue past it. "It doesn't really matter, does it? The government's prosecuting you, not me. And you just keep giving them more reasons. Like this."

"I'm public enemy number one. I don't think they need any more reasons."

"You destroyed the Javits Center," he said.

"All the things I'm accused of, up to and including assassinating the president, and you go straight to destruction of property?" I glared at him. "What do you know? *Actually know,* not the made-up crap you're feeding the people around you."

He met my gaze. Phillips was not a guy who was easily intimidated, and right now, hard as it was to tell, he was pretty pissed off that I was holding him against his will. "It doesn't matter what I know or don't know. All that matters is that you have been charged with a series of crimes that you're going to answer for."

"You know I didn't do any of it, don't you?" Something about the thought was vaguely reassuring, even though he didn't so much as blink when I asked him.

"I know what you're charged with," he said. "The court may consider leniency if you were to turn yourself in—"

"Listen, jackass," I said, "I'm not going to the Cube for things I didn't do. Because you'd be forced to try and restrain me, and I think you know from experience, I'm not really the restrained type, in any sense of the word. I'm out here. I've been steering clear of conflict with your people, and you've been continuously running me through the mud. All right, I got it. When Harmon was in charge, you had to follow his lead. Fair enough. Now that he's not, though—"

"Now that he's not," Phillips cut over me, "if you think you've made things better for yourself, you're even more delusional than you were when you thought you could run a federal agency. I think we all know how that turned out."

"Marvelously, compared to what you've done," I said. "Let's do numbers. How many metas work for you again? After you fire Scott, I mean? And how many men did you just send into a situation where they got their asses kicked? How many state lines did Elliot Lefavre and June Randall make it through before you actually decided to get off your butt and start treating them like a federal case? How many meta incidents are state and local governments having to farm out to private contractors—" I meant my little organization here, of course, "—because you don't have the manpower, the expertise, or the inclination to help with them? How many times did headquarters get destroyed on your watch, oh brilliant administrator? Because I count two. And finally … how many most-wanted fugitives are standing in front of you right freaking now, with you unable to do a damned thing about it?"

He burned quietly in front of me.

"Yeah," I said. "That wouldn't have happened when I was in charge." I just shook my head at him pityingly. "I'd tell you to stay out of my way, but we both know you're too dumb to heed my advice. I'm not a threat to anyone but the same people you're supposed to be chasing."

"You can't really believe we're just going to let you wander around out there, doing whatever you like," Phillips said. He never knew when to shut up, either. "That's not how this works. The noose will tighten. It has to."

"By all means, keep dedicating all your limited resources toward catching me," I said. "The last president tried it, throwing entire teams of metas, my friends—telepathically brainwashed, I might add, drones, planes, missiles …

everything he had, basically."

It almost worked, too, Harmon said.

"You could see how that goes," I said. "Or you could stop wasting my time and yours and get on with the business of actually, I dunno, policing people committing crimes that you know are happening rather than the made-up ones I'm charged with that you apparently know didn't happen." He flushed a shade of pink. "Up to you, really. But don't be surprised if someday soon, your failures become so flagrantly obvious, and your successes so distant that even you can't keep your job any longer. Best of luck, Mr. Phillips."

And with a friendly wave, I stepped off the roof and shot off into the distance, leaving him there to find his own damned way down and back to the police cordon.

72.

Scott

The paperwork was going to be a nightmare, Scott realized, and wondered if turning June over to the locals might mitigate his part in any of it. "I'm out of here soon, anyway," he murmured to himself as he lurked outside the command van, keeping an eye on June. She was sitting, head down, in the back of a police cruiser, for the time being. She'd been in there for about an hour and hadn't shown any sign of wanting a fight.

A car came squealing up and disgorged Andrew Phillips, so furious that Scott fancied he could almost see a wavy cloud of steam forming over his scalp. Scott watched him with barely disguised amusement; Sienna had made it plain she wanted to have a conversation with him, and Scott had a suspicion he knew how well it would have gone.

"Do you know what just happened to me?" Phillips came stomping up, the perma-frown on his face so tight that it would have taken liters of Botox to relax it.

"You took your first Uber?" Scott tried to hold in the smirk. It was hard. Phillips had never been anything other than an ass to him.

Phillips got right up in his face, shaking a fat finger. "You listen to me ... you're done."

Scott looked back at the special tactics team, some of whom were still drying out from the soaking. "I suppose you've got your new boys now ... the, uh ... wave of the future." He kept a straight face while delivering the pun, but not easily.

Phillips's face contorted. "I may not be able to prove you attacked them … but I won't forget this."

"It's okay," Scott said, "I was going to resign anyway. And, judging by how quickly you drive people away, your new team of badass strongmen will last about six months before they realize you're an assclown and resign, too. So … enjoy." He waved at the driver of the car that had brought Phillips, trying to flag him down before he drove off.

"We'll be watching you," Phillips said, as Scott pulled open the car's door. "If you're helping her … we will eventually prove it."

Scott just shot him a smile. "How? You just lost your last investigator, dumbass." And he got in the car, giving a little wave as he drove off, putting an end to another chapter of his life.

73.

Sienna

"Hey," I said as Scott walked into the hotel room where I was waiting for him. I'd showered off, changed into something very un-Sienna in preparation for losing myself in America again. Ahh, the glamorous life of a fugitive. "How'd it go with Phillips?"

"My days of government service are over," he said, wandering in to lean up against the door frame to the bathroom, his tie loosened and his collar wide open. It was a much better look for him than the buttoned-up facade he maintained while a stooge. "Again, I mean."

"Just as well, the culture in that place had gotten pretty crappy," I said as I carefully applied eyeliner. I had to be extra, extra careful, even with my meta dexterity, because I had almost no experience applying the stuff. "Or so I hear. Obviously I haven't worked there in a long time."

"Yeah, it really went downhill after you left and they folded it into the FBI," he said, treading the line between well-delivered sarcasm and stock seriousness so effectively I couldn't tell which he was being.

I put down my eyeliner, because this was about as good as it was going to get. It was heavy black, made me look kind of old-school Goth … which I wasn't actually sure was a thing anymore. The black wig waiting in my bag would help sell the look, though, and probably give people the illusion that I was searching for myself or something.

Hahahahahaha. As if … could have … lost … myself.

You are lost, Harmon said quietly.

"I'm sorry, Scott," I said again, drawing a look of surprise from him.

He tried to wave it off. "You already said—"

"No," I shook my head. "What I did to you … was so grossly wrong. I made the unilateral decision to spare you the pain of our relationship, to try and cut the cord, and I told myself for months … years… afterward that I was doing it because you told me you wished you could just forget me and move on.

"But I did it to spare myself the pain of not being able to just say … 'We're not right for each other. We've grown apart. It's over.' Because I was more afraid of coming home from long trips and finding myself alone than—I don't even know."

He stayed silent for a little while, mulling over what I'd said. "I'm not going to say it's okay, because … obviously it's not. It's enough not okay that Harmon was able to use it to twist me against you, but … I will say that you do seem genuinely sorry, which is not something I've always felt from you, so … thank you."

You're welcome seemed a dumb thing to say, so I didn't say it to him. *You're right,* Harmon said, *that would be dumb.*

"I don't hear you coming up with any better suggestions," I said, tossing my eyeliner into my bag. Swish! Dexterity won that one.

I do have one thing I could say that might make you feel better, Harmon said.

"It creeps me out when he does that," Scott said, frowning.

Well, would it creep you out more or less if I showed Sienna here how to use my power in order to move these stolen memories of yours into that water-swollen gourd you call a head?

I blinked. "You can do that?"

My business is the mind, Harmon said. *This is as easy as downloading porn from the internet.*

"Why that analogy?" Scott asked, pursing his lips in distaste.

Just buckle your safety belt, fool, and soon you'll be experiencing the complete and total lack of joy that will come from those missing memories, Harmon snarked.

"Thank you," I said to him as Scott settled in a nearby chair. "To ... both of you, I guess."

"This doesn't settle everything," Scott said, sounding a little more guarded. "But ... it's a start, I guess."

"I'll take a start," I said, taking a seat of my own on the bed. "I just hope ... that now I have enough time to see it through to whatever end it takes."

"Amen to that," Scott said, and closed his eyes. The memories started to flash in front of mine as they left my head ... and went home to his.

74.

Scott

He lay on the bed for a while after Sienna left, going through those old memories—new again, now—like he was taking his time going through one of his mom's photo albums. It felt weird, those unrecalled things, like holes in his mind had been filled, colored in, bright and vivid where before only grey nothingness had been.

The knock at the door surprised him; she'd been gone for quite a while and he doubted she'd returned. He padded over to the peephole in bare feet, cold against the tile, and peered out.

A second later he unlocked the door and greeted his guest with a smile. "Didn't expect to see you here, Reed."

Reed Treston came in, his long hair back in a tight ponytail, but that perpetually windblown look still about him. He lacked the beard he'd sported in the shots Scott had seen of him online, since he'd re-emerged from the skies or whatever he'd done after South Dakota. "I was in Daytona to consult and figured I ought to stop by."

"Consult, huh?"

"Well, I figured I'd drop by and twist Andrew Phillips's tail until he went red with apoplexy," Reed said with a muted grin. "He's inscrutable at first, but once you get to know him, it is really damned fun to push his buttons."

"How'd you find me?" Scott asked, shuffling his way back toward the bed. His head still felt stuffy, swollen, from the memories returning. In a way, it was like rediscovering himself, and it felt ... weird.

"Well, I run a kind of detective agency now," Reed said with a faint smile. "It's sort of our job."

"I heard about that," Scott said with a smile of his own, sticking his hands in his pockets. "Did you get a P.I. license? A for real one?"

"I did," Reed said. "I'm a bounty hunter, a private investigator ... the whole nine yards."

"Twelve-year-old me would be very impressed."

"How's it strike twentysomething-year-old you?"

Scott froze. "You heard, didn't you?"

"Why, whatever do you mean?" Reed asked innocently.

"You know I left the FBI ... don't you?"

"I'd be a pretty lousy detective if I missed something as big as that, don't you think?" Reed asked. "It's sorta what I'm here about."

Scott stayed in place, almost afraid to move. He knew what was coming next, like a train coming toward him, but he felt stuck in place. "Is that so?"

"Come on, Scott," Reed said. "You're not going to go back to work for your dad now, are you?"

"It's the family business," Scott said with quiet gravity. "There are certain expectations—"

"You have the power to control the waters of the world," Reed said. "And not only that, you're a more powerful Poseidon than has walked the earth since ... I dunno, maybe the original, based on what Hera told me. If you go back to Minnesota and just move money around for your dad ... that sounds like a real waste of talent to me."

There was some tender thread in Scott's mind that resonated to that. Why had he left the government? And why had he come back? Even with his memory restored, some parts of that were fuzzy. Something about the idea of the life he would have had drove him away from it in the first place, and some push from a mind-manipulating schemer had brought him back. Trying to do the right thing had kept him there a little longer, though.

And it had felt good.

"We've got a pretty big team growing," Reed said, with obvious enthusiasm. "If you join, we'll have eight metas on staff full time. Good people, with experience. You know most of them. And since you've been with the FBI … you know the need is not getting smaller for what we do."

"No, there seem to be more metas out there today than there were yesterday," Scott agreed. "A suspicious mind might wonder why that is."

"Trust me," Reed said, turning serious, "we're suspicious. We're wondering. And we're working on it. If you join us … you could be working on it, too."

What do I want out of life? Scott wondered, staring at Reed, earnest, the offer before him.

I came to the Directorate, youthful, naïve, wanting to do good.

I left the agency, burned out, tired, jaded, wanting to be free.

I came back to the government without a mind of my own, wanting to crush Sienna.

I stayed because I wanted to help Sienna, to do what was … right. And now …

Now …

"We could really use you, Scott," Reed said. "And this thing we're doing—we make a difference. We genuinely help people. You know that if you've seen the aftermath of some of the things we've been on, like Orlando."

"Yeah, I know," Scott said, nodding along. "You're righteous."

And maybe I want to do what's right for a while longer.

"What do you say?" Reed asked. "We have donuts in the break room."

"Well, hell," Scott said, his decision made before that even came in, "if there are donuts …" And he extended his hand to take Reed's, giving it a solid pump. "You can count me in."

75.

Sienna

The phone rang in my ear as I waited for the person I'd dialed to pick up. It rang once, twice, three times, and then a female voice on the other end—staid and reserved—answered.

"Hello?" Curious, because she didn't recognize my burner phone's number.

"Oh, hi," I said, probably sounding excessively breezy, "is, uhm … Steve there?" I made up a name out of thin air.

"There's no Steve here," she said, her voice laced with amusement.

"Oh, well, thanks," I said.

"Have a good one," Ariadne Fraser said, and hung up.

I could tell she didn't recognize my voice at all.

"Part of me thought you might have lied about what you did to her mind," I said aloud, looking around the darkened room. I was in one of my safe houses, a one-bedroom apartment in Hutchinson, Kansas, that had absolutely no décor and only a thin, single-width mattress on the floor for furnishings.

No, Harmon said simply. I had a feeling it was as close as I'd get to an apology from him. I didn't have any more venom in me to be angry with him, especially after all that had happened this last day. I was alive, after all, and I'd made it through another ordeal.

My phone buzzed in the darkness with a text message

from Miranda Estevez. *Mission accomplished,* it read, *Poseidon has signed on.*

It hadn't even required much of a push, I suspected, on either end. Scott may not have wanted to admit it when we were dating, but he'd always gotten a righteous rush out of the police work we did. He never felt it as much as I did, and he took some hits along the way that threw him out of it. But given a few years for the world to knock him around … yeah, he was tough enough inside to do the job now.

In fact … I didn't know if I could see him doing anything else.

I have a question I think we all need an answer to, Zack said, uneasily. *What now?*

"Now … I think I need to sleep for a little while," I said, punting on truly answering it.

You sure about that? Bastian asked. He sounded awfully uneasy for a man who couldn't actually die.

We worry about you, Wolfe said.

"Been talking to Harmon?" I asked.

There's very little else to do in here besides talk, Harmon said.

"I'm fine, guys," I said. "Or … I will be. Promise."

It is not good to go through life keeping at a distance all those who care for you, Gavrikov said. *I should know. We could feel it—that warmth you had when you knew Klementina had come to help you.*

"I know," I said, nodding in the darkness, where no one could see it. "It was … a good feeling."

It would be a true shame if you didn't feel it again for a long time, Gavrikov said.

"Guys … let's talk about it tomorrow," I said, and lay my head back on a pillow that was so thin it could have been measured in micrometers, and closed my eyes, fixing my mind on one very particular person in the moments before I drifted off.

When the darkness claimed me, and I felt myself slide into sleep, it came with a warmth that I'd almost forgotten, outside of the moment when I'd known that Kat had come to save me. It was an almost unfamiliar sensation in a world gone cold, a world I pushed away from myself, kept at arms' length.

For their safety, I said.

But that wasn't true.

"Hello, Sienna," Doctor Zollers said as he stepped into the light of my dreamwalk, his old office represented around us in this fictional world, complete with the fish tank that used to rest in the corner of his waiting room. He looked out at it curiously, then smiled at me. "I've been a little worried about you lately. How are you feeling?"

I tried to keep a stiff upper lip, but ... it was so damned hard. "I think ..." I struggled with the words. What the hell was it about my pride that made it so difficult for me to just say it?

I'm lonely.

I'm scared.

I've lost all my hope.

He waited patiently, not speaking, the silence between us an untrimmed thread he left for me to cut.

And finally I did: "I think you were right. I can't do this alone anymore ... can't ... carry the weight *alone* anymore.

"I think ... I might need some help."

Sienna Nealon Will Return in

SMALL THINGS

Out of the Box
Book 14

Coming May 16, 2017!

Author's Note

Thanks for reading! If you want to know immediately when future books become available, take sixty seconds and sign up for my NEW RELEASE EMAIL ALERTS by visiting my website. I don't sell your information and I only send out emails when I have a new book out. The reason you should sign up for this is because I don't always set release dates, and even if you're following me on Facebook (robertJcrane (Author)) or Twitter (@robertJcrane), it's easy to miss my book announcements because...well, because social media is an imprecise thing.

Come join the discussion on my website:
http://www.robertjcrane.com!

Cheers,
Robert J. Crane

ACKNOWLEDGMENTS

Editorial/Literary Janitorial duties performed by Sarah Barbour and Jeffrey Bryan. Final proofing was once more handled by the illustrious Jo Evans. Any errors you see in the text, however, are the result of me rejecting changes.

The cover was once more designed with exceeding skill by Karri Klawiter of Artbykarri.com.

The formatting was provided by nickbowmanediting.com.

Once more, thanks to my parents, my in-laws, my kids and my wife, for helping me keep things together.

Other Works by Robert J. Crane

World of Sanctuary
Epic Fantasy

Defender: The Sanctuary Series, Volume One
Avenger: The Sanctuary Series, Volume Two
Champion: The Sanctuary Series, Volume Three
Crusader: The Sanctuary Series, Volume Four
Sanctuary Tales, Volume One - A Short Story Collection
Thy Father's Shadow: The Sanctuary Series, Volume 4.5
Master: The Sanctuary Series, Volume Five
Fated in Darkness: The Sanctuary Series, Volume 5.5
Warlord: The Sanctuary Series, Volume Six
Heretic: The Sanctuary Series, Volume Seven
Legend: The Sanctuary Series, Volume Eight
Ghosts of Sanctuary: The Sanctuary Series, Volume Nine*
(Coming 2018, at earliest.)

The Girl in the Box
and
Out of the Box
Contemporary Urban Fantasy

Alone: The Girl in the Box, Book 1
Untouched: The Girl in the Box, Book 2
Soulless: The Girl in the Box, Book 3
Family: The Girl in the Box, Book 4
Omega: The Girl in the Box, Book 5
Broken: The Girl in the Box, Book 6
Enemies: The Girl in the Box, Book 7
Legacy: The Girl in the Box, Book 8
Destiny: The Girl in the Box, Book 9
Power: The Girl in the Box, Book 10

Limitless: Out of the Box, Book 1
In the Wind: Out of the Box, Book 2
Ruthless: Out of the Box, Book 3
Grounded: Out of the Box, Book 4
Tormented: Out of the Box, Book 5
Vengeful: Out of the Box, Book 6
Sea Change: Out of the Box, Book 7
Painkiller: Out of the Box, Book 8
Masks: Out of the Box, Book 9
Prisoners: Out of the Box, Book 10
Unyielding: Out of the Box, Book 11
Hollow: Out of the Box, Book 12
Toxicity: Out of the Box, Book 13
Small Things: Out of the Box, Book 14* (Coming May 16, 2017!)
Hunters: Out of the Box, Book 15* (Coming July 2017!)
Badder: Out of the Box, Book 16* (Coming September 2017!)

Southern Watch

Contemporary Urban Fantasy

Called: Southern Watch, Book 1
Depths: Southern Watch, Book 2
Corrupted: Southern Watch, Book 3
Unearthed: Southern Watch, Book 4
Legion: Southern Watch, Book 5
Starling: Southern Watch, Book 6* *(Coming June 2017 – Tentatively)*

The Shattered Dome Series
(with Nicholas J. Ambrose)
Sci-Fi

Voiceless: The Shattered Dome, Book 1
Unspeakable: The Shattered Dome, Book 2* *(Coming 2017 – Tentatively)*

The Mira Brand Adventures
(with a Co-Author to be named later)
Contemporary Urban Fantasy

Mira Brand and the World Beneath: Mira Brand Adventures, Book 1* *(Coming April 2017!)*
Mira Brand and the Tide of Ages: Mira Brand Adventures, Book 2* *(Coming April 2017 - Tentatively)*

*Forthcoming, Subject to Change

Made in the USA
Columbia, SC
15 May 2019